DANCING THE SKIES AND FALLING WITH STYLE

Calvin Shields

DEDICATION

To Daniel Bernoulli who kept me safe from Isaac Newton

ACKNOWLEDGMENTS

To my long-suffering wife and family.

To the Arvon course of '18 for supporting me and giving
me confidence to write.

To John Gillespie Magee Jr for the poem 'High Flight.'

To Buzz Lightyear whose chin is even bigger than mine.

High Flight

Oh! I have slipped the surly bonds of Earth
And danced the skies on laughter-silvered
wings;
Sunward I've climbed, and joined the tumbling
mirth

Of sun-split clouds, — and done a hundred
things
You have not dreamed of — wheeled and
soared and swung
High in the sunlit silence. Hov'ring there,
I've chased the shouting wind along, and flung
My eager craft through footless halls of air . . .

Up, up the long, delirious burning blue
I've topped the wind-swept heights with easy
grace
Where never lark, or ever eagle flew —
And, while with silent, lifting mind I've trod
The high untrespassed sanctity of space,

Put out my hand and touched the face of God.

John Gillespie Magee Jr

"That wasn't flying, that was falling with style!"

Woody to Buzz Lightyear.

Toy Story 1995, Disney/Pixar

Prologue

It started with a small gathering of red blood cells in an artery leading to my brain, along with an unhealthy dose of misplaced belief in my own invincibility. I wonder what the noun of congregation of red blood cells is? A clot, an idiot or a stroke perhaps?

We approached the top of Monte Renoso on the Alta Strada in Corsica. It was snowing hard and the wind whipped up the heavy snow into curls of cold, white wetness.

My fellow skiers were some distance ahead of me, smudges of colour barely visible in the sulphurous view of my goggles. There was little definition, sky and snow blurred into one, outcrops of rocks and slurries of ice dotted the slope. I was climbing with skins on my skis, the heavy back pack dug into my shoulders.

We had climbed from the ski station of Val D'Ese, accompanied by two Corsican guides, to trek one hundred kilometres north to Monte Cinto. The trip was planned to last seven days, overnighting in mountain refuges on the way. The Alta Strada is recognized as one of the more difficult and challenging high Mountain ski trails in Europe.

More red blood cells accumulated in the artery and slowly moved towards my brain as a clot. Tumbling in the accelerated blood stream, the clot reached a point where it was too large to proceed. It slowly blocked off the blood supply and cells gradually started to die.

I was finding it difficult to keep up. One of the guides, fell back to accompany me. He sported a patchy black beard a long thin nose and olive skin burnt by the sun. He lifted his goggles, his close-set dark eyes peered at me. Was there a look of distain, I wondered? After all, he was about half my age.

My mind was in turmoil.

I didn't want to make a fool of myself. I could do this, this wasn't difficult. What was I trying to prove for God's sake? And to whom? For Christ's sake I should have acted my age rather than pretend to be something I'm not.

I felt the first twinges of panic in my stomach.

"I can't understand it," I said in French, taking whooping gulps of air "this isn't a difficult climb."

"Suivez-moi," he said curtly with a heavy Italian accent.

The artery was now completely blocked. I had three to four minutes before the certain death of brain cells. I focused on his skis. He was climbing slowly, exaggerating the steps. I followed doggedly, but without energy.

"Wait!" I called, my voice curiously dampened by the snow. "I have to rest!"

I turned sideways and suddenly my head swam. There was no horizon and I was completely disorientated. I pitched forward and lay down, mouth full of snow.

Laurent scrambled over to me.

"Take your helmet off. We have 100 metres to go, can you make it?"

"Ta gueule!" I replied, sitting up to undo my skis and shrug off my backpack.

"I have to lie down".

My head was spinning, I turned sideways, lay down and was vomited violently, the brown patch of steaming puke melted into the snow. I slid slowly down the mountain through the brown éjecta.

Laurent skied below me and stopped my premature descent with his poles. He called up to the team leader to come down, with a hint of panic in his voice.

The snow was beginning to drift around my head, tickling my nose. It was cold after the sweat of climbing up. The sound of skis scraping through the snow came from above me.

Disembodied voices demanded. "Colin, are you OK? Do you know where you are? How many fingers can you see?" and so on. They took my sleeping bag from my pack and started to stuff me into it.

"Colin, can you hear me? It's Jeff". I nodded. What did he expect? He was bellowing into my ear. "The weather is too poor for a helicopter, we're going to make a sledge and lower you down to a bergerie. A mountain rescue unit is trekking up to take you to hospital."

I was sick again. This time someone supported my head and I managed not to cover my sleeping bag with vomit. The brown snow was immediately shovelled away. I quickly realised the best option was to keep my eyes shut, and not move my head too much. My recollection of the descent is limited to sounds only. Urgent worried voices muffled by the blizzard, faint tinkering noises of the sledge being constructed interspersed with French expletives and the impotent hissing and crackling of the walkie-talkie carried away by the wind.

After an interminable delay, the improvised sledge was ready. They lifted me onto the crude structure and strapped me firmly to it. One of the ropes was wrapped tightly round my bladder, and I felt certain I was going to piss myself. Four skiers belayed me down the mountain. The sledge was unstable and swayed and rolled from side to side as we careened down the slope. At one point the sledge rolled over and turned upside down. I was face down in the snow with my chin acting as a snow plough. My sleeping bag opened and scooped up the snow like a polar basking shark. I was very cold, wet, nauseous, uncomfortable and concerned.

Eventually the slope reduced, and the helter-skelter descent slowed to a halt. The blizzard had strengthened, the wind tugged at our clothes and the snow stung our exposed skin. The visibility was very poor, but I was able to make out what appeared to be a shingled roof on top of a large mound of snow. The bergerie was almost completely entombed in a huge snow drift, like a frozen wave with the crest jetting streams of sleet into the turbulent atmosphere.

Jeff untied my ropes and with the help of two others, dragged me towards shelter. The bottom two thirds of the doorway was blocked by snow. They manhandled me through the small opening, and I fell to the stone floor in a heap. I was in a cramped, stone-walled ante room filled with broken furniture, tools and cobwebs. It was very dark, had one small unglazed window and smelled of damp. In the gloom I was surprised to see a whiskered old man in a peasant smock. He was short and stocky with a mop of white wiry hair; his face was round with the texture of a walnut. Laurent tumbled through the opening, wiped away the snow from his face and spoke quietly to the man. They removed bundles of rags from a clear plastic covered bed, and I gratefully collapsed on it facing the rough stone wall. They covered me with the moth-eaten, foul smelling rags, I curled into a foetal position and started to warm up slightly.

Jeff and his team could not help any further, so they put on their skis, wished me luck, and continued their journey. Laurent stayed with me as we waited for the mountain rescue team. I felt a drip of water on my head. With great effort I looked up at the ceiling, my head swam, and my vision briefly inverted. I closed my eyes and when I opened them again, I noticed that the roof was made from planks of wood pushed together. There were big gaps between the uneven edges, it was leaking like a sieve. The snow was forced into the cracks where it melted, and I started to shiver violently.

'At least I should be out of here soon,' I thought.

Drip,

Drip,

Drip.

A few hours later, I was jolted from my stupor as four mountain rescue gendarmes spilled through the small opening. They looked the same. They were young, bearded and muscular with rosy cheeks. They gathered round me, their breaths froze into a milky brume as they spoke.

"It took us four hours," said one of the quartet in passable English, "the storm is too bad. Too dangerous. We will have to stay here the night."

My heart sank.

"There may be a window in the morning when a helicopter might land."

"What happens if it can't?"

"We will take you over the mountain to the nearest village. About five hours"

I groaned.

The night was interminable. The gendarmes set up camp in the room and attempted to light a small fire with damp wood and only succeeded in filling the hovel with acrid smoke. They covered me with a gold thermal plastic sheet and checked on me at regular intervals. I did not move apart from vomiting into an ornate china bowl and to piss into a bucket.

I was very wet and very cold.

Drip,

Drip,

Drip.

The raging wind abated as the first glow of dawn appeared through the window. The radio crackled into life.

"The helico will be here in 15 minutes. You need to get up. Now!" Someone yelled.

It was easier said than done, I had no balance and I struggled with my jacket. I had problems putting on my boots and kicked over the bowl full of vomit in the process. I was unceremoniously bundled through the opening into the soft snow. I heard the helicopter approaching. The light hurt my eyes, the wind had died down and I sunk to my knees in the snow. I squinted and saw a small yellow and red helicopter hovering just above the snow. The visibility was zero in a maelstrom of powdered snow and ice crystals.

The helicopter aborted the landing and climbed with a noisy clatter.

I sat back, utterly dejected.

"It's having another go!" shouted one of the gendarmes, and sure enough, it turned around and approached us again.

The volume of the rhythmic whump of the blades increased and a waft of snow-laden air hit me as the helicopter settled unevenly on the soft snow. Two gendarmes dragged me through the snow and manhandled me into the back of the helicopter. The heating was on, warmth at last. The gendarmes loaded the skis, equipment and backpacks into the helicopter alongside me. Laurent jumped in, and we took off for Corté.

I spent one night in the small hospital in Corté in the centre of Corsica. I was still wearing my ski boots when I was placed on a bed in the emergency room. The young man in the bed next to me stared at me with wild vacant eyes. He was a hallucinating drug addict. The emergency doctor examined me and told me that I had had a stroke. I had already guessed, but I was devastated to hear it confirmed.

How could I possibly have had a stroke? I have never smoked, I didn't drink much, and I was exceptionally fit. Obese, sedentary, smoking friends of mine weren't having strokes; it was not fair.

I threw up into a grey cardboard receptacle. God I was tired. A nurse took a blood sample and attached a drip to a tube protruding from my arm. I closed my eyes, all I wanted to do was sleep.

The following day, half awake, I was taken by ambulance to the larger hospital in Bastia where I was subjected to scans, an echograph and an MRI.

Perhaps it was an after effect of the stroke, but all the nurses looked stunning. One olive skinned nurse, dressed in pale green scrubs, leant over me to adjust my drip. She had short auburn hair with dark evenly spaced eyes and sensuous lips. Her bouncy breasts strained the buttons of her blouse.

I was pleasantly pleased to note that my stroke hadn't affected me where it mattered most.

I was flown to the Centre Hospitalier Universitaire de Nice and admitted to the stroke unit.

My balance had improved sufficiently to allow me to go to the bathroom unaided, but I hated being confined to my bed, to my room, to that hospital. I had bouts of claustrophobia and wanted to run away.

I thought no one was watching, I unhooked my saline drips, held them in my arms and tiptoed out of my room with my arse hanging out of my hospital gown. I managed a very wobbly two-kilometre jog, interspersed with star jumps, up and down a corridor near the ward.

I was elated, I felt free. I felt normal. I could do this. I would be OK.

I received a serious bollocking from the doctor who observed my momentary bid for freedom, and I was confined to bed again.

My room in the Pasteur was clean and modern. It had two beds and I shared it with another patient.

Instruments, tubes, bottles and other medical paraphernalia hung on the wall behind the beds. The window overlooked a small courtyard, it was impossible to see the sky.

Sounds from the corridor tumbled into my room. A television, nurses talking, bottles chinking, trolleys squeaking, someone gently moaning in the distance.

Smells from the hallway wafted in the air, stale cooking, floor polish, antiseptic sprays, faeces and urine.

Surely, I wasn't supposed to be there? This was for frail old people, smelly people. Sentient saggy old gits. Boring, mundane, bumbling old men.

I reminded myself that I was the same age as them. This was my world, and maybe my future. How could that be? I wasn't like them, was I? The spectre of my own mortality flitted before my eyes.

Gilbert was about 75 years old, lanky, with swept back, thinning long grey hair. He had a round, lined, sunken face and a vivid purple birth mark on his left cheek. He had a pronounced hooked nose and small, wild, milky blue eyes which darted nervously about.

He was brought into the room in a wheelchair and the female nurses quickly undressed him. One nurse brandished a large nappy while they crowded around him, methodically stripping him of his dignity. He protested in a rising, fractured voice.

"Putain! Ho La la!"

There was no dividing curtain between our beds, so I turned over to face away from him, to give him a little privacy.

As the nurses left the room, they informed him brusquely that he was not allowed to sit up or get out of bed. He had lost his freedom, privacy and respectability.

The door closed with a slam, and Gilbert sat up, his thin arms and pale parchment skin accentuated by the looseness of his hospital gown. His eyes narrowed in defiance as he looked at me.

"Help me to the toilet" he said in French.

"C'est interdit. You are not allowed to move."

"Rubbish", he replied and mumbled something, his lack of teeth and strong accent made it impossible for me to completely understand what he was saying.

Gilbert looked up imploringly, his pale eyes brimmed with tears.

"Please" he croaked.

I turned away.

He eventually fell asleep, murmuring and farting next to me.

Gilbert awoke just after midnight and shouted,

"Lisa, Lisa viens avec moi! Où es-tu Lisa?"

He thrashed about and shouted for Lisa at the top of his voice for over an hour.

Who was Lisa? I wondered, looking at him in the dim light. His body twisted awkwardly with each shout. What part did she play in his life? Wife? Daughter? Lover?

No one came.

In a flurry of sheets, grunts and creaking bed springs, Gilbert turned on his side and started to snore as loud as a chainsaw.

I pulled the pillow over my head.

The snoring eventually subsided into a faint babble of incoherent mumblings.

The thin light of dawn leached through the curtains as Gilbert's journey drew to a close. With a muted sigh, the word "Lisa" escaped gently from his lips, and slowly evaporated in that last stuttering breath.

A beautiful young black nurse called Beatrice sat on my bed wearing a bright red cardigan over her hospital scrubs and talked about my future. She was from Burkina Faso and had a round even face, with smooth dark skin, full lips and a wide nose.

"Imagine that you have arrived at two doors on the road of your life. One door is closing but the other is opening. You must go through the opening door. Who knows where it will lead? Perhaps it will join your original path? Either way the direction of your life has changed. Think of it as an opportunity to do something different."

Her voice was deep, her large round dark eyes mysterious, alluring and smiling.

"Profite, mon ami."

Profite in French means so much more than 'profit' in English. It means embrace, welcome, take advantage of and enjoy.

Beatrice was right of course. Who knows what was going to happen?

The young doctor sat on my bed. She looked uncomfortable. Her blonde hair was tied back in a pony tail revealing the stethoscope which hung around her neck. She looked at me through her purple rimmed glasses.

"Monsieur. I'm sorry to tell you but we have found a smudge on your MRI in your brain."

She held up a black and white film to the light and pointed to an insignificant dot on the glossy negative. I was surprised, and my heart sank.

"What does that mean?" I asked, full of foreboding.

"We think it's a glioma."

I said nothing.

She put her hand gently on my arm. I liked the feeling of warmth.

"Gliomas can be an aggressive form of cancer which is difficult to treat"

I paused, trying to absorb this frightening news, I needed to know.

"In the worst case, how long might I have?" I asked, my voice trembling.

"It could be less than six months."

She slowly removed her hand from my arm.

I lay back and closed my eyes. Ghastly fingers of alarm wrapped their clammy talons around my neck, chocking me slowly. Claustrophobia overwhelmed me, a surge of apprehension engulfed me, and I wanted to run. Incomprehensible random thoughts cascaded through my mind and evaporated without resolution.

There must be a mistake?

How could this happen to me?

I opened my eyes and stared blankly at the ceiling.

If my time is up, at least I can honestly say that I have taken every opportunity life has lobbed at me.

It is said that when faced with near death, one's life flashes before one's eyes. It's not true, mine slowly unfolded into a soap opera of epic proportion.

My birth certificate shows that Colin Fairdale was born in a garage in North Piddle, Worcestershire in 1949 to an RAF Officer.

My father was sent to Singapore in 1960 and I was bundled off to a crumbling boarding school in the Midlands.

Later, in 1966, my father was posted to Aden in the Yemen to help with the transition to independence and I flew out to join my parents for the Easter holidays.

Aden

Bullets smashed through the louvered windows and embedded themselves in the soft plaster of the ceiling. Glass cascaded onto the red floor tiles in an eruption of spangling shards, and the air was filled with thick choking dust.

More bullets hit the outside walls with dull thumps.

"Keep your heads down!" my father shouted.

The ceiling fan was wrenched from the ceiling with a direct hit, and still rotating, demolished the small table by the front door. An ashtray from the splintered cabinet rolled towards me and spilled its obnoxious contents. I glanced up. Helen and John lay face down on the floor with their eyes closed and hands over their heads.

The lights flickered and went out. Dull light from the security lamps in the street outside, washed through the shattered windows.

The staccato crack of firing from the street below faded as the flatbed truck carrying the rifle toting terrorists accelerated away.

My father stood up covered in white plaster dust and ran into the bedroom to ensure our African Grey parrot was OK before returning to check on us.

This was our welcome to Aden.

We lived in a top floor flat in Ma'alla overlooking the bay of Aden where oil tankers and dhows plied the stagnant waters. Sometimes, when the wind was from the west, it was possible to smell the acrid smoke from the vast BP oil refinery at Little Aden. To the south, the jagged rocks of an extinct volcano encircled Crater Town. Crater was terrorist controlled and strictly out of bounds.

Ma'alla Straight connected the town of Aden with the British Forces headquarters at Steamer Point. British forces and MPBW families were quartered in five story blocks of drably painted flats which lined both sides of the road. It was difficult to secure, and incidents occurred regularly which is why the road was known as 'Murder Mile'.

Once, my father stumbled on a terrorist planting a bomb under a car below our flat. He chased after him, shooting wildly with his service revolver.

He missed of course, I'm surprised he didn't shoot someone else.

We had to be vigilant. The Air Commodore at RAF Khormaksar had recently held a birthday party for his daughter, Louise.

The family's Yemeni manservant rolled a grenade into the middle of a group of children gathered around the birthday cake. Louise was killed, and four other children were badly injured.

She was just 15-years old.

A dull rumble rattled the broken window and dislodged a piece of glass which fell to the floor and shattered. A flash of light briefly illuminated the flats opposite and large drops of rain sploshed on the balcony. A louder crash of thunder and dazzling zig-zags of lightning heralded an advancing armada of storm cells.

It hadn't rained for 26 years, but it poured all night. It cascaded through the shattered windows, puddled under doors and dripped through the roof of our flat. The rain eased in the early morning and Ma'alla Straight was flooded to a depth of 2 or 3 feet.

It was All Fools Day, the sky was dark, sulky and brooding.

Baka Mousa pirouetted in a *Danse Macabre* mopping up the rainwater from the red polished floor tiles with cloths tied to her feet. She was Somali with wonderfully smooth olive skin. She smiled at me, her large, sooty eyes glanced in my direction. Her long dark hair was bundled under a bright yellow turban accentuating her enormous circular silver earrings. She was only 25, but her large breasts made her look much older. I was confused, I couldn't make out if I was attracted to her or not.

The still air was humid and uncomfortably warm, the electricity had been off for some time, and the one remaining ceiling fan was not working. Our flat had a spartan, cheap, furnished-in-a-hurry feel about it. The rattan sofas were uncomfortable, and the chairs spindly and fragile. The beds had thin mattresses and squeaky springs. I shared a room with my brother John, and my sister Helen had a small room to herself. Baka Mousa slept in an airless maid's room the size of a cupboard adjoining our tiny kitchen.

"There's a curfew today so you can't go out." My father reminded me before he departed for Steamer Point.

He was strikingly handsome and tanned with black slicked-back Brylcreamed hair. He had a pronounced chiselled jaw, and remarkable pale grey eyes. In his khaki RAF uniform, desert boots and peaked cap he looked like a Hollywood matinee idol. The lanyard of a Webley .45 revolver holstered on a blue webbing belt hung around his neck.

The door closed softly behind him.

My father was 9 when his father died in a skirmish with Afghani tribesmen on the North West frontier of India in 1928. He was raised by his redoubtable mother in a terraced house in Gravesend. He was from a long line of tough, hard-as-nails soldiers and had the same true grit, no nonsense approach to life. Unfortunately, he saw emotion as a sign of weakness. He never hugged me or showed any affection. I craved his attention, and I was constantly trying to please him, hoping to achieve some recognition. I felt I wasn't good enough for him. My mother was beautiful, dark haired and free spirited. She was the life and soul of the party and was often the centre of attention for the many unattached officers, which led to rows with my overly jealous father. Our apartment was small, and their raised voices regularly echoed off the walls late at night.

24

I turned on the Grundig radiogram and tuned it to the British Forces Radio, it buzzed into life as the valves warmed up.

FLOSY and the NLF had called for a one-day strike. The strikes crippled the economy and acted as catalysts for rioting and violence. Troops were on high alert and we were confined to quarters.

The announcer claimed that Allah had brought the rain because he disagreed with the strike. I was sure none of the terrorists would pay the slightest bit of attention, but unless they were good swimmers, I couldn't see much rioting happening.

I turned the radiogram off and sloped to the bathroom.

My father had given me an electric shaver, although I didn't really need it. I had a shave for the first time and made a show of patting on the sandal wood scented talcum powder and shaving off the virtually non-existent whiskers. In the steamed-up mirror, a deeply tanned, jet-black haired boy stared back. I was proud of my thick hair, and I painstakingly combed it into a Beatle mop. I wiped my prominent chin. My pale hazel eyes were a striking contrast to my generally swarthy features. I looked closer. I had an unattractive, sulky looking pout. My mother said I was very handsome, but she would, wouldn't she?

Baka Mousa wrung the cloths in a bucket and started to clear up the Kitchen.

She tipped the egg shells into the waste bin, placed the dirty plates in the sink and secured the lid of a large glass Kilner jar. Our eggs were preserved in jars of isinglass and tasted of fish. The milk for my soggy cereal was made from 'Klim' powdered milk and tasted of chlorine. The freighter from Mombasa managed to dock between strikes and unloaded its precious cargo of frozen meat. Spam wasn't on the menu for the first time in ages. Everything was tinned, frozen or powdered, nothing was fresh.

How I longed for school food! I never thought I would ever say that!

I went downstairs to investigate the flood. The rain had eased to a persistent drizzle and the sky was sullen and oppressive, the road was submerged by murky brown water to the middle of my thighs. An old Yemeni with his robe tucked above his knees, drove a camel pulling a green cart through the rubbish strewn sludge. Cardboard, wooden pallets, turds and a dead rat floated by, people stared down from the balconies in bemused silence. I turned to move away when the bow wave of a passing armoured troop carrier nearly drowned me.

A squaddie shouted.

"You're breaking the curfew! Get the fuck inside! You could have been shot, you prick!"

I was completely confused about girls! Nobody prepared me for the confusion.

26

My parents didn't discuss it with me and certainly no one at school had tried. It was perfectly OK to engage in mutual masturbation behind the bike shed at school, or have feelings towards a blond 4th form schoolboy, but anything to do with girls was strictly forbidden. I had feelings towards some girls which I couldn't explain, it was a sort of empty-stomach, yearning excitement.

Yvonne lived in one of the flats opposite. She was about the same age as me but so much more sophisticated. She was tall, slim and elfin. The fringe of her bobbed blonde hair partially hid her heavily freckled face and her clear grey eyes were a striking contrast to her sun tan.

I was very attracted to her and wanted to see more of her, but I didn't have enough courage to ask her out.

We caught the same bus to the beach club at Gold Mohur or to the Officers Club at Tarshyne. The buses were military vehicles with wire mesh over the windows to prevent grenade attacks. An armed soldier and a military escort of two Land Rovers guarded each bus.

I climbed on the bus and realised the seat next to Yvonne was vacant. I pushed my way through and sat next to her, I hoped she hadn't noticed me jostling for position. She smiled as she moved over for me and my heart leapt. She wore a tie-dye cotton beach wrap pulled up into a sort of mini dress revealing the faint down of hair on her legs. I was wearing shorts, and occasionally our bare legs touched as the bus bounced along.

The same soldier from the Northumbrian Fusiliers guarded our bus each day. He was rugged, muscular and wore a red and white cockade on his beret. The SLR rifle gave him an air of authority, maturity and invincibility. He was probably only two years older than me, but what a difference. How I envied him.

Yvonne flirted with him and I was consumed with jealousy. My emotions were difficult to cope with or understand.

How could I make my feelings known to her? I tried to talk to her, but I sensed she wasn't really listening.

"Hey what do you think of The Beatles 'Penny Lane'?" I asked trying to sound cool.

She glared at me as if I was an imbecile.

"What? They're a load of prats. The Stones are groovier. Check them out."

With that, she turned and stared out of the window grille.

I was strumming my guitar on the balcony one day when the wind suddenly increased. My music score flew over the balustrade and glided down in the swirling dust to the street. In the distance, white caps appeared on the mottled sea and waves crashed onto the shore. The sky behind me was turquoise but in front a purple-brown wall of sand 500ft high drew menacingly nearer across the harbour. It soon enveloped the flats on Ma'alla in its gritty embrace and reduced the visibility to a few yards. We spluttered and rubbed our eyes as we closed the windows and doors.

For a moment it was as dark as night, but it disappeared as quickly as it arrived.

An off-duty sergeant from the Argyll and Sutherland Highlanders had his jaw shot off by a terrorist in the souk at The Crescent after the sandstorm and two mortar bombs landed in the sea just off the beach at Gold Mohur. No one was hurt but it made a mess of the diving platform.

Langham's

My father returned from Steamer Point and handed me an aerogram from my Housemaster Mr. Liebert.

"Greasy" Liebert shuffled around the school in heavy brown brogues, worn tweed suit and faded black gown. His grey, wiry, hair and eyebrows were in complete disarray, a black pipe was perpetually clenched between his teeth and a thin yellow line of tobacco juice stained his chin. Black, thick rimmed, round glasses perched on his bulbous veined nose.

Greasy taught me Latin in the second form when I was 12 years old. I hated Latin, I never did my prep and I often clowned around in class. Greasy lost his patience with me one day and hauled me to his study

"You're stubborn and wilful, Fairdale," he growled as he bent me over a chair, "and I intend to teach you a lesson!"

He picked up a thin bamboo cane from behind his desk and beat me three strokes on my behind. Greasy wasn't strong and his technique wasn't very good, so it didn't hurt too much, but I pretended it did, and burst into tears. Poor Greasy! Full of remorse, he gave me an orange and a soft cushion to sit on until I felt better.

Old fool!

I was beaten on two other occasions at school.

The first was in the junior school.

My parents were in Singapore and I was 11 years old.

The housemaster, Dr Bradley, was a squat, odious reptilian bully who liked little boys. He tried to put his hand down my underpants at wash inspection one day in full view of the matron. I instinctively pushed him away, and after that, he took every opportunity to make my life hell. He frequently rapped me hard on my head with his knuckles, kicked me, or shouted at me incessantly.

It was my first term, and I decided to run away to Singapore. I had 5,999 miles to go, when the kindly village Bobby spotted me and escorted me back to school. Dr Bradley was sweetness and light until the policeman left, then he kicked me into his study. He dragged me to a chair, bent me over it and pulled down my shorts and underwear. I can remember clearly the absolute silence before he beat me that first stroke. He was a sadist and knew how to use a cane with maximum effect. It whistled through the air and hit my exposed arse with a solid thwack! It hurt like hell and I yelped. A second stroke hit the same spot. Shit that hurt! With the third stroke, I pissed myself, the acrid yellow puddle spread under the chair and soaked into the carpet. He was panting and breathing loudly, and I couldn't understand why. I screamed loudly as the three remaining strokes fell. Crying, I stood unsteadily and staggered to the door.

It was locked!

I frantically scrabbled at the key and he beat me four more strokes on my back, grunting with each stroke.

I fell through the door and scampered away as fast as I could from that demon.

The last time I was beaten I deserved it. Mr Portman was the coach of the second XI hockey team, he was young with curly black hair and had absolutely no sense of humour at all.

It was a gloriously clear crisp winter afternoon, and I was bored with hockey practice.

It's amazing how versatile a hockey stick can be. It can be a guitar, a machine gun, a sword, a microphone, a club, and indeed, a hockey stick.

We were huddled round the goal area, when I shouted 'En Garde!' at the befuddled goalie and despatched him with a lunge of my hockey stick-épée.

Mr Portman didn't see the funny side of it.

He sent me off.

Trailing my stick behind me, I trudged towards the side line where an inviting tracksuit lay folded on the grass. It was too tempting, I pummelled it into the mud with my hockey stick-cudgel. The sun was behind me, and as I pounded, I noticed the growing shadow of someone behind me. I turned around. It was Mr Portman and unfortunately it was his tracksuit.

I received three of the best for my troubles.

It's an interesting fact that being beaten attracts a certain admiration and respect, particularly if the strokes are in a tight grouping. As was the custom, I dropped my trousers in the washroom, and two witnesses confirmed that my three strokes had landed within a band of one inch!

"Ouch!" They exclaimed. "That must have hurt"

"Nah!" I said, lying.

I swaggered off. It was almost worth it.

I picked up the aerogram and unfolded it into a single sheet of pale blue tissue paper. Almost every inch had been written on in spidery black ink.

Master Colin Fairdale	*Prof. J Liebert*
c/o Flt Lt R M Fairdale	*Devon House*
156 Ma'alla Straight	*Langham's School*
BFPO 69	*Market Langham*
Yemen	*Leics*

4ᵗʰ April 1967

Dear Fairdale

With reference to the incident during the CCF night exercise against Stowe School last term, the Headmaster, RSM Tucker and I met to discuss the event, and it was decided that there is no logical explanation as to why a pencil was in the barrel of your rifle, while loaded with a blank cartridge. The conclusion is that the pencil was placed there intentionally. This is a dangerous violation of the weaponry regulations of the CCF. The farmer, whose

*cow you shot in the behind with the said pencil, has
accepted our apologies and will not take it any further.*

*Considering this, and the fact that next term is
thankfully your last term at Langham's, you will not be
made a prefect for the last trimester. The case is now
closed.*

*However, I'm pleased to inform you that you have
been offered an apprenticeship at Petters Machinery
Company in Ely, subject to achieving 3 C grades in
your A levels.*

*Mrs L sends her regards. She has been busy dead-
heading roses in the garden. You should notice quite
a difference on your return at the end of the month.*

Yours sincerely

Professor J Liebert MA Hons

I was relieved. I was dreading telling my father about the
incident, although I think he might have been a little amused.

The Combined Cadet Force was a load of crap anyway.
Amazingly we had an armoury stocked with fully functional
World War I Lee-Enfield .303 rifles, Sten guns, Bren guns
and even two 25-pound field cannons!

Every Wednesday afternoon we pretended to be soldiers,
dressed up in World War I uniforms, and paraded around
with rifles and hob-nailed boots.

We looked ridiculous! The locals must have laughed their tits off at our bunch of privileged poofs, poncing around like a dysfunctional and obsolete home guard. Most of us hated it, but some thrived on it such as the head boy, who strutted around in his immaculate Under Officer uniform with a swagger-stick tucked stiffly under his arm.

I was still a lowly Private, even some fifth formers had been promoted Corporal or Sergeant ahead of me.

Once a term we held an all-night CCF exercise with a neighbouring public school. This normally involved one school trying to capture the other's command post, ammunition dump or some other strategic objective. It was a great excuse to escape school, visit a pub, have a fag or muck around.

Our last opponent was Stowe School. Stowe is almost a self-contained village so a quick snifter in a pub was out of the question, we would have to make our own entertainment.

At the beginning of the exercise our platoon was issued with five blanks and a thunderflash each. The exercise began at 10pm and we easily slipped away from our Corporal in the dark. We sheltered in the Palladian Bridge for a couple of hours smoking, goofing around and sleeping.

At midnight as the moon shone brightly between scudding clouds, we silently crept towards the main school buildings. We cautiously crawled past the enemy defences and tiptoed into the dormitory quadrangle. We detonated our thunderflashes and fired a few rounds into the air. The noise was deafening! Lights flickered on and windows opened in a flurry of concerned voices. Laughing our heads off, we scarpered into the night. They must have thought it was an IRA attack. We made our way through woods, over fences and across sodden fields towards the rendezvous point when we stumbled upon a herd of cows standing quietly in the corner.

It's amazing how fast a cow can run with a pencil up its arse.

I was encouraged to know that Petters Machinery were interested in me, but I had absolutely no intention of working for them.

I applied for every career which required an interview, anything which got me out of school. I went for interviews in London with Westminster Medical College, Clarks Shoes in Somerset and Imperial Chemicals in Slough. The best was for British Overseas Airways Corporation pilot training at the College of Air Training in Hamble, near Southampton. They gave me a return rail warrant, and the two-day interview included a night in the college. A taste of freedom at last.

Better still, I passed the first interview which required me to sit a further two-day interview.

Heaven!

I screwed up the aerogram and threw it in the waste bin. I picked up a towel and went to the beach.

A'isha

I hung out with some of the MPBW kids at Gold Mohur. We swam to the mangled diving platform and returned to play table tennis on the beach. It had been an unusually clear day and the sea breeze brought merciful respite from the heat. The waiters were setting up the cine projector by the pool for the screening of 'Doctor Zhivago'. A group of Yemenis and their children arrived in an armed convoy of cars and trucks. The women wore heavily beaded, colourful Sana'ani dresses and yashmaks, the men white robes and loose fitting finely embroidered turbans.

One of the girls detached herself and walked gracefully towards us. She was stunning, her pale skin was soft and flawless. She smiled broadly. Her almond eyes were divided by a petite, slightly retroussé nose and her dark hair was covered by a brightly coloured Hermes scarf. She was slim and wore dark slacks and a white blouse. Her eyes were obsidian and so dark her pupils weren't visible. She wore heavy eye liner.

She ambled over to our band of misfits and started talking to one of the MPBW boys. A few seconds later they walked over to me.

"Colin, this is A'isha" said Matt, his blotchy, pimply face flushed as he spoke.

"She's in the same class at school," he stuttered, his curly blond hair waved in the breeze. "I told her you were a fan of that weird group, The Young Tradition."

A'isha turned to look at me, her eyes turned me to jelly.

"Is that true?" she purred with a heavy Yemeni accent.

"Defo. They're far out." I replied, my throat strangely constricted.

"You really like them? Their harmonies are like our music, they're familiar to me."

"I think the Beatles and the Stones are cool as well." I blurted out. "I'm learning how to play the guitar, you know," I added trying to impress her.

"Look," she murmured, "I have to go, my Mum and Dad are waiting for me. Would you like to come to my place and listen to some music? I've got all the Tradition's singles and loads of other LPs."

Would I like to go to her pad?

Is a duck's arse watertight? I thought.

"That would be amazing!" I said, all too eagerly. "Where do you live?"

"My mother's in the Federal Assembly. We live in Crater"

"But Crater is out of bounds for us, It's dangerous." I replied as my heart sank.

She stepped closer, I could smell the sweet perfume that the Yemenis prefer to wear. She looked at me intently.

"Where do you live?"

I told her.

"Good, I'll send my mother's body guard to pick you up after prayers on Tuesday evening. Is that OK?"

Dazed, I managed to croak.

"Fab."

The sun shone mercilessly through the windows of our apartment and I was bored. FLOSY had called for another strike and we couldn't go out.

A strange thing happened.

An explosion rattled the windows with a thud, rifle fire and shouts from the street below reverberated among the closely packed buildings. We lay down facing the floor and waited. Helen didn't look up from her book, John fiddled with a jigsaw puzzle, I glanced at the repainted ceiling and crossed my fingers. The attacks were so frequent that we were becoming inured to the shock.

A captured soldier had recently been decapitated in the Radfan and a photograph of his severed heat on a pole appeared on front page of a local Arabic newspaper.

Tensions ran high and it was rumoured that the SAS had been deployed to help with the crisis.

The concussions eventually petered out and an eerie silence ensued. In the distance, a faint murmur ebbed and flowed with the rumble of vehicles crawling along the street.

We edged onto the balcony and cautiously peeked over. A convoy of open-backed, camouflaged army lorries approached, heading towards Steamer Point. In each one lay a heap of white robed bodies splashed with blood. In the distance I heard a cheer, and then another. I carefully stood up. The balconies were crowded with onlookers and soon Ma'alla Straight echoed with the frenzied hullabaloo of their cheers as each truck drove by.

I cheered with all my might until I lost my voice.

The curfew wasn't lifted so we went to bed early.

John snored gently in the bed next to me with just the top of his hair visible above the sheet. It was strange that he was fair when the rest of the family were so dark. The slowly rotating ceiling fan cast a kaleidoscope of shadows on the walls and the crickets softly chirped behind the shutters. I watched a chit-chat stalk and catch a fly. It was amazing how graceful a little lizard like that could be when it stalked a fast-moving prey.

Sometimes I felt that I was that fly.

Thankfully there wasn't a strike on Tuesday. Baka Mousa prepared Spam fritters for dinner which I ate without interest. I told my father I was going to the Youth Club and slipped out of the apartment. I wore my tight-fitting drainpipe trousers, winkle pickers and a blue striped shirt. I shaved with my new razor and splashed on some Brut aftershave. I thought I looked pretty cool, but I didn't feel it. I was incredibly nervous.

The bus for the Youth Club came and went and I waited behind a pillar looking nervously around for any sign of trouble.

A big black Mercedes with heavily tinted windows appeared in the distance. The bright street lights reflected off the shiny chrome causing the car to shimmer as it approached the bus stop.

The door opened and a balding white man wearing sunglasses emerged holding a small pistol. He was short, muscular, and every move was slow and deliberate. He looked around, his white linen suit was sweat stained and crumpled. He saw me cowering in the shadows and hissed.

"You Colin?"

I nodded.

"Come" he said. He walked round to the far side of the vehicle and opened the left front door.

I sprinted over to the car and jumped in. He closed the door. It was air-conditioned! What a luxury! Jimi Hendrix's 'Hey Joe' blasted out from the 8-track and the noxious smell of stale cigar smoke filled the air. The car was a mobile arsenal. Guns, rifles, machine guns and pistols were strapped everywhere. The body guard jumped in the driver's seat, slammed the door, and we sped off in a cloud of dust.

Crater wasn't far, I guessed it would take about fifteen minutes.

"Putain, what you doing with A'isha?" he asked with a strong French accent. He took off his sun glasses and his tiny eyes bored into me. He had a livid scar on his cheek and tattoos on his knuckles. What little hair he had was slicked back, he had no neck, his head just seemed to fuse into his shoulders.

"Nothing, just coming to listen to music." I replied meekly.

"You better be careful" he said menacingly, "I've been in the Congo, I see bad things and I don't want bad things happen to you."

We turned away from the airport road and there weren't any more street lights. Huts and hovels lined the rubbish-strewn road, some made from cardboard, some from corrugated iron. Moth-eaten camels grazed in the scrub. There wasn't much traffic and we seemed to attract a lot of attention as we shot past.

"We come to check point soon. Lie down. Don't move" he barked.

I wound the seat down as far as it would go and lay there staring through the glass roof of the car. I could make out a few stars. That was unusual, dust and pollution from the BP refinery normally obscured the sky. The car stopped, and I heard English voices. We were waved through.

We entered Crater. I peered through the bottom of the window. There weren't many lights, but there were people milling around, some carrying bundles on their heads, others holding small children or pulling donkeys and camels. The crude mud walled streets narrowed which slowed our progress. It was a confusing warren of dark alleys and forbidding passage ways. No wonder so many British soldiers had been murdered there in the last few years.

We approached a large red steel gate set in a high mud wall where two Yemeni guards lolled in the shadows. They stood to attention to let us through. I wound down my window. We were in another world, an oasis in the desert. Grass lawns stretched either side of the drive, formal flower beds and palm trees shivered in the breeze. A lily covered ornate pond with a cascading fountain stood in the middle of the driveway where the baleful sounds of croaking frogs disrupted the still night. The house wasn't a palace, but it wasn't far from it. It was an immense modern white building with a pillared marble façade and a grand staircase leading to the front door. The car stopped and I got out. Brass lanterns hung from the eaves, the scent of incense floated heavily in the air and wind chimes jingled faintly. A wizened old man came down the steps. He wore baggy pantaloons with a broad cummerbund and pointed leather slippers, which I thought were remarkably like my winkle-pickers.

"Salaam." I said.

He bowed, said nothing, and led me up the stairs. At the top of the stairs A'isha stood smiling at me.

"Hi" she whispered. "Follow me."

My heart pounded. She wore the same clothes she had at the beach club without the head scarf. Her lustrous black hair cascaded in curls to her shoulders. She looked ravishing.

I had absolutely no idea what to do or say. I was tongue tied.

The entrance hall had a highly polished patterned marble floor, high ceilings and drapes covered the walls. Plants and flowers stood in colourful pots on small tables and to one side was a small ante-room. We walked in and sat down on sofas facing each other with a small ornate gilded coffee table between us. A servant with an oddly shaped flat hat approached with a tray of lemonade, stuffed dates and sponge cake.

"Help yourself" said A'isha, "I'll go and get the records and the Dansette."

A'isha stood up and sashayed through the far door. I felt a rising excitement as I watched her glide through the wooden door with its exquisite marquetry. 'I'm in for a bit of fun tonight' I thought, gleefully rubbing my hands.

I turned to pick up my glass and noticed the old hag sitting on a chair by the entrance. She was clothed in black with only her leathery face visible. She stared intently at me with her hawkish eyes.

'Oh fuck' I thought 'what the hell is she doing here?'

I moved towards her to see if I could close the door. She dragged her chair to block the doorway without averting her eyes for a second. Then it dawned on me.

She was a chaperone!

I sat down, dejected.

A'isha returned with her record collection and her red Dansette.

When it was time to go home the crone was still there, watching me like a hook-nosed hawk.

Ascot

I didn't hear from A'isha, in fact, she didn't turn up at school or the club again. Colonel 'Mad Mitch' Mitchell and The Argyll and Sutherland Highlanders stormed Crater, booted the rebels out and it was discovered that A'isha's house had been attacked by terrorists and partially destroyed. There was no sign of the family and it appeared they had all been massacred.

Poor A'isha. What a tragedy, what a waste, what an awful shame.

I returned to Langham's for my final term. I lay in the warmth of the sun by the boundary of the cricket pitch idly chewing a piece of grass. My last term had been interminable, I had outgrown the school, its petty rules, and it was time to leave.

Cricket was an enigma; how could a game be so unbelievably boring and last all day?

The batsman hit the red leather ball with a satisfying thwack, and it sailed through the air in my direction. A fielder sprinted towards the ball with his hands outstretched and caught it in mid-air. He held the ball high in the air, turned towards the umpire and fell heavily on the grass. A bright green grass stain ran the length of his pristine white trousers.

Polite applause wafted over from the pavilion.

What a stupid game.

I sat my last exam in the ancient ironstone school house in the church grounds. I had been in that Dickensian backwater so long I felt I must have been there when it was built in 1584.

I pissed on Mrs Lieberts' roses the night before the end of term as a farewell present and poor old Greasy was positively tearful when I said goodbye. He probably danced a little jig as soon as I closed the door.

I got that bastard Bradley.

I called the NSPCC before I left school and told them my sorry story. The police raided the Junior House and caught Bradley in bed with a 10-year-old boy and arrested him on the spot.

I caught the train home to Ascot.

We lived in a 1950's beige bricked bungalow with a green copper roof, surrounded by pine trees and rhododendrons. It was dark, damp and not much else grew in the sandy acidic soil. I had buried a Quink bottle of nitro-glycerine mixed with chalk somewhere near the compost heap. It was enough to blow one's foot off I suppose. My study mate at Langham's had made it in the labs and, incredibly, he sent it to me in the post. I used to pack my air rifle pellets with the paste and blow the heads off squirrels.

The uneven oak parquet tiles were loose, and the windows were ill fitting and draughty. A large circular shag pile carpet with vivid rings of black, red and orange was in the centre of the lounge, the sofas were bright orange and the curtains lime green. The colours were as subtle as a train crash.

My father returned from Aden after independence and was posted to RAF Strike Command at High Wycombe.

I scraped through my A Levels and I had to decide my future. I had narrowed it down to Medical school at Westminster College or Pilot training at Hamble.

I could imagine myself as an eminent gynaecologist on the cutting edge of medical science, surrounded by swooning pretty nurses. I could also see myself as a dashing, daring, aeronaut battling the elements surrounded by adoring beautiful stewardesses.

Which to choose? They both ticked a lot of boxes.

Super Hero? Yes. Centre of attention? Yes. Respect? Yes. Lots of money? Yes. Sex appeal? Without doubt.

The difference really boiled down to the length of training. For a Doctor it was five years, for a pilot it was two. That was a big difference

Then I noticed an advertisement in 'The Telegraph' for pilot training at Hamble. *'Earn £1,500 a year after 2 years'* it proclaimed in large letters. Alongside the text was a drawing of a steely-eyed pilot walking down the aircraft steps towards a blonde stewardess waiting for him in an MGB sportscar.

She looked amazing. I was sold.

The problem was that I didn't have much interest in, or knowledge about aeroplanes. I only applied to get out of school. I was sure I would be able to bluff my way through.

I wrote to Hamble to accept their offer, and by return of post I was told that my course would start in six months.

I needed a job.

Oakleigh Animal Food Products were advertising for labourers in 'The Ascot Gazette.' They hired me, the hours were 5am until 3pm six days a week at 10/6 per hour.

I also found a job as a wine waiter at the 'Coach and Horses' from 6pm until midnight. I knew absolutely nothing about wines, but I needed to save as much money as possible.

The Oakleigh Animal Food Products factory was in the old goods yard behind Ascot station. It produced dog food from the carcasses of livestock after the butchers and tanners had finished with them.

The factory was a collection of prefabricated metal buildings, chimneys and delivery bays. Steam continuously rose from vents and smoke stacks which condensed on the metal and fell as a fine drizzle. The concrete floors were covered in patches of moss and green mold. The stench of rotting meat and burnt flesh was appalling and permeated every corner of the factory. It was a requirement to be inoculated against all sorts of diseases to work there, even as an office secretary.

It was a dark satanic mill by any account.

I worked in all three stages of the production process.

Lorries from abattoirs dumped the remains of animals in a steaming heap in the holding bays. The first stage was to sort the remains into bins.

Depending on the '*menu du jour*', the second stage was to load the remains from relevant bins into a mincer-crushing machine. Bones made a frightful noise as they were crushed, showering us with tiny osseous splinters. Mincing livers didn't make much noise but sprayed us with a fine '*mousse au chocolate.*' We used meat hooks to lift cow's udders into the machine as they were slippery and very heavy. Cows' vulvas were slippery too but only weighed about 1lb. The resulting effluent was piped across the factory to the freezing bay.

Finally, in the freezing bay, the effusion was squirted from an overhead nozzle into trays on conveyor belts. When the trays were full, they were lifted into industrial quick freezers. Two conveyor belt systems were installed 15 feet apart. The trays weighed about 25 lbs. It was back breaking, monotonous work.

About twenty people of all ages worked with me and we didn't talk much. There was a remarkably strong old man, a pair of twins, Frank, who said he was ex SAS and a Nigerian called Odogwu, who everyone said slept on the sacks in the storeroom and ate the dog food for dinner.

Frank was about 30 years old, tall and thick set with huge tattooed muscular arms. He had short dark hair, a slight lisp and he didn't like me. He pushed me around, teased me about my accent and ribbed me for not keeping up with him when we were loading the freezers together.

Frank was a bully, and I didn't like him either.

One day I was freezing cow's vulvas while on the other belt, they were freezing liquidised liver. We wore rubber gowns, aprons, boots and long red gloves. It was hot in all that rubber and I was tired and bored.

Really bored.

For some reason our conveyor belt stopped. I had a cow's vulva in my hand, and I looked over and saw Frank by the other conveyor belt bending over a tray of liquidised liver. I slipped my hand inside the vulva, it fitted like a glove, and I hurled it at Frank. It described a graceful arc through the air and fell dead centre in the tray of minced liver. A tsunami of hepatic goo covered Frank from head to toe.

Everyone stopped working and stared at him.

Spluttering, Frank looked around and saw me laughing my head off. He wiped the liver from his eyes and spat it out from his mouth.

"You bastard!" he yelled and picked up a cow's udder.

Cow's udders were very heavy, probably about 10 or 15 lbs, but he was very strong, and he managed to lob it in my direction. It bounced off the conveyor belt and hit the old man next to me in the stomach. Winded, he fell backwards and knocked over a bin of sheep's gall bladders. I picked up a pair of pig's lungs, and with one lung either side of my fist, I threw it at Frank.

It was amazing how aerodynamic a pair of lungs were. They soared towards him, but missed, and hit one of the twins in the face. Mayhem ensued with one side of the floor throwing projectiles at the other. Bladders, penises, kidneys, vulvas, bones and testicles filled the air. It was chaos. Frank had been hit multiple times and stood with intestines in his hair, chopped liver down his vest and a lung on his shoulder.

He strode angrily towards me with his fists raised. I tried to run away but he cornered me between the freezers. He threw me to the floor and was pushing my face in my tray of slimy fetid cow's vulvas when the foreman burst in.

I got the sack.

They taught me a lot about wines at the Coach and Horses but my career as a wine waiter was short lived. Diners complained to the manager that I smelled. It was probably true, as no matter how thoroughly I scrubbed myself in the bath each day, I could not completely wash away the putrid smell of dog food.

I was relegated to the kitchen as a *'plongeur par excellence'.*

Ab Initio

The College of Air Training was located on a grass airfield at Hamble near Southampton. It was acquired in 1960 by BOAC and BEA to meet the requirements for future expansion, and to replace retiring wartime pilots. Fading patches of camouflage on the control tower and rusty Bofor anti-aircraft gun emplacements evoked the airfield's wartime heritage; the mess and parade ground its military roots.

I stepped from the train at Netley station. It was a cold, overcast February afternoon with a raw wind from the Solent whistling through the leafless trees. I wrapped my new college scarf tight around my neck and fastened the top button of my navy-blue trench coat. I made my way towards the exit holding my heavy suitcase as the big diesel engine throbbed into life and slowly pulled away. Squealing and clanking it carried off my childhood in belching clouds of dark smoke.

The college bus was waiting for me in the car park. I was the lone passenger.

In silence, we drove alongside a weed covered, dilapidated perimeter fence. I wiped away the condensation and peered at the windswept grass airfield through the steamed-up window, 'what was I letting myself in for?' I wondered.

A guard in prison-warder black uniform pushed open the heavy white entrance gates and waved us through.

I hauled my suitcase into the stuffy guard house.

"Ah, yes, Fairdale."

The guard wore his hat tipped forward on his closely cropped head and peered at me with tired eyes from beneath the shiny peak.

He handed me a clipboard.

"Fill out this form. You're sharing with Kelly until we can find some more room."

He tapped the form with a pencil.

"You're in Leo block, room 4, just past the squash courts, on the right."

He pointed towards the door with his pencil and handed me a key with a wooden fob.

"Sign here. Visitors need to sign in and out in this book, and girls are not allowed in the college at all after 2000 hours. Is that understood?"

I nodded and signed, wondering which block Al Capone was in, or how easy it would be to dig a tunnel under the fence.

I made my way to Cell Block 'H.'

The biting wind funnelled down the alley by the squash courts making my eyes water. I quickened my pace towards Leo.

I opened the door to room four. A young man sprawled on one of the beds with a glass in hand, a half empty bottle of whiskey on the bedside table, and an open copy of 'Tit-Bits' on his lap. He had long black sideburns, a round face, mischievous eyes and was smiling from ear to ear. He rose and shook my hand vigorously, looking at me intently with his clear green eyes.

"Haloo." He said in a lilting Irish accent, "I'm Kelly, Ciaran Kelly. Nice to meet you. Most people call me Keir. We're roommates for a while. Sorry about that, but we're going to have a blast. Have a drink."

He flopped back on the bed and picked up the bottle, splashed some whiskey in my toothbrush glass and handed it to me. I sat down on the empty bed.

"Bloody Hell! This place is worse than my school." I moaned.

"We need to do something about that" he said. "We'll liven it up with loads of girls, but I think they're a bit thin on the ground round here. Maybe we could get a job lot in from St Mary's Girl's School in Portsmouth?"

He picked up the 'Tit-Bits' and pointed to a scantily dressed, long legged girl lounging against a bar stool and grunted.

"Look at the tits on her"

I warmed to him straight away.

We were slightly hung over as we listened to the droning introductory address by AVM Hesketh in the college cinema the next day. I looked at the forty-seven other aspiring pilots who had been selected for the course. Most were clean cut and sat ram-rod straight concentrating on every word of

Hesketh's codswallop. Head boy types every one of them I thought.

I glanced at Keir beside me, he was asleep, slouched in his seat snoring quietly.

We had been streamed into three groups of sixteen, Keir and I were in group C. I asked one of the head boy types how the grouping had been decided.

"Group A is for those who have A levels in Maths and Physics, B is for Physics and Sciences and C is for macramé or needlework." He smirked.

Next up was the Chief Pilot, Captain Roope. He walked up and placed his hands firmly either side of the lectern. He was short with a crew cut and had a severe expression on his face, very military.

He announced the course content.

The first four months was to be spent in ground school learning aerodynamics, meteorology, propulsion, communications, navigation and so on. Only those who passed the final technical exams would progress to the flying stages of the course.

50 hours general flying was planned on the De Havilland Chipmunk, 100 hours intermediate flying on a single engine Piper Cherokee, and 75 hours advanced flying on the twin-engine Beechcraft Baron B55.

He finished his talk.

"Gentlemen, you may liken me to a pair of secateurs. I'm here to prune out the deadwood, so be warned."

Keir grunted and sat up.

Welcome to Hamble I thought.

After a month Frank Gizzard packed his bags and left. He was very homesick and decided to leave, just like that. He was billeted in Leo, and Keir moved into his room.

The ground school was very difficult, it was just like being back at school only ten times more intense. Rob Overton was a timid, inky-fingered swot whose desk was next to mine. I can't imagine why he was in group C as he seemed to know everything. He lived, ate and farted aviation. I paid him to do my homework and my Post Office savings account took a hit.

Keir lived in Bracknell and had a school friend on our course. 'Chase' Williams was of average height and solid with fair hair. His rectangular face had deep set small eyes, high cheekbones and uneven teeth. He was scruffy, had dirty shoes and never tied his tie properly. He had an evil sense of humour, smoked and drank a lot. He and Keir were as thick as thieves.

One evening we gave up revising and Keir drove us to 'The Bugle.' The place was packed, some of our course were there, but no head boy types I noted. I bet they were swotting and masturbating over their flying manuals.

We got absolutely plastered.

We were thrown out of the pub at closing time and as we staggered to the car, Keir said he was going to try to beat the perimeter record. A twisting narrow road runs around the airfield for three or four miles and each intake tried to beat the unofficial lap record. Six of us somehow managed to squeeze into his aubergine Mini and we set off. Pissed as a parrot, Keir threw the little car round corners, onto the verges with wheels spinning and brakes screeching. We arrived back at the entrance gate and tumbled out. One of the back wheels was on fire. The six of us, full of beer, pissed on the wheel and quickly extinguished the fire in clouds of pungent steam.

We were nowhere near the record.

The next day I found an old Matchless 600 motorbike in pieces in one of the hangers. I reassembled it and managed to get it going. It was been great fun tearing round the airfield. I persuaded Keir to come for a ride and we had a hoot. It was difficult to see without goggles, and on the way back, I accidentally rode up the steep embankment of the water reservoir and Keir flew off the back with his arms flailing impotently as he splashed into the water.

He didn't speak to me for two days.

The incessant tedious lectures were interminable. Dr Fallon fell asleep in Meteorology class and left the blackboard covered in what looked like Egyptian hieroglyphics. What the hell was a tephigram? Who sodding cared about Saturated Adiabatic Lapse Rates? I wanted to stove his head in with his precious Ashram Whirling Psychrometer.

I was in the back row next to Rob who was carefully copying notes from the blackboard while Keir and Chase smoked and perved over the latest Playboy Magazine. Some of the class were reading notes, others stared out the window. It was a sunny clear day outside.

Ground School had been almost impossible and despite the help from Rob, I was finding it difficult. The subjects were hugely boring, and I hated being hemmed in and constrained by rules and regulations. It was just like being back at school only worse.

I watched the Chipmunks and Cherokees flying overhead with envy. I wanted to sue BOAC for misrepresentation in their adverts, there were no gorgeous blondes in sportscars anywhere near Hamble.

Four more people were terminated including Jim Smythe from our class. His desk was removed, and the other desks were shuffled around so there wasn't a glaring gap. At that rate it wouldn't be long before Rob was all on his own in the middle of the class room.

I had been told that I was on the Vice Principal's 'Grey List.' The VP was head of ground studies. He was a humourless, colourless ex RAF Navigator and not many people who found themselves on his list completed the course.

I tore a page from my Meteorology reference book and constructed an elegant, aerodynamically perfect paper aeroplane. It was an aeronautical extravaganza, DaVinci would have been impressed. I set fire to a wing with my lighter and launched it at Keir. It flew like a bird, trailing flames and smoke but unfortunately not in a straight line. It landed on Fallon's chest, woke him up, and almost set fire to his tie.

We were set extra homework and I was cold-shouldered by the class for the rest of the week.

Our final exams loomed, and I invited Rob Overton to join us for a quiet drink in the pub. He seemed genuinely surprised and pleased to be invited as he didn't often venture out. The real reason had nothing to do with friendship, I wanted to butter him up make sure that he would let me cheat from him if necessary, during the exams.

Keir drove us to the 'White Hart'. The bar had a low ceiling stained yellow from cigarette smoke. Old oak beams were strategically positioned in the ceiling to inflict maximum injury to anyone walking to the bar. The bright red patterned carpet was frayed at the edges and smelled of stale beer. Rob sat down on a chair by the roaring fire as I pushed my way to the bar. Keir and Chase were playing darts with Ben Phillips, a lovely Australian guy who was the shortest person on our course. He was the minimum acceptable height for a pilot at 5ft 1 inch, and he was the only person who could walk straight to the bar without ducking his head. I had to raise my voice to be heard above the babble of voices, chinking glasses and the whirring of the fruit machine in the corner.

"Two pints of bitter please." I shouted at the lad behind the bar.

He had a bright pink floral kaftan, tight fitting red hipster jeans, bulbous eyes, an enormous afro hair do and a bushy moustache. He looked like a parrot inflated by a straw up its arse.

He drew two flat pints of warm amber ale.

Over by the darts board, Keir shouted "Far out!". He'd scored a triple twenty.

"That'll be three and six, man" the barman said with a Liverpool drawl.

I counted out the coins, picked up the beers and joined Rob by the fire. He was sitting quietly trying to light his pipe. With each flick of the zippo he sucked noisily, until eventually, the tobacco started to sizzle. The sweet-smelling smoke rose to the ceiling and mingled with the pungent haze.

We took a few sips.

"So, how's it going?" I asked gently, wafting away his smoke.

He settled back in his chair, flicked some specks of imaginary ash off his brown corduroy jacket, and frowned, looking down at his pipe.

"I'm not like you lot" he said, with a strong northern accent.

He made a face, took out his lighter and relit his pipe. Drawing hard he blew out a cloud of smoke and peered at me.

I realised that I hardly knew him at all. He was older than me, the same height but his face was so non-descript that I hadn't really looked at him closely before. He had an even oval face with small jaw and long straight nose. His mousey brown hair was short, tidy and combed to one side.

His eyes nervously darted around as he took another sip. His eyebrows moved in sympathy.

"I'm not privileged like you. We don't have much money, I've worked bloody hard to get here" he continued, "I was given a rough time at school. I had ideas above my station. What people don't realise is that it doesn't matter where you come from to be a pilot. All that matters is if you have the temperament. I mean, look at our course."

He waved his pipe in the vague direction of the group standing at the bar.

"I know half are posh, but the rest are a real mixture. Ben over there is the son of a vicar and is 25. How old are you, 18? John Bishop's dad is a brickie. My dad's been on the dole for ages. My Dad and Mam are so proud of me, I can't let them down."

With that he downed his pint and wiped his mouth on his sleeve.

I stared into the murky depths of my empty glass and thought. Christ, I'm only here because I fancied the blonde in a sportscar.

I stood up, hit my head on the beam, and went to the bar for a refill. While I was waiting, I looked over to the dartboard. It was Ben's turn. Ben had short curly black hair, long heavily stubbled chin and dark smiling eyes. He was one of nature's true gentlemen. He didn't have a nasty bone in his body, he was a bonzer bloke. He missed the dartboard completely and collapsed with laughter.

We were all a bit subdued driving back to college. I sat in the front with Keir. He turned to me and with a puckish smile said, "If we pass these exams, I dare you to invite Knocky-knees out for a drink. Fat chance you'll get her to your room, but if you do, you can borrow my car to take her home."

Surprised, I hesitated and then looked at him and replied, "You're on!"

I passed! How the hell I did it, only God and Rob knew. I scored two points above the pass mark and Keir passed by one. Rob was top of the class of course. There were two failures, both from B, and they left the next day.

We were scheduled to start flying the following week and Keir and I were teamed together. Our instructor for basic training was Captain Dai Edwards who had a reputation for being a nice guy.

The mess had a canteen refectory where we ate each day. The food wasn't too bad, and at least there was plenty of it. Three intakes were run consecutively at Hamble each year, so there was space for more than 100 people to sit down. The mostly male kitchen staff were hired locally, and generally did a good job. There were a couple of women, one was probably 60 years old, but the other called Lillian, was in her mid-twenties. She was quite pretty, tall, as skinny as a rake and had short curly blonde hair. She wore heavy eye makeup which accentuated her doleful eyes, and bright red lipstick which emphasised her pout. She wore very short miniskirts which showed off her long matchstick legs. I must admit that I had seen better looking legs on a chicken. Unfortunately, she was noticeably pigeon-toed, and when she walked, her knees knocked together, hence her nickname 'Knocky-knees'.

Lillian was serving in the mess, and emboldened by the presence of Keir and Chase, I asked her if she fancied meeting us at 'The Bugle' some time. To my surprise she agreed. We fixed a date for the following Saturday.

First Solos

Dai Edwards was one of the youngest instructors in the College, and the only one who hadn't been in the RAF. Most of the Instructors had fought in the Second World War and could be overbearing and impatient, but Dai wasn't like that at all. He was slim with short swept back dark hair, an uneven mouth and square chin. He was Welsh, and his sing-song accent was pronounced and sometimes difficult to understand. He was a gentleman.

Dai spent hours briefing Keir and me in the class room before, at last, I followed him out to the Chipmunk. I was wearing pale grey overalls, a leather helmet and throat microphone. Thankfully it was a perfect day to fly, the wind was calm with good visibility and high cloud. The Chipmunk was a single-engine, low wing, monoplane with fixed undercarriage. It was silver with stripes of dark blue, light blue and red along the sides. The top of the nose was painted black and the College coat of arms was emblazoned on the tail. It was a two-seater in tandem configuration; the pupil sat in the front seat and the instructor in the rear. The sliding canopy was fully open, and I clambered onto the wing and lowered myself carefully into the front seat. I sat there looking at all the dials, switches and levers. It smelled of petrol, oil and sweat. I adjusted the rudder pedals, strapped in tight and tried to get comfortable. I plugged in my headset and heard Dai running

64

through the checklist behind me. He started the engine, and with a vibrating roar the propeller burst into life. We taxied out to the take off point, he opened the throttle and we bounced down the grass strip.

Suddenly the bouncing stopped, and we were airborne. We hardly seemed to be moving as we slowly climbed over the Solent towards the Isle of Wight. What a sensation of freedom I felt, there was nothing but sky all around apart from little puffs of cloud, so close, I felt I could touch them. The azure blue of the Solent was scored with scratches of white from the wakes of ships far below.

I heard Dai's voice in my ears.

"OK Fairdale. You have control."

Those immortal words!

Gingerly, I grasped the joy stick, and following the soothing instructions from Dai behind, I steered the fragile craft towards the south.

Towering cumulus clouds were building up in the afternoon warmth over the island as we levelled off at 5,000ft near Cowes.

"I have control, follow me through on the controls," crackled in my headphones

He lowered the nose and the speed increased. We pulled the stick back and I was pressed into my seat. The nose rose higher and higher, the engine laboured and we were briefly upside down. The ships and the patchwork of little fields were now above my head. We continued round our loop back to level flight. My heart raced, and I was breathing heavily into my throat microphone.

Dai laughed.

"Let's attack that cloud!" he yelled hurling the Chipmunk onto its wing tip.

The amorphous white, pink and grey cloud towered over us. We dived in a spiral towards the billow of water vapour, turning tightly to keep one wing tip in the mist. We soared up inverted to chase floating strands of cloud, stalled and tumbled vertically earthwards in a spin. Dai levelled us off at 3,000 ft and we turned to head for home. I was exhausted, ecstatic and elated. My mundane existence had changed forever. From then on, my soul would be in the skies, and I would live forever in three dimensions instead of two.

The purpose of the basic flying course was to develop skills sufficient to fly solo without an instructor. Two students from our course had failed so far. Most 'C' course had already gone solo, a few hadn't, including Overton and myself.

Dai briefed me for an hour, discussing the finer points of circuit work. A circuit was simply a race track pattern. Take-off into wind, turn left or right onto a reciprocal track downwind, then turn on base leg to join the approach path to landing. Once the aircraft was safely on the ground the aircraft throttle was opened and we took off again without stopping. The circuit was then repeated. We called them circuits and bumps.

On the way to the apron I went to the washroom to relieve myself. Someone was vomiting repeatedly in one of the cubicles. The door opened and a pale-faced Rob Overton emerged holding his leather helmet. He wiped his mouth on his sleeve. His grey flight suit was a little too big for him, it was baggy, and the trouser cuffs covered his shoes completely. He looked very vulnerable.

Rob was surprised to see me as he walked to the sink and splashed water onto his face. I touched him gently on the shoulder.

"You OK?" I asked.

He turned around and looked at me. "I'm like this before every flight. I really work myself up. It's ridiculous."

I put my arm around his shoulder. "I often feel the same."

Which isn't true at all. The only time I ever felt sick was the day after a session in 'The Bombay Curry House', and Dai decided to demonstrate an inverted spin from 10,000ft.

Rob visibly relaxed and a slight smile spread across his face.

"Really?"

"Really" I replied.

We strolled towards the aircraft parked on the apron. Keir was checking over his Chipmunk as Ben walked past.

"Hey, Ben!" Keir called out, "Is it true they've had to put extender blocks on the rudders for you, and given you a booster seat?"

Ben ignored the comment and Keir dissolved into guffaws.

It was warm but overcast with high clouds and a slight crosswind. I completed one circuit with Dai, and was about to open the throttle for another, when he told me to complete the landing roll and taxi to the control tower. The slipstream buffeted me as he slid back the canopy. The noise was deafening, and I could only just hear him as he said.

"Right, Fairdale you're on your own. Don't prang it!"

He unbuckled, climbed out onto the wing, and walked towards the control tower. He didn't look around, he didn't even give me the 'thumbs up', there was nothing.

I waited, perhaps waiting for instructions from behind, or maybe a friendly pat on the shoulder, waiting for anything.

But I was on my own.

The sun peeked through the overcast and a startled flock of seagulls flapped into the air as I opened the throttle for take-off. I could see some people gathered on the apron watching me as I slowly climbed away.

I've been told that I'll never forget my first solo. Time will tell I suppose, but I'm sure I'll never forget looking behind me downwind over the Hamble River and seeing nobody there. An empty seat! The biggest "Oh shit" moment of my life.

I somehow managed a smooth landing and taxied to the apron where I parked and shut down the engine. I completed the post flight checks, climbed onto the wing and jumped onto the tarmac. I took off my helmet as Keir, Chase, Rob and some others crowded around me clapping me on the shoulder. Smiling, Dai pushed his way through the mob and shook my hand.

"Well done boyo. Well done indeed, Colin"

It was the first time he had called me by my first name.

Knocky-knees was as good as her word. She turned up at 'The Bugle' and joined us at the bar. Looking very self-important, Keir slouched on my left with his elbow on the counter, smoking a black Sobranie. To my right Ben and Chase were deep in conversation about who knew what?

We all said hello as Knocky-knees squeezed in-between me and Ben and asked the landlord for a Babysham.

Knocky-knees wore a bright yellow, short-sleeved mini dress with oversized white lapels, a thin white belt and knee-high white PVC go-go boots. She had straightened her blonde hair and styled it in a bob. She wore heavy eye-liner and her cheeks were accentuated by a dab of rouge. I wondered if the beauty spot on her cheek was real. Knocky-knees towered over everyone in her high heels. With a modicum of imagination, she looked a bit like Twiggy, and believe you me, I had a very fertile imagination.

Keir whispered in my ear.

"Bloody hell! she's scrubbed up well."

He leered at her over the froth of his beer.

"She's not bad looking." he added, "for a giraffe," downing his pint in one go.

"Is that a fan belt?" he asked, nodding at her short dress, "It's about an inch below sea level for God's sake!"

"I prefer Asian-looking girls" said Chase wistfully to no one in particular, toying with his glass.

Keir ordered another round while Knocky-knees sipped her Babycham and talked to Ben. More accurately, she was talking down to Ben as he only came up to her waist. Keir turned to me, pulled me closer and spoke softly.

"A couple of beers, and I'm beginning to fancy her." he said lubriciously in my ear, while giving her the once over.

I moved closer to Knocky-knees, my thigh touched hers. She didn't pull away, she moved closer.

"I wonder if I can get her into my room?" Keir continued.

Knocky-knees slipped her hand in to mine and gently squeezed.

"It's worse here than being in a monastery" Keir moaned, "I haven't had a shag in ages."

Lucky you, I thought, I haven't had a shag in my entire life.

Knocky-knees took my hand and gently placed it between her legs just below the hem of her dress. The pub was filling up, and we were pressed together against the bar. She started moving against me. I didn't know what she was doing but it felt good, and she was clearly enjoying it.

Keir leaned across me to talk to Knocky-knees.

"Lillian, you're looking very pretty, doll" he slurred.

I raised my eyebrows and groaned. What a load of claptrap! I moved my hand higher, my fingers caressed the soft skin between her thighs. She pressed harder against me.

Keir continued to chat her up while my hand continued its upward journey. Her head was close to mine and I could hear her breath in my ear.

Keir put his hand on my arm and murmured in my other ear.

"I think I'm in with a chance, Colin, I hope you understand?"

He turned his attention back to Knocky-knees.

Keir prattled on smoothly and reached across me to take her hand in his. He started to stroke her hand. I slipped my fingers under the elastic of her panties.

Keir lifted Knocky-knees' fingers to his mouth and gently kissed them, looking intently into her eyes.

"Do you want to come back to the college Lillian? I've got plenty of booze."

"Yes. OK" she replied, her sultry voice loud in my ear.

Keir winked at me with a look of triumph.

Keir stopped the car two hundred yards before the main gate.

"There's a hole in the fence Lillian, just there, climb through." He pointed to a gap in the tangle of wire. "I'll come and get you on the other side."

She got out and unsteadily tottered towards the fence.

Ten minutes later, I made my way from my room past the dustbins and through the long grass towards the fence. Keir arrived at about the same time. He looked astonished.

"What the fuck are you doing here, Colin?" he blurted out.

I looked at him and smirked.

Knocky-knees slowly walked up, looked at Keir and took my hand.

"I hope you understand?" I said gleefully, as we sauntered towards my room.

Keir stood forlornly, making his best impression of a goldfish without a bowl.

I'm not sure what happened.

I locked the door. Knocky-knees threw me on the bed, it collapsed with a crash and she burst into a fit of high-pitched giggles.

'Shit! the whole camp will hear'. I thought.

Hurriedly she took off her dress and bra and threw them in the corner. I don't know why she bothered as she was as flat as a pancake. Growling, Knocky-knees leapt on me, ripped off my shirt and smothered me with kisses. In a tangle of arms and legs, she hit me in the eye with her elbow. I tried to keep up, but it was all too quick and confusing.

She dug her nails into my back and bit the lobe of my ear hard.

"Ouch!" I cried.

"Touch me down there" she demanded. "Play with me now!"

She turned onto her back, took her panties off.

"Here let me show you", she gurgled impatiently and guided my hand.

Faster and faster we went, with her hand holding mine. She started to buck and yell, her free arm thrashed around and knocked the lamp from the bedside table onto the floor where it shattered. The curtain tangled round her flailing arm.

"Yes, yes!" she shouted at the top of her voice as she pulled the curtain rail from the wall.

It ended as soon as it started.

Knocky-knees lay panting in the debris of my room. Suddenly she sat up. Her eyes flickered.

"I need to get back home to Southampton, now!"

She slipped her panties on.

'What?' I thought. 'Is that it? What about me?'

She looked very irritated and pulled the yellow dress over her head.

"Come on. Hurry up. It's too late for a bus, you'll have to drive me."

Confused, I started to protest, but she glared, and cut me short.

"For fuck's sake let's go!".

"OK, OK, Lillian" I reluctantly agreed, "you'll need to go back through the hole in the fence and I'll pick you up on the other side."

I put on a clean shirt, got dressed and we opened the door. Two or three doors in the corridor were already open and anxious faces peered out. I'm sure they thought I'd murdered someone. It was cold and raining slightly as I walked her to the fence. She stood shivering with mascara running down her face.

"I'll get the keys to Keir's car, Lillian. I'll be as quick as I can."

I banged on Keir's door. No reply. I banged harder. More doors opened. More noses poked out.

"Keir!" I shouted. "Wake up!"

A blurry eyed Keir opened the door and stared uncompassionately at me.

"What do you want?" he snarled.

"Can I have your car keys? I need to take Knocky-knees back to Southampton. You said I could?"

He glared at me with pure venom in his eyes.

"Fuck off!"

"I hope you understand," he said and slammed the door in my face.

Shit! The only other person I knew who had a car was Ben. It was a Ford Prefect front-half welded to a Ford Escort rear. It was a death trap, it drove sideways and had big holes in the floor. But at least it was a car.

I sprinted over to Ben's block. He opened the door wearing striped pyjamas and holding a very worn teddy bear.

"No problem" he said, yawning, looking confused. "But it doesn't start very easily." He handed me the keys.

I tried for twenty minutes to start the car without success. Eventually the battery died.

There was nothing else I could do, so I gave up and went to bed.

We had made so much noise that the whole college knew that she had been in my room.

I had a black eye, a bitten ear and scratch marks down one side of my face. I looked as if I'd done twelve rounds with Mohammed Ali.

Of course, I intimated that this had happened during a mutually satisfying shagfest, and my reputation skyrocketed.

Two days later I swaggered into the canteen and the room erupted in cheers. Keir glowered and refused to speak.

Knocky-knees stood behind the counter serving out mashed potatoes. She went bright red and looked daggers at me.

I strutted to the queue, piled my plate high and sauntered towards her.

The room fell silent.

She scowled at me with her face in a rictus of repulsion.

"Wanker!" she snarled and threw a ladle-full of mashed potato onto my plate.

The gravy erupted from my plate, covered me from head to foot and dripped from the end of my nose.

Everybody howled with laughter and hammered the tables with their fists.

There but for the Grace of God

R ob Overton was the only one from our course who hadn't gone solo. He was unlucky with the weather but had logged more than twice the average number of hours needed to go solo. Rumours spread that he was struggling.

It was hot and sunny, and Keir and I had our sleeves rolled up completing the pre-flight inspections of our Chipmunks on the apron when John Bishop ran over to us.

"Overton's on his first solo!" he puffed.

We walked over to join a small group of people standing on the edge of the apron. A Chipmunk passed over us climbing, and we all waved.

"At least he got the bloody thing into the air", muttered Keir without looking up.

The aircraft disappeared into the haze.

"He'll be back in five minutes," said Chase, "We'll have a better view from over there."

We moved towards a patch of grass covered in white daisies and buttercups and sat down. Fieldfares chirped in alarm as a sparrow hawk flew overhead, and the faint clanking of a train could be heard from Netley. I chewed on a stalk of grass with my face towards the warm sun.

"There he is" said Ben shielding his eyes from the sun.

"Stand up, Ben" grunted Keir.

"I bloody-well am!", retorted Ben.

"Tosser!"

We looked towards the south and sure enough, through the shimmer, a small silver speck slowly evolved into a plane.

Rob's flight path was erratic as he approached the field. The sound of the engine accelerating, and decelerating echoed off the hangers behind us. He was too high over the boundary fence and he increased his rate of descent. The wheels hit the ground hard and he bounced high in the air. He decided to go around, the engine roared into life and he staggered away.

Perhaps it was the sun in his eyes. Maybe he hadn't given himself enough space from the preceding aircraft, or he was overloaded. Either way, he didn't see the red and white Cherokee which was climbing below him.

With a loud crunch, Rob's right wing touched the tail of the Cherokee.

He overreacted and turned steeply away to the left, heading towards us. The Cherokee turned to the right, and missing half a tail, managed to crash land on the far side of the field.

Rob's nose dropped in the steep turn, he pulled it up hard and the Chipmunk stalled. He managed to level the wings as he fell out of the sky and hit the ground with a hollow thud. We stood open mouthed.

"Christ!" I shouted. "Bloody hell!"

Nobody moved for a few seconds before we all rushed towards the wreck. The Chipmunk was mainly intact, the nose and tail were twisted, and the undercarriage legs had pushed up through the wings puncturing the fuel tanks. The smell of aviation fuel was overpowering. The engine clicked as it slowly cooled, and the siren of a fire engine started to wail behind us.

Rob was moving in the cockpit.

He had managed to force the shattered canopy back and was trying to unfasten his seat harness as we approached.

"Hang on, Rob!" I shouted at the top of my voice. "We're here!"

He turned to look at me. His right arm was at a grotesque angle, and a trickle of blood ran down his forehead from beneath his helmet. He opened his mouth to say something, his eyes imploring, wide with fear.

We were suddenly hurled backwards by a blast of hot air. My ears rang, bits of grass and earth rained down on us and it was difficult to breathe. The fuel had ignited and exploded. Angry orange flames engulfed the aircraft and a black ball of smoke rose in the air.

Rob screamed terribly above the roar of the inferno.

I got to my knees. The heat was intolerable, the firestorm pushed us back.

Rob was writhing in his seat, screeching inhumanly, with one arm flailing wildly. Jerking convulsively, he half rose out of his seat and turned towards me. Suddenly, his head flopped forward, and he fell silent.

His left arm reached out to me in supplication, fingers twitching, as the flames consumed him.

Final Approach

Flying was suspended for a few days after Rob's accident. An enquiry was held, and no blame was apportioned. Luckily the occupants of the Cherokee escaped with nothing more serious than cuts and bruises.

Rob didn't have many friends at College, but his dramatic death shocked us all, and we held a subdued wake for him at 'The Bugle' sombrely toasting him with frothy pints of best bitter.

When we were off duty, we relaxed in the pubs or in the mess. The refectory and kitchen were in the northern wing of the mess. The lounge and bar were in the east wing. The bar had three full size billiards tables and two dartboards in a corner. The walls were lined in dark oak panelling and the floor was covered with beige lino. Bottles of spirits were stacked at the back of the bar alongside shelves of dimpled pint glasses. Students' pewter tankards hung on hooks above the counter, in the centre of which, stood a solitary beer tap flanked by beer mats and ashtrays. A portrait of The Queen dominated one wall.

The lounge in the mess was spacious with metal framed windows and a heavily patterned red carpet. A red brick fireplace was flanked by photographs of unfamiliar aeroplanes. Dark brown leather armchairs with wooden arms filled the room. Most of the chairs were occupied by students in uniform, smoking and reading the papers.

I was carefully carving my name in the arm of my chair with a penknife, when a guard approached and told me that the Principal wanted to see me in his office.

'Shit!' I thought. 'I've got the chop!'

The Principal's office was in Aries House at the end of the entrance road, close to the mess. The long arms of the ornate clock on the front of the building showed 4pm as I climbed up the stairs.

Nervously, I knocked on the heavy oak door.

"Enter", came the gruff response.

I pushed open the door and gingerly walked into the cluttered, stuffy room. Charts hung on the walls and books and manuals were scattered around.

AVM Hesketh sat at his desk with an unlit pipe in his hands. He had a large head with straight dark eyebrows and balding sweptback grey hair. He peered at me over his half-moon glasses.

"Ah Yes", he muttered and looked down at a note pad on his desk. He looked up at me again.

"Ah Yes. Fairdale. Fairdale, this is Mr and Mrs Overton", and with the end of his pipe pointed to two middle-aged people sitting on the other side of his desk.

"They've come to pick up Overton's personal effects and they asked to meet you."

I walked over and shook their hands. They sat round shouldered and looked small and uncomfortable.

Mr Overton was almost bald with a stubble of hair on the sides of his head. He sported a bushy grey moustache, and his semi-circular, bristling eyebrows perfectly followed the curve of the thin-rimmed glasses balanced on his protruding ears. He had bags under his eyes, and his forehead was deeply wrinkled. Mr Overton wore an open, collarless lightly-striped shirt with cufflinks and thin waistcoat. He leaned forward, placed his elbows on his knees and looked at me with his sad red eyes.

Mrs Overton's brown curly hair was hidden by a purple knitted beret. She wore no makeup and her face was puffy and lined. She wore a dark blue coat with a large silver brooch on her left lapel. Mrs Overton dabbed at her eyes with an embroidered cotton handkerchief.

Mr Overton looked at his fingernails and then glanced up.

"Rob often mentioned you in his letters," he said, chewing the corner of a nail. "We just wanted to meet you."

Mrs Overton sniffed gently behind her handkerchief.

"Yeah." I stumbled, feeling very uncomfortable, "Rob was my best friend. We all liked him. He was a part of our group."

I fidgeted with a button on my blazer.

"Sometimes I helped him with his homework, but he worked really hard and got top marks in the finals," I continued hoping Hesketh would take notice. "He talked about his Dad and Mam a lot."

Mrs Overton stifled a gentle sob, Mr Overton bit his lip.

"He was a great pilot." I paused, not sure what to say, "it was just rotten luck," I almost whispered.

An uncomfortable silence followed. Hesketh fiddled with his pipe, I looked at the ceiling and Mrs Overton sobbed intermittently.

Hesketh cleared his throat.

"Thank you." He looked down at his notes again. "Ah Yes, thank you, Fairdale."

I shook everyone's hand, bade them farewell and left the room. I leant against the closed door and let out a sigh.

For once I wasn't feeling very pleased with myself.

It was decided to reduce our course by six months. Leave was reduced to two weeks a year and Saturday flying would commence with immediate effect. I wondered what the local noise abatement committee would think about that.

There would be only one non-flying Instructor on duty on a Saturday, and in order to cram in the hours, two students could fly together in the same aeroplane for the first time.

This was the most wonderfully stupid thing they could do.

Keir and I flew together the following Saturday. The day was hot, hazy and with thunderstorm activity forecast over the Isle of Wight in the late afternoon. Our brief was simply to fly to the Isle of Wight, stooge around for a couple of hours and return home. Aerobatics were strictly forbidden.

Keir overheard Chase and Ben planning to fly to Bembridge to do some circuits.

We had no plan.

We sauntered out to our Chipmunk. We'd had a Japanese meal in Warsash the night before and finished it off with a couple of bottles of Sake. Keir hid a half bottle of whiskey in his flight suit and packed his dark blue Roberts transistor radio in his flight bag. I sat in the back seat and Keir turned his transistor volume to maximum as we taxied out. He lit a fag and puffed the smoke in my direction. My stomach began to churn.

John Bishop was on his own and decided to see how high he could go. He climbed in a spiral for nearly two hours and got to 19,000ft before he fell unconscious from oxygen deprivation. He tumbled out of the sky for nearly 12,000ft before recovering and returning to Hamble.

Stupid idiot!

Half an hour later we were at 5,000ft over the Isle of Wight. It was hot and stuffy in the bright sunlight, the cockpit smelled of oil and petrol. The back of Keir's head was just visible over the cracked leather coaming as we bounced about in the turbulent midday air.

Keir said on the intercom.

"Let's surprise Chase at Bembridge," and with a flourish, plunged towards the south east.

We saw them daintily poncing about from about 10 miles away. We hid behind a towering cumulus cloud and pounced on them diving at full speed. Just before we got there, Keir rolled the Chipmunk into a diving spiral and shot passed them upside down, with only a few feet to spare. We were so close we could see that Chase had almost crapped himself. Keir's bottle of whiskey and transistor fell onto the canopy and slithered down its side. Chase came after us and we spent the next twenty minutes pretending to be in a dog fight, swooping and rolling over the countryside.

After that I was not feeling at all well.

I puked heavily into a sick-bag.

"Bloody Hell, Col" said Keir, "that stinks. Get rid of it."

"Sorry, Keir" I spluttered, "I haven't got anywhere to put it."

Keir coughed, sniffed and complained about it for a while, and eventually said.

"Wait a minute, I've got an idea. Let's go to Sandown and surprise her."

Sandown airfield was a grass strip just to the west of Bembridge where sheep grazed. It had an air traffic controller and her job was also to chase the sheep away. Someone said that she sunbathed topless by the tower.

Keir's plan was to give her a present.

He descended to fifty feet and flew towards the tower as fast as we could go. Trees and buildings flashed past in a blur as we bounced about in the thermals. I wound the canopy slightly open. The wind roared and sucked out a checklist and some charts, the buffeting was ferocious as we neared the tower.

Keir banked the Chipmunk steeply to the left and I'm sure I saw someone lying on the grass by the base of the tower.

I launched the sick bag out of the opening, and it curved gracefully towards the ground, spinning slowly as it went.

I doubt we hit her, but I have a wonderful image in my mind of her suddenly sitting up covered in half digested sushi, sashimi and noodles.

Intermediate Flying Instruction was on the Piper Cherokee single-engine, four-seater aeroplane. Keir and I were teamed together for the whole course.

Our Instructor was Nick Boycott, a tall, rambunctious man from Yorkshire. He had unkempt black curly hair with a long face and small penetrating eyes. An elongated nose swept towards a mean mouth and prominent thin chin. He was very untidy and sloppy, and his threadbare overcoat was plastered with stains. He was an unpleasant bully.

We had to learn to fly the aircraft on instruments without reference to the outside world. This was achieved by a device made from angled slats fixed to the windscreen which allowed the instructor to see out but not the pupil, who also wore a contraption known as a hood to restrict his view further.

Boycott's instructional skills were honed to a fine art.

I was flying under the hood one day, but not accurately enough for Boycott. To reinforce the point, and to illustrate his coaching finesse and communicational skills, he hit me repeatedly over the head with the checklist the size of The

Encyclopaedia Britannica while shouting in a strong Yorkshire accent.

"Fairdale. If yer don't ferkingwell get this raight I'm goin' to stuff my prick in yer ear and fuck some bloody sense into yer!"

Keir sniggered in the back.

On another occasion, he said that he had had enough of me, and told me to land at Chichester. He opened the door and kicked me out.

"Fuck off. Find your own way home." He snarled in his most encouraging tone, and promptly took off with Keir leaving me behind.

Two hours later he returned to pick me up by which time I was thoroughly wet and miserable.

In the autumn Captain 'Secateurs' Roope took delivery of a new upgraded Baron B55. He decided to land on the shortest grass runway after a shower of rain. He skidded and went through the hedge at the far end of the strip. Only his pride was hurt, but I haven't laughed so much for a long time.

Advanced flying was on the twin-engine Beechcraft Baron B55. We learnt procedures required to fly commercial air routes and we regularly flew to international airports.

Our instructor was a Polish ex RAF wartime pilot. Piotr Gustyn was a larger than life impulsive character, with a mischievous sense of humour and wicked smile. He was short with fair hair, blue eyes and spoke in broken English. He once barrel-rolled a Baron down the airway from Southampton to Gatwick.

One day, during the cruise, the right engine seized up and the propeller spinner flew over the wing with a clatter. The propeller didn't feather, and the drag made the aircraft difficult to handle. We trained for engine failure so frequently that the actions to control the aircraft were completely automatic. Piotr didn't interfere or say a word until after landing, when he clapped me on the shoulder.

"Well done, Colll!"

Towards the end of our course, Piotr announced that we would fly to Luxembourg and spend the night there.

"I know Kid Jensen," he said nonchalantly, "we will visit him at Radio Luxembourg."

We were fans of Radio Luxembourg and tuned to 208 most evenings. Astonished, Keir and I looked at each other. How on earth can this ancient old fart know one of the most famous British DJ's?

"If it's true," whispered Keir, "perhaps we could mention our graduation ball and get a bit of totty to come along?"

"Good idea." I murmured.

Piotr bluffed his way through the doors of the art deco Villa Louvigny and we marched upstairs. Dressed in a bright striped sweater, Kid Jensen sat behind a glass wall speaking into a microphone suspended from the ceiling. Baby faced and skinny he had permed blond hair with a centre parting. The Kid stopped talking, the red light went out and Piotr tapped gently on the glass. The Kid glanced up, looked surprised and beckoned us in. I'm certain he had no idea who the hell we were. Hairy, hippie types were lounging about in the studio looking very trendy. I've never felt so self-conscious in my life with my short hair blazer and tie.

Piotr introduced us and explained who we were. Confused, The Kid said hi. I mentioned our upcoming ball and he said he would give it a 'mench.'

"I've got a couple of square weirdos here who want a mention," he drawled into the microphone, suppressing a fit of giggles.

Our open invitation to our grad ball resulted in one middle aged biddy and a bespectacled, spotty teenager turning up.

The morning that a man walked on the moon for the first time was the morning I was awarded my wings. Forget Armstrong, I felt I could reach for the moon or even the stars.

'That's one small step for Man and a giant leap for Colin-kind' I thought.

The twenty-six students who had passed the course traipsed into the boardroom in Aires House. I looked around, their faces were so familiar, we were comrades-in-arms, survivors of eighteen months of intense and stressful study. The atmosphere was surprisingly subdued, we were almost shell-shocked.

The heavy double doors opened. Hesketh walked in steered by the VP and flanked by Chief Pilot Roope.

All eyebrows and jowls he stood and examined us over his halfmoon glasses.

"Gentlemen, welcome," he announced, waving his pipe around.

"Welcome to The College of Air Training. You have overcome great odds to be selected for pilot training. The next eighteen months will be....."

The VP nudged him and whispered loudly, "Wrong speech."

Startled, Hesketh shuffled his notes.

"Yes, of course. Gentlemen, congratulations." he continued.

In turn we received our wings and a certificate from Captain Roope. I looked down at that small almost insignificant piece of cloth and gold braid and thought how much blood sweat and tears had been shed to win them.

It was almost an anti-climax.

Cadet

We hurtled towards the immense, dull sepia sandstone cliffs towering above us, just visible in the spray between each frantic stroke of the windscreen wiper. The gusting wind blew across the ocean current below us, stirring the slate-grey sea into a frenzied chop, from which spray was flung high in the air. We were flying at 50ft above the Atlantic at our maximum speed of 280 knots directly towards the 700ft high foreboding Cliffs of Moher in a BOAC VC10 airliner. The noise from the slipstream was deafening, the air was turbulent, and the aircraft shuddered and shook. It was difficult to read the instruments, but the Flight Engineer called out the altitude from the radio altimeter.

"52 feet, 50 feet, 48 feet!" he squeaked.

The pitch of his voice on the intercom rose as our altitude decreased. If we had flown any lower, I'm sure he could have sung Castrato in an Italian opera.

The massive stratified rock face virtually filled the whole windscreen, casting us in its shadow. I could make out O'Brien's Tower perched on the precipitous summit with flocks of seagulls circling and wheeling around it. Atlantic rollers crashed into the base of the cliffs in an explosion of spume.

In the seat beside me was a bemedaled, ex RAF ace who had flown on the famous 'Dam Buster' raid during the war.

He sat ram-rod straight, hands firmly on the controls, staring intently ahead with a manic grin on his face.

Who was I to question him? A mere Cadet? I didn't dare.

We were going to crash into the cliffs, but I said nothing.

My sphincter was going 'half-crown, thrupenny bit, half-crown thrupenny bit' as I closed my eyes.

But I'm getting ahead of myself.

We left Hamble at the end of July for three weeks leave, and I was happy to see the back of it. I had made some good friends and we had had some fun on occasion, but the relentless pressure and the lack of time off really got to me.

I received a letter from BOAC stating that Cadet Officer Fairdale was to report to BOAC Training Centre, Cranebank at London Heathrow in August to start a conversion course on the Vickers VC10.

The VC10 was a British built intercontinental airliner with a T-shaped tail and four engines at the back of the fuselage. I thought it the most beautiful commercial aircraft in service, even though it was probably not as efficient as its main rival, the similarly sized Boeing 707. It was faster than the 707 but had an inferior range. More importantly for me, it was easier to land, and the stewardesses were rumoured to be more attractive than on the 707 Fleet.

The hero's welcome I was expecting when I returned home to Ascot did not materialise, and when I proudly showed my mother my wings, she peered at them and said dismissively.

"They're not as good as the RAF wings, are they?" and turned back to her cooking.

I hardly saw my father. He often disappeared for weeks without notice and returned as suddenly as he departed. My mother said he was involved with undercover work for the RAF, but I thought he was busy working under the covers with alluring dusky maidens at some forgotten RAF outpost.

I was still a virgin, although most of my friends assumed otherwise. In fact, they thought I was a champion sexual athlete who once trashed a room while indulging in mind boggling sado-machoistic practices. It couldn't be further from the truth. My brief encounter with the fairer sex remained an enigma which exacerbated my feeling of inadequacy and ineptitude. Knocky-knees had scarred me for life. Would I ever get over it, I wondered?

I walked down the road to a phone box to call Keir. Bracknell was just a few miles from Ascot, and we arranged to meet at his local watering hole, 'The Stag and Hounds' at Binfield. I managed to soft soap my mum into borrowing Dad's car for the evening.

I parked Dad's tatty white Austin A40 under the creaking 'Stag and Hounds' sign on the triangular green, between Keir's aubergine mini and a gleaming convertible pale blue E-Type Jaguar. It was a warm evening and drinkers were standing outside the front door of the pub catching the last rays of the setting sun. Children were played on the green, their shrieks of high-pitched laughter punctured the still air. The pub was an ancient white-washed coach house with a prominent gable end and red clay roof tiles. The bulging facade had black iron 'S' stays and the beige painted windows were at differing levels.

I pushed my way through the group by the door and walked inside where I saw Keir, surrounded by girls, propping up the bar with Chase by his side. He wore drainpipes and elasticated boots, a white shirt and bootlace tie, he had grown his sideburns and his crooked teeth spread in a grin when he saw me.

"Col" he said as he put down his beer.

"It's good to see you too Keir." I smiled.

He reached out his hand which I shook vigorously.

Chase turned towards us, he was wearing shabby pale blue dungarees with white grubby plimsolls, his hair was untidy, and his forehead glistened with sweat. He seemed to be putting on weight.

"Hi, Col. This is Jasmine." Chase indicated the young Asian looking girl with long black hair and short white mini skirt standing close to him.

Keir introduced me to everyone. They were mostly friends from school. One man was tall with long curly mousey hair, large circular glasses and thin smile. He wore a charcoal tight-fitting double-breasted pinstripe suit with broad lapels and a bright blue handkerchief in the top pocket. He had a white, long-collared shirt with cuff links and a blue and white polka dot tie. He was smoking a cigarillo and had an arm around a gorgeous blonde who was a dead ringer for Jean Shrimpton.

"Meet Charles. He's a jeweller in London."

I said hello.

"Didn't do well at school but he's got a bloody E-Type," Keir muttered, taking a drag on his cigarette, looking a bit pissed off.

Bloody Hell! I thought. I've worked hard at school and have just spent nearly two years in a flying Gulag and I've nothing to show for it. Even the ailing Austin, that rusty piece of crap in the car park, wasn't mine.

I drank a couple of pints and caught up with Chase's news. Keir wandered over and introduced me to Annie.

Annie was short, perhaps even shorter than Ben, with red hair, cheeky grin, freckles and enormous knockers. She wore a floral loose-fitting smock and jeans; her titian hair was backcombed in a gentle beehive making her appear taller. She looked at me with her small deep blue eyes.

"Keir says your dad's in the RAF. Mine was too, a fighter pilot in the Battle of Britain. He's just retired."

There was something about her eyes, something inexplicable, indefinably subtle. Desire can be conveyed by the smallest inflexions or movements, the merest parting of lips, a slight widening of the eyes or a raised eyebrow. Whatever it was, I immediately felt a connection and more importantly it seemed reciprocated. I felt flushed and confused. I wasn't really concentrating on what she was saying but I understood the basics. She was an art student in Reading, she lived with her parents in a small thatched cottage in

Bracknell, didn't get on with her Dad and she didn't have a boyfriend.

Keir handed me a pint and gave Annie a gin and tonic.

"Thanks." I said.

We continued talking. She wasn't beautiful in the strict sense of the word, but she was attractive. Her eyes sparkled, she flirted and when she laughed, she closed her eyes and her whole face creased up.

Drinks came and went, and at closing time we wandered out to the car park. Charles was drunk and argued with the Jean Shrimpton lookalike. Keir took a piss against the pub sign and by the bushes Chase had his tongue down Jasmine's throat.

"Do you have a telephone?" I asked Annie. She nodded.

"Give me your number and I'll give you a call"

She told me her number and clambered into the back seat of Keir's car.

Charles shot off in the E-Type with a roar, his tyres spat gravel over the car park. I crawled away ignominiously in my kangarooing, misfiring, apoplectic A40.

I invited Annie to dinner at the Bernie Inn in Bracknell. I wore my best corduroy jacket and chinos and she wore a mid-length dress with a frilly neck and black leather boots. Her hair was tied up and little ringlets fell on her freckled cheeks. She wore a white choker around her neck and pearl-drop earrings.

She was in a bit of a state as she got into my car.

"Charles is dead," she said, her voice choking, "he fell asleep on his back. Bloody idiot! He puked in the night and fucking-well drowned in his own vomit."

I was shocked, I hardly knew him, but I couldn't suppress the thought that without Mr E-Type there would be a lot less competition around.

Our fingers touched over the table as we ate our meal in silence.

She wasn't in the mood after dinner, so I dropped her off at her tiny thatched cottage. I wondered if her parents were gnomes as the house was so small. We arranged another date. She had recently passed her driving test and wanted to practice, so she said she would pick me up in her Mum's Minivan and take us out.

Two days later she picked me up on the Ascot road. I opened the door of the tiny olive-green car and squeezed in. Annie was smoking a cigarette which she flicked out of the open sliding window.

"Do you fancy going to the Finchampstead Ridges?" she asked, looking at me with her impish eyes. "I've got some beer in the back."

How could I turn down an offer like that, so we sped off towards Finchampstead.

It started to drizzle as we pulled into the carpark on the Ridges. It was a typical English all-pervading, irritating drizzle. Annie switched off the engine, tuned the radio to Radio One and lit up a cigarette, filling the little car with smoke. I opened my sliding window and the left shoulder of my denim shirt turned dark from the drizzle. Annie reached round to the back seat and grabbed two bottles of Double Diamond which we quickly swigged. John Peel's velvety voice on the radio murmured in the back ground.

Annie was an only child and was constantly fighting with her father. She was a talented artist and experimented with dark inks and bright acrylics. Her father thought art was a complete waste of time and that she should ditch her lefty, hippie course and pursue a proper degree.

Annie wore a simple minidress and sneakers; her hair was tied in a ponytail with a white ribbon. She slipped off her sneakers and put her feet up on the olive dashboard either side of the steering wheel, her dress rode high up her thighs.

The cigarette glowed brightly as she took a drag and slowly exhaled the smoke through her nose. She stared wistfully through the windscreen, the drizzle turned to rain and the drops thrummed lightly on the roof. The windscreen started to mist up and she wiped it with her sleeve,

"Bloody English weather!"

Annie exhaled and stubbed out the cigarette, the embers in the ashtray glowed in the twilight. She finished her beer, put the empty bottle behind my seat and turned towards me.

It happened just like that. Without a word, she cupped my head in her hand and leaned over to kiss me. Our lips met and I wasn't sure what to do, so I followed her lead, but It wasn't quite what I expected. The intimacy of the kiss was arousing, the texture of her lips on mine induced a frisson of pleasant sensation, but not the explosion of pure passion I was expecting, after reading Playboy or watching too many romantic films.

I felt her tongue push into my mouth and move in and out. 'Was this a metaphor for shagging?' I wondered, 'was I supposed to suck it or return the favour?' I gently prised her lips apart with the tip of my tongue and entwined it with hers. It was like a sack of ferrets fighting in a beery ashtray.

Slightly alarmed and bewildered I stared at the windscreen. She whispered sultrily,

"Close your eyes"

I obeyed.

Annie kissed me harder, moved closer and put her hand on my leg, tenderly stroking my thigh. How she managed to move closer in that confined space with her legs either side of the steering wheel, I have no idea, she must have been a contortionist. I wanted to stroke her as well, but I couldn't find her thigh in the jumble of limbs and clothing. She took her hand off my thigh and started to unbuckle my belt. 'This is interesting' I thought. I was wearing my tight jeans and in the confined space she was having difficulty in unzipping them. I shifted up and down trying to help her and hit my head on the roof.

With a sigh, Annie moved away from me into her seat. I opened my eyes and saw in the light from the radio, that her legs were still either side of the steering wheel and her dress had ridden up to her waist.

I unzipped my fly, shuffled down my jeans and underwear and turned towards her, placing my hand on the inside of her thigh. She kissed me passionately, and her breathing quickened as I slowly caressed her. She stopped kissing me and reached behind her back and un zipped her dress. She slowly pulled it over her shoulders and sat back wearing only a voluminous white bra. I wanted to free her enormous freckle free breasts, but I didn't know how. I scrabbled at the back of the bra. Annie sighed again and unfastened the clasp at the front. Unleashed, they were humongous, smooth and silky. I buried my face in them.

The rain pounded on the roof of the van.

Annie fondled me. She tugged me towards her, frantically I rolled over in her direction and caught my scrotum in the handbrake. Gingerly I extricated myself and tried again. I was half astride her with her breasts squashed against my chest and one of my legs sticking out of the sliding window, when my bum became stuck under the steering wheel. I tugged myself free while the horn blared. Annie unwound her legs and tried to straddle me, but there wasn't any space for her feet and the gear lever looked positively dangerous.

Eventually we admitted defeat and picked up another beer.

Two weeks later I started my course with BOAC at Cranebank.

BOAC was the British state-owned airline created by the merger of Imperial Airways and British Airways Ltd. in 1939. It operated VC10s and 707s on international flights out of

London Heathrow. BEA operated European flights from Heathrow.

I spent four months in the classroom learning about the VC10. It was so thorough that I'm sure I could have built one myself by the end of the course. I somehow passed the final exam, but before I could be let loose on the unsuspecting public, I had to learn to fly the aeroplane itself. Keir, Chase, a few other Cadets and I went to Shannon to learn how.

'The Old Ground Hotel' was in Ennis, the County Town of Clare, by the banks of the River Fergus in the west of Ireland. It backed onto a narrow medieval street in the centre of town.

We checked in, and the receptionist told us that the crew would be in 'The Poet's Corner' later that evening.

With some trepidation we pushed through the swing doors into the smoke-filled bar. The walls were panelled with dark mahogany, and a wooden cubicle with an ornately carved pediment stood opposite two green leather-buttoned ottomans. Oak Windsor chairs and tables were scattered on the scuffed, planked wooden floor and dim tiffany lights hung from the stuccoed ceiling. Two Captains were holding court at the bar.

We made our introductions.

One of the Captains shook my hand and introduced himself.

"Les Owens."

He looked me up and down.

"I hear your father was in the RAF?"

"Yes sir" I replied, "Bomber Command. He was shot down in 1942. POW."

"Bad show." He replied, swirling his gin and tonic, "I was lucky. 617 squadron, you know, The Dam Busters, and all that."

I nodded. I couldn't imagine him on that famous bombing raid. He didn't look like a hero. He was short with receding brown hair which accentuated his protruding ears and square jaw. He turned slightly to stub out his cigarette and I noticed a swathe of medal ribbons on the left breast of his uniform jacket. I recognised a DFC and a DSO. His penetrating eyes continued to stare at me as he blew out the last of his smoke.

"OK, Fairdale you can fly with me along with," he looked at a notepad lying on the bar and scratched his long nose with the end of a pencil, "along with Kelly, Williams, Phillips and Brunt."

He folded the notepad, put it in his inside pocket and pointed with his pencil towards two men chatting over a pint.

This is Ed Edwards our Engineer and First Officer Nigel Gillespie. They will be helping me."

We said our hellos.

Ed was rotund, with a round beaming, moustached face and circular wire framed glasses. When he spoke, he thrust his dimpled chin forward and peered over his thin greying moustache. He fidgeted with a beer mat while lightly bouncing on his toes.

Nigel was tall, dark haired and reserved. He had an elongated, narrow face with prominent chin and bags under his eyes. He had medal ribbons on his jacket so he must have served in the war. He didn't look at me when I shook his hand and seemed awkward and uneasy.

"Righty-oh, it's late, I'm off for a kip," said Les. "Pickup will be at 6 am sharp in the lobby. I'll brief you lot at the airport."

With that, he turned and marched out.

The atmosphere palpably lightened and I ordered a round of drinks.

Ed took a gulp of beer, wiping his moustache on his sleeve.

"You'll be all right," he said in a high-pitched voice looking at me, "you're RAF, you'll be OK."

"He's got a name as a chopper," he said menacingly to the others, "so be careful. He's bonkers and re-enacts the raid every time he comes back to Shannon. Flying under the radar, pretending to bomb the tower and all that sort of stuff."

He took another swig. He nodded towards a couple of men seated at a table in the shadowy corner of the bar.

"You see those two? That's Robert Mitchum and Leo McKern. They've been filming 'Ryan's Daughter' round here for ages. The producer got really pissed off when he was filming a First World War love scene on the beach and Les' VC10 shot past in the background at 50 feet!"

He dissolved into a fit of girlish giggles, finished his beer and strolled off to bed.

A group of people including a blonde girl, who looked like Sarah Miles, crowded round Robert Mitchum's table laughing and talking. The barmaid approached them and timidly asked for an autograph.

Nigel sat back, took a drag on his fag and flicked the ash on the floor.

"He's a queer one, that Ed," he commented with a Geordie drawl, "he's known as 'Electric Ed'. Mad as a box of frogs. We drove to the Cliffs of Moher the other day and he stood on the edge with his arms out and leaned right over, into the wind. Nuts!"

He made a circular motion with his finger pointing at his head and rolled his eyes.

"Yesterday we were doing circuits and the landing gear didn't indicate down, so Ed went down into the lower hold, opened the floor hatch and poked his head out to have a look. We were at 2,000ft doing 200 knots for God's sake!"

He paused.

"Welcome to the BOAC circus."

The VC10 had the most spacious cockpit or flight deck of any modern airliner. The Captain sat in the left front seat, the co-pilot in the front right, the Engineer behind him at his panel on the right and the navigator had a table facing backwards at the rear of the flight deck. The cockpit was large enough for a crew toilet cubicle and a teleprinter was installed under the navigator's desk.

Modern jet aircraft are designed to fly at speeds approaching the sound barrier. The VC10 cruised at 86% of the speed of sound, or Mach .86 with a maximum of M.93. It was necessary to demonstrate that no undesirable flight characteristics occurred close to the speed limit. Keir was at the controls with Les in the late afternoon when the high-speed run commenced. I sat in the cabin looking out of the window at the wing. The aircraft started to buffet gently as the speed increased. In the evening haze a small shock-wave appeared at the front of the wing, which slowly moved backwards as the buffeting increased in intensity. We shook violently as the shock-wave reached the trailing edge of the wing.

We had gone supersonic!

A small amount of yaw in flight will cause the aircraft to roll. The VC10 had a divergent Dutch roll which meant that if the roll was unchecked it would increase in amplitude until eventually, the aircraft would turn upside down. The VC10 was fitted with automatic yaw dampers to stabilise the aircraft, but we had to learn how to control the Dutch roll without them. The demonstration allowed for a maximum bank angle of 45 degrees.

Les instructed me to go to the rear of the aircraft and view the enormous T tail through the rear, roof-mounted inspection 'scope. He turned the dampers off, kicked the rudder and the oscillations began. The rolls slowly increased to over 110 degrees and the massive tail twisted with each roll, as the rudder slammed from side to side. It was hard to ignore the enormous stresses that the tail was being subjected to.

In the event of a pressurisation failure we had to demonstrate proficiency in descending the aircraft rapidly to a lower level from high altitude. We closed the throttles, extended the speed brakes and descended the aircraft at its maximum speed to 10,000ft. The most comfortable way to commence the dive was to bank the aeroplane first, but of course Les didn't consider that. Ralph Brunt was at the controls with Les when he started his emergency descent. I was having a crap in the loo when Ralph pushed the nose down hard into the dive. I flew off the crapper and hit my head on the ceiling, followed by two steaming, turds.

And so, it was, towards the end of my course in Shannon, that Les Owens tried to kill me.

I was certain we were going to die. Les suddenly slammed the throttles fully forward.

With a roar from the four Conway jets, Les pulled back hard on the stick. I opened my eyes as the G force pushed me into my seat and we pitched up violently. I could make out the top of the cliff above us, we were very close to the rock face and seagulls scattered frantically in all directions. Our speed dropped rapidly, and the aircraft started to buffet with an impending stall as we shot over the rim with just a few feet to spare. We accelerated in the valley behind the cliff, and with a triumphant look on his face, Les turned towards Shannon.

Downwind for landing, Les shut down three engines and we landed with just one operating.

The engine was smoking as we climbed down the steps and walked across the tarmac.

Les informed us that, apart from Brunt, we had all passed.

I was now a fully qualified Second Officer.

Poor John Bishop died in an air crash at Lomé. Air Togo bought a VC10 to operate a daily flight to Paris using BOAC seconded pilots. For some reason, they flew into the ground 13 miles short of the runway killing everyone on board.

What a pity.

John was a square jawed, softly spoken gentle giant who would be sorely missed.

I returned to Ascot with my dark blue double-breasted uniform with one thick, proud gold stripe on the sleeve.

I picked up Annie, we had a few celebratory drinks in the 'Stag', and I drove Annie home to Hobbit House. We chatted in the car for a while before she asked me if I would like to come in for another drink. I hesitated. I couldn't imagine we would have any privacy in the miniscule cottage, but when she told me that she slept in a shed in the garden, I quickly agreed.

Annie, the art student, was a bit of a Hippy. The walls of her cabin were painted in psychedelic colours and posters of pop bands were pasted on the ceiling. Oversized beaded cushions lay on the floor and strings of small bells hung on the back of the door. A king-sized bed dominated the room, and a curtain of tassels led to a small bathroom.

Annie locked the door and turned on the transistor. She paused to light some candles and joss-sticks and the sickly-sweet smell soon filled the room. She took off her suede afghan jacket and hung it on the back of the door. She sat on the bed and carefully tied her hair with a rubber band, then rolled over and switched off the lights.

'Leaving on a Jet Plane' drifted from the radio as Annie took off her boots and slowly started to undress. In the dim light she stood facing me with her mouth slightly open and her eyes fixed on mine. Annie watched my reaction as she reached behind her back and unzipped her dress. Looking at me with wide eyes, she steadily pulled her dress up from the middle and the hem rose to her waist. She paused and opened her legs a little.

I was mesmerised.

Crossing her hands, Annie gradually pulled the dress over her shoulders and dropped it on the floor. She undid her bra and let it slide from her shoulders. She stood completely naked for a while with her arms by her side, letting me look at her. She lifted the covers and calmly climbed into bed. She watched me as I undressed in front of her. Her eyes widened when she saw how excited I was.

I crawled into bed alongside her and we embraced at once. It was wonderful to feel her naked body against mine, to stroke the smooth skin of her neck, to feel her lips on mine. We explored each other gently, unhurriedly. Our legs entwined, and I felt her excitement as she moved herself against my thigh. Rapid flutters of breath caressed my neck as she buried her head in my shoulder.

We made love in the candlelight, our pavane gently gaining tempo until fulminating in a crescendo of passion.

We lay breathless and clasped each other closely as the joss sticks sputtered and died.

BOAC

I walked across the tarmac at Heathrow towards the VC10 which towered over me in the bright apron lights. The royal blue livery swept purposefully towards the massive tail where, barely visible in the late-night mist, the gold 'Speedbird' flash was emblazoned on the fin. The words 'BOAC' and 'CUNARD' in gold shone brightly in the harsh light.

I paused in awe, it looked so large, foreboding and overwhelming. I glanced at my single, Second Officer stripe on my sleeve, I was 19 and about to fly passengers for the very first time

I had come a long way in two years.

My first flight was to Lagos and Les Owens was the Captain. We had a cabin crew of three stewards and three stewardesses. The stewardesses wore dark blue knee-length pencil skirts with short tapered jackets and open necked white blouses. The stewards had dark blue double-breasted uniforms with thin stripes on the sleeves to denote rank. The men wore caps and the girls forage caps.

The Biafran War had ended but Nigeria was on high alert. The secession of the Biafran State failed, which resulted in widespread suffering and starvation among Igbos. Security was tight at Lagos airport and armed, emerald-green uniformed soldiers guarded our aircraft. An officer with a bright red belt and cravat rifled through my suitcase in the customs hall, he wore dark sunglasses, a pistol and a sneer on his jet-black face. Two armed soldiers escorted us to the hotel in our minibus.

The Ikeja Arms Hotel in Lagos had chocolate brown carpet covering the walls. The floor was deep red clay tiles and the ceiling was a dirty yellow colour. Loose wires hung from tarnished brass electrical fittings and the grimy white tiles in the bathroom were cracked and stained. I drew the thick hessian curtains. Outside, the airless, threatening sky was heavy with rain. The swaying fan creaked overhead, the room smelled musty and damp.

I went down to the swimming pool. The sun was fierce and the air extremely humid. Two of our girls were sunbathing but didn't want to be bothered with a 'junior-jet' like me. I felt so young and inadequate.

The retirement age in BOAC was 50 years old. Pilots were recruited from the RAF after the War and most would soon retire. There was a considerable age difference between the Captains and co-pilots, and consequently, there was a yawning social disconnect. Captains were from a different generation. A generation which saw the horrors of War, privation and destruction. A generation of rigid mores and disciplined inflexibility. Most Captains had difficulty in accepting that the soft, long-haired, 19-year-old liberal Hippy sitting in the right-hand seat could actually be a pilot.

We returned to London via Kano. I was co-pilot from Kano to London and my duty was to do an external pre-flight inspection of the aeroplane. I was walking round the aircraft on the apron in Kano when I heard a shout. The refueller ran from the plane with an armed soldier chasing him. The soldier shot him in the back from almost point-blank range, just like that. He lay on the on the ground moaning and tried to crawl away. The soldier walked up to him and shot him in the head. I was horrified, and I stupidly shouted.

"What the hell did you do that for?"

The solider turned and pointed his rifle at me and snarled.

"He am Igbo. Dey is filth!" and spat on the ground.

I nearly shat myself, put my hands up, shut my mouth and backed off ignominiously. I reported it to the Captain, but he told me to forget it, there was nothing we could do, this was Nigeria, and this was a consequence of war.

I was relieved to be on our way home.

At 5,000ft, climbing out of Kano, Les got out of his seat and went back to first-class to eat his dinner. He returned a few moments later and indignantly announced that the first-class was full, and that he was going to have a sleep in the crew toilet. He took off his jacket and tie, lit a cigarette, and with a shrug, disappeared into the WC on the flight deck.

Chris, the First Officer, sat in Les' seat.

We were climbing through 24,000ft when the aircraft lurched, the engine fire warning bell sounded, and red lights flashed.

I called for the Engine Fire checklist.

A few seconds later the fire extinguished, the bell stopped ringing and relative calm returned to the flight deck.

We waited for Les to come rushing out of the loo, he must have heard it, he must have felt the aircraft yaw. But Les didn't appear.

We waited anxiously but nothing happened, and we continued our merry way towards London on three engines.

Jeff, the Engineer, motored his seat forward and leaned over the centre console and said.

"I think we'd better write him a note."

I agreed. I tore the corner off the flight plan and scribbled:

'Dear sir, we've lost an engine' and handed it to the Engineer.

Jeff motored his seat back and carefully pushed the note under the door of the toilet.

It disappeared, we waited with bated breath and still nothing happened.

We looked at each other, mystified.

Then, slowly, the same piece of paper was pushed back out from under the loo door. Jeff picked it up, unfolded it and written on the other side was.

'Well you'd better bloody-well find it then!'

Les finally emerged a couple of hours later and we continued without further incident to London.

I was fed up with living at home, but I couldn't afford to rent anywhere. A deduction was made every month to cover the cost of my training at Hamble and, after taxes and all deductions, I received the grand sum of £92 three shillings and five pence each month. I could expect flying pay once I started flying regularly, so my situation would improve, but until then I was stuck at home.

Annie's parents were away, and I wanted to stay with her, but my parents disapproved, and it wasn't worth arguing. I was still a child in many ways I suppose, but I worked in an adult world. I was old enough to fly 200 people to New York, but I wasn't old enough to have a drink when I get there.

I was extremely jealous of Keir, although I didn't want him to know.

Keir had saved enough money to buy a plot of land in Weybridge and he was going to build a house.

Keir met an old couple who owned a little wooden summer cabin on the River Thames near Weybridge. They were considering selling it as it was too expensive for them to maintain. Keir told them he was getting married and that their wonderful home would be a perfect place to raise a family. Teary eyed and sentimental they sold it to him.

He was going to knock it down and he and his father were planning to build a bachelor pad in its place.

How I envied Keir's close relationship with his father.

I returned from a Singapore trip with 'Electric Ed.'

On the approach to Changi, the Captain knocked out his pipe in the wastepaper bin and it burst into flames. I politely pointed out the conflagration by his elbow, and he calmly replied.

"Oh Shit! Not again."

"Fire Checklist, number one wastepaper bin!" he announced.

He poured his tea into the bin and we continued the approach with steam and flakes of ash filling the cockpit.

'Electric Ed' bought some expensive tropical fish in Singapore and connected their little glass tank to the aircrew oxygen system for the long flight to Bahrain.

Ed was obsessed with dirt and dust. The cockpit was difficult to keep clean and the cleaners were reluctant to come onto the flight deck for fear of damaging something.

Ed designed a cockpit vacuum cleaner.

He bought a length of flexible pipe which was the same diameter as the sextant housing, and he jury rigged a temporary coupling for the sextant port. The sextant port was an airlock in the roof of the cockpit through which the sextant was inserted during astro-navigation.

It was a calm clear starry night. The full moon shone on the Bay of Bengal, casting long shadows from scattered candy floss clouds, thousands of feet below.

Ed eased himself and his oversized stomach out of his seat and reached up to the sextant port to connect his Heath-Robinson contraption. The pressure difference between inside the aircraft and outside was 8-9 psi. and the diameter of the pipe was about two inches. Ed calculated that the hose would have suction of about 25 psi, but he didn't realise that that was about ten times the suction of a domestic vacuum cleaner. He paused and adjusted his glasses before switching it on.

He pulled the lever to open the port.

A whoosh filled the cockpit and the open end of the pipe snapped up into the air. It flailed about like an indignant writhing snake and sucked up everything in its path. Pages from Ed's technical log disappeared down the twisting tube, charts were plucked from the centre console and it devoured the stilton from the cheeseboard. There was a sudden silence as it digested the Captain's hat and, with a gulping belch, disgorged the tattered titfer into the void.

Ed tried in vain to shut the port, but the flimsy pipe started to ingest itself, and with a farting spasm, the tube disappeared up its own orifice. Still attached to the vent, the pipe beat loudly on the first-class roof until it disintegrated somewhere over Madras.

The Captain wasn't happy.

We landed in Bahrain and to Ed's dismay his tropical fish were bloated and floating upside down. His over oxygenated ocellated cardinalfish had drained the crew oxygen tank. We were delayed two days waiting for a replacement to be flown from London.

The Captain was apoplectic.

Alcohol was forbidden in Bahrain, but the authorities turned a blind eye to a small crew bar tucked away in the bowels of the 'Gulf Hotel'. Ed waddled up to the bar, threw his voluminous stomach on the bar, and demanded.

"Fill 'er up"

A couple of rich Bahrainis in the bar invited the crew to a beach house for a party. We jumped in the pool naked and frolicked in the water. As we were getting dressed one of the stewards said he thought he saw and underwater camera.

I wondered if our very own blue movie would be for sale in the souk?

It was only a few years since shipping lines scaled back their passenger operations. Flying was expensive, noisy, uncomfortable and fraught with danger, but passenger numbers were rising. Surprisingly, travel by air was still seen as romantic and exclusive. Our passengers tended to be Royalty, movie stars or government officials. The British Empire was crumbling, and BOAC was tasked with operating to flash points throughout the Empire and beyond. We were often affected by global events either directly or indirectly.

I operated a Hajj charter flight from Karachi to Jeddah. It is a religious duty for Muslims to make the pilgrimage at least once in a lifetime. Poorer Muslims spend a lifetime saving for the trip and the flight to Jeddah was often the first time that they have ever been anywhere near an aeroplane. It was always chaotic in the cabin, they ignored the cabin signs, and I have heard stories of primus stoves being lit in the aisles to cook lunch.

During the cruise the chief steward reported that someone had crapped in the sink in one of the loos, and that the crew weren't going to clear it up. We told him to lock the door and I wrote in the technical defect log.

'Sink used as arsenal.'

It now became the responsibility of the ground engineers to sort it out on our arrival in Jeddah.

On the return sector to Karachi, the engineer had signed off the defect in the log by writing.

'Rectumfied'

I flew over Da Nang in Vietnam on the way to Hong Kong from Delhi as the USA invaded Cambodia. In the distance to the north west, flashes from explosions lit the night sky with a flickering pale-yellow hue. It was disturbing to be in my seat drinking a cup of tea, while 35,000ft below, young men of my age were dying for a country, and a cause most of them knew nothing about.

Flying was structured, rule-based and reasonably predictable. I couldn't say the same about the stewardesses and I still wasn't sure how to approach them. Perhaps it was my innate shyness, over-eagerness or lack of experience, but I didn't feel accepted or welcomed by them. I was on the outside looking in. I thought that by then I would be fighting them off, but unfortunately, I was more likely to be chased by the stewards.

Tabasco da Gama the Red-Hot Navigator

My Commercial Pilots Licence was blue. It was a small booklet about six inches by four inches and contained my medical certificate, radio licences and aircraft and instrument ratings. Captains had an Airline Transport Pilots Licence which was green. The Flight Engineers licence was brown, and the Navigators licence was red.

I now had blue and red licences.

The navigation course was hard, but interesting. We studied spherical geometry, star recognition, meteorology and astronomy.

We navigated the aeroplane flying at 600 knots using a thousand-year-old technique developed for boats sailing at 10 knots. The new Boeing 747 was going to have an inertial system which would dispense the need for navigators, but I doubted that the VC10 would be retrofitted.

Navigating by the stars was simple in principle but not necessarily in practice. The elevation of three equally spaced stars was measured by a periscopic sextant inserted through the roof of the fuselage at the rear of the flight deck. The sextant was like a mini submarine periscope with two handles which could be rotated to look for the stars. The position of the aircraft was on a line drawn on the chart calculated from the elevation of a star. The position lines from the two other stars were plotted on the chart, and where the lines intersected denoted one's position. However, depending on the accuracy of the calculations and angle measurement, the lines rarely crossed at the same point. The resulting triangle was known as a 'cocked hat', the centre of which was assumed to be the aircraft's location.

Regrettably my cocked hats often seemed to be the size of Africa.

The star-shot calculations were comprehensive and only three three-star fixes could be made every hour which meant, at best, we had some idea of where we were 200 miles ago.

Astro-navigation was time consuming, and even experienced navigators only had one or two minutes every twenty minutes to relax, eat or go to the loo. Once the actual shooting of the stars commenced, each star was 'shot' for two minutes without break and could not be interrupted.

When available, other navigational aids were used as well such as Loran, long range radio beacons and sometimes radar. Astro was consistently reliable so long as we were clear of cloud. If the sky was obscured, we used dead-reckoning to calculate our progress, applying forecast winds and temperatures as a best guess scenario. The jet streams over the Pacific had been observed at up to 300 knots, so it wouldn't take much of change in windspeed or direction to throw us far off course. During the day it was possible to use bright stars, planets, the Sun and the Moon for fixes.

With my red licence I was now qualified to fly across the Atlantic and The Pacific. The world was at my feet.

The Atlantic routes were very popular because the meal allowances were high, the destinations were civilised, and the trips were short. They were flown by the senior old buffers who didn't like the Fuzzy-Wuzzies of Africa or the Chinks of Asia, they didn't like Indian food and they didn't like operating into airfields with minimal navigational aids and safety equipment. The Captains who plied the Atlantic were known as the Atlantic Barons, they could be bullies, arrogant and self-important.

I apprehensively introduced myself to my first Atlantic Baron in the ops centre before my inaugural New York trip. Captain James Salmon was of average height with short salt and pepper hair and shifty eyes. He sported an RAF handlebar moustache above his mean thin-lipped mouth and his face was sallow and pitted with little acne scars. He didn't introduce himself and his handshake was limp and cold; perhaps that's why he was known as Jimmy the Fish.

The operations room was bisected by a lengthy, wide counter. Fluorescent lighting illuminated the room in a ghostly pale glare, bookshelves lined the walls and flight bags piled on top of each other in the corners.

Telephones rang and teleprinters chattered as the Duty Officer approached with our flight plan. Jimmy pored over the papers on the counter, carefully turning them over and making notes with his pen. A front was forecast mid-Atlantic and we could expect thunderstorms for our arrival in New York. We had 122 passengers and five tonnes of diplomatic mail, but otherwise all was in order. Jimmy decided how much fuel he wanted, picked up the paperwork and thrust it at me without looking. He grabbed his briefcase, put on his cap and strode out of the door. I took a sextant from the rack, signed for the ship's papers, and I followed them down the corridor. Jimmy turned to the First Officer, Johnathan and said gruffly.

"Mister Frazier, tell mister Fairdale to get his hair cut."

We were ready to start the engines when the first-class stewardess came onto the flight deck to introduce herself. She was about 30, feisty, and all bosom and hair. Her tight white blouse and blue pencil skirt accentuated her curves, and her blue forage cap was dwarfed by the back-combed, lacquered hay-stack of blonde hair.

"I hear we have a new Junior-Jet up here?" she purred, looking straight at me.

I haltingly tried to explain that I wasn't exactly new, but she brushed that aside and continued.

"Well, we had better give you a good time in New York then." She winked and pinched my cheek. I blushed as she turned to address the front seats.

"I'm Joan, gentlemen. If there's anything you need just call me." With that, she blew me a kiss, and walked out.

As soon as we were airborne, I started the preparations for my first fix which was beyond the west coast of Ireland, at 15 degrees west. I pulled the navigation table out, spread a plotting chart and sharpened my pencils. I switched on the teleprinter below my desk, turned on the Loran oscilloscope and opened the Air Almanac at the appropriate page. The aircraft master clock was set by observing the sun and Johnathan kindly offered to set the sextant up while I did the calculations. When the calculations were complete, I squinted into the eye-piece of the sextant to take a shot of the sun. I checked for parallax errors by shooting the sun again with my other eye.

I corrected the clocks and started to work out the calculations for my first fix. Joan barged onto the flight deck.

"Hey, JJ" she said, "would you mind having a look at a seat at the back of first-class, it's having trouble reclining?"

The Fish gave me permission to leave the flight deck, and I went aft through the curtains into first-class. The passengers were eating canapes, drinking champagne and smoking. I smiled as I walked through the curtain, and to my surprise everyone smiled back. Someone sniggered, and soon the whole of first-class was laughing or giggling. I felt very confused, and luckily Joan intercepted me to say that the seat had fixed itself, so I wasn't needed after all. Bright red, I scampered back to the flight deck and went to the WC for a nervous pee. I looked in the mirror and to my horror, I saw that I had two huge black panda eyes. I scrubbed my face, and it dawned on me. That bastard Johnathan had smeared the sextant eye-piece with black boot polish. I tip-toed back into the flight deck. Joan stood smiling at me with her hands on her hips and they all burst into laughter. Embarrassed, I sat down at my desk. It's the first time The Fish was known to do anything other than scowl.

I took my first astro shot over the Atlantic. I kept the tiny pinpoint of Jupiter in the crosshairs of the periscope and pressed the collimator button while keeping the sextant level with the bubble of a tiny inbuilt spirit-level. Each reading was averaged over two minutes and if interrupted the fix would be ruined

I heard the flight deck door open and I smelled Joan's perfume. She came up behind and tried to distract me by nuzzling my neck, breathing in my ear and pressing her tits into my back.

Jupiter started to wobble, but I doggedly tracked it.

Unphased by my lack of reaction, Joan ran her hands down my chest and started to tug at the zip of my fly. She slipped her cold hand into my underwear.

Jupiter made circles in the viewfinder and the collimator whirred wildly as I tried to keep track. I persevered, but Joan didn't. With a hard squeeze of my balls Joan gave up, withdrew her hand and walked out. I finished my shot and plotted our position.

My cocked hat was enormous; it wasn't the only cock that was.

She was so wild. I had never met a stewardess like that before and it's a pity I didn't fancy her. I decided in future if I liked the look of the first-class stewardess, I would set up the periscope and pretend to take a fix even if it wasn't a navigation sector. I could live in hope.

We drove to the Berkshire Hotel on 52nd Street in a violent thunderstorm. The roads were in an appalling state of disrepair and the bus lurched and crashed over potholes and the uneven tarmac. It was early evening New York time, but I was very tired. The traffic was heavy, and as we slowly descended from Jackson Heights towards the Midtown Tunnel, the city appeared across the East River. A sunburst from the setting sun appeared behind the purple-black thunderstorm towering over the city, radiating outwards in a mimicry of the Statue of Liberty. Flashes of incandescent lightning illuminated the labyrinth of rectangular skyscrapers. It was raining heavily as we entered the Midtown tunnel.

The city was a cacophony of noise and motion. Blaring yellow and black cabs crashed over steaming raised manhole covers, people scurried on the sidewalks, lights flashed, and sirens wailed mournfully. We dropped the cabin crew off at the Lexington Hotel and arrived at the Berkshire.

We rode the elevator up to our rooms and Johnathan suggested that we meet up in his room for a drink.

Twenty minutes later, I knocked on Johnathan's door bringing with me two cans of beer. Jimmy and the Engineer lounged in chairs and Johnathan perched on the edge of the bed. The room was stuffy from smoke and noisy from the traffic outside. On the bedside table stood three nearly empty half-bottles of spirits. The conversation was about the War and the stories got taller the more they drank. I was ignored but when everyone got up to leave, Johnathan said to me in a slightly slurred voice.

"Meet in the lobby at midday? We'll have a quick drink to help us sleep before our flight back."

"You'll probably wake up very early. If you do, check out the crew library," he continued.

I looked a bit puzzled.

"Ah yes, of course. Open the ventilation grille in your wardrobe and you'll find dirty books in the ducting. That'll keep you amused," he laughed, "goodnight."

I went to my room and even though I was dog-tired, I decided to have a look at the library. It was easy to pull the grille off, and with mounting curiosity, I reached inside and pulled out a well-worn book. It seemed familiar and I slowly turned it over. It was a VC10 Flight Manual! Some wag had removed the naughty stuff and substituted it with that!

It was however a sure-fire way to send me to sleep.

I met Johnathan and the others in the lobby, and even though it was a hot muggy day, I wore my suit and tie. We walked a few blocks to McCanns Irish Pub.

I asked Johnathan a question as I sipped my second pint of beer.

"What are the rules about drinking and flying?"

Johnathan put down his glass, took a drag on his fag, and looked at me with a twinkle in his eye.

"Hm. I'm not sure, but I think there's an eight in there somewhere. It's either one pint eight hours before a flight, eight pints one hour before a flight, or any alcohol within eight feet of the aeroplane."

Smiling, he picked up his glass and finished his beer.

By the time we reached London The Fish had not said one word to me throughout the whole trip.

Churchill has a lot to answer for.

The Ottomans ruled Palestine peacefully for 400 years until they were kicked out by the British at the end of World War I. A Palestinian state was defined by the Balfour Treaty of 1917 but in 1922, as Colonial Secretary, Churchill was instrumental in the establishment of a Jewish state west of the River Jordan. During the Second World War many Jews escaped persecution in Germany by fleeing to the nascent Israel. The British left Palestine in 1948 and the fledgling state of Israel declared independence. A war quickly ensued, and the vastly outnumbered Israelis defeated their Arab neighbours and annexed 60% more land than had been agreed in 1947. 700.000 Palestinians were displaced into Jordan and the Jordanian controlled West Bank

The Palestinians were homeless and a little more than pissed-off.

In 1964 the PLO was formed with the sole intention of recapturing their stolen land. They swiftly resorted to terror tactics to achieve their aims.

A series of terror attacks and border disputes led to the six-day war of 1967. Israel routed the Egyptians, Jordanians and Syrians and took control of the West Bank and Gaza.

The Palestinians were now angrier than a nest of wasps.

A BOAC VC10, en route from Bombay to London, was hijacked by the Popular Front for the Liberation of Palestine and blown up in the desert at Dawson's Field in Jordan. Luckily no-one was killed, but as hijackings were easy, attention-grabbing and fashionable, I sensed there would be more to come.

I wiped away the condensation from the window in my bedroom at Ascot. Autumn was on its way, it was getting cooler, and I could see the squirrels laboriously burying nuts for the winter. A murmuration of starlings performed their aerial ballet in the twilight. A billowing, nebulous, chiffon scarf of birds, wheeled, swooped, twisted and turned in perfect harmony, their clamorous screeching ebbed and flowed with each turn. The 'season of mists and mellow fruitfulness' was upon us, but the view from my window wouldn't change much as the pine trees and rhododendrons were deciduous. The windows in my bedroom were ill-fitting, the icy drafts froze on the inside of the glass and the ancient central heating struggled to cope. I didn't like the cold.

Keir, Chase, Ben and I occasionally played rugby for a local rugby club, it was a good excuse for keeping fit and having a few bevvies. Flying permitting, we went to training as often as we could. Chase was a good player and tackling him was like trying to stop a Sherman tank. Keir liked to call himself 'snake hips', but in my view, he was effete and easy to catch. The second team Captain, Norman, was a mountain of a man, he was all brawn and no brain but made a very effective human battering ram. He was quite handsome, and his rugged appearance was emphasised by a chiselled chin, steel blue eyes and broken nose. He married a Latvian girl ten years his junior. Sofija was a stunning brunette with long straight hair, legs up to her arm pits and flirty bottomless green eyes. Some unscrupulous cards suggested that Norman found her in the personal ads of Titbits, but whatever, they seemed to get on very well. Norman was a builder and Keir and I helped him renovate the rugby club house. We got to know them well and they regularly joined us at the Stag and Hounds.

Annie became very clingy and jealous. Maybe it was because I was more confident with women, and I was aware that women were attracted to me. It was a powerful feeling.

Jenny was the daughter of a Shell executive who lived in Wokingham. She had been giving me the eye, and I increasingly wondered what it would be like to be with another woman. It excited me but worried me in equal doses. I liked Annie, but I felt I was too young for a long-term relationship. Ben had been with Alice ever since he left Hamble. They would probably get married and Ben might spend the rest of his life wondering what other girls were like.

I didn't want that.

I cared about Annie, and I didn't want to hurt her, so why was I tempted by Jenny? I didn't know. Perhaps it was just curiosity? I considered taking Jenny out just to see what it was like. Would my conscience let me do that I wondered?

The gang met up at The Stag and Jenny was there. She was curvaceous with mid length blonde hair, full lips and small moles dotted her rosy cheeks. She looked at me suggestively. I was sure I was getting the green light. She was listening to Keir who stood by the bar holding court with a beer in hand, telling an interesting story in his gentle Irish brogue.

Keir had been called out at short notice to fly the most coveted trip on our route network. London to LA, across The Pacific to Honolulu and Fiji, onwards to Australia, and return by the same route. It was coveted for many reasons, the allowances were sky high, it was a very sociable and a long duration payment was made. The downside was that for navigation, it was extremely challenging. The upper winds were always very strong and unpredictable, land-based radio beacons were virtually non-existent, thunderstorms often obscured the sky, and after 4,000 miles of open ocean, a couple of degrees of error could cause the aeroplane to miss an island destination by hundreds of miles. I assumed Keir was called out to cover someone more senior who called in sick.

Perhaps he had gone sick because the Captain was none other than my nemesis, Jimmy the Fish.

Jimmy only spoke to Keir via the First Officer. He gave him a continuously hard time and grumbled or shouted about any minor infraction. By the time they left Fiji, on the way home, Keir had had enough, and Jimmy still hadn't uttered a single word to him.

Climbing out of 5,000ft, Jimmy carefully took off his white gloves, stubbed out his cigarette and walked to the back of the flight deck. He put his coffee cup on Keir's desk, adjusted his tie in the mirror on the back of the flight deck door and proceeded towards the first-class for his meal. A few moments later the door burst open and he returned in a foul mood.

"There's only one seat available, and it bloody-well won't recline!" he fumed through his moustache at the First Officer. "I'll have to sit up here instead," he wailed with flecks of indignant spittle spraying all around. He stomped to his seat and sat down heavily with his arms crossed.

As the most junior, and often the youngest, members of the crew, the only time we had any real responsibility was when we navigated. No one else knew exactly where we were, and most of the ancient Captains had absolutely no idea at all. If a heading correction was required after a fix, the new heading was written on a 'heading correction' form and passed to the pilots at the front. Nothing needed to be said.

Normally the correction was a few degrees.

The flight deck was dark except for the red glow of the back-ground lighting as the flight settled down for the long haul to Honolulu. Flickers of lightning flashed in the distance and the whirring of the instruments was barely audible above the hiss of the slipstream. Keir worked at his desk under his map-light while Jimmy sulkily read a newspaper.

Twenty minutes later Keir finished his first fix.

Keir scribbled the new heading on the heading correction form and placed the card on the centre console, between the two pilots. The First Officer was busy trying to call San Francisco on the HF radio, so Jimmy picked up the card and held it under his map-light. It was a heading change of nearly 45 degrees! Astonished, Jimmy turned around, looked at Keir, and begrudgingly altered heading.

Twenty minutes later after another fix, Keir pushed the heading correction form forward with a flourish. It was a similarly large heading correction. Jimmy looked incredulous but said nothing and altered course again.

Keir completed the third fix and presented the enormous heading correction to Jimmy.

Jimmy couldn't contain himself. Flabbergasted, he turned around and with a wild look yelled at Keir.

"Boy! What the bloody hell is going on? Hrumph. What's all this jinking about? Have you any idea where we bloody-well are?" His voice rose menacingly.

The Engineer and First Officer silently turned to look at Keir

"Yes sir" Keir replied, "I'm absolutely sure where we are."

"Damn it, Boy! Why are we flying all over the place?" he replied in exasperation.

"Well sir," continued Keir smugly, "I didn't dare ask you to move your mug which you placed on my chart, so I navigated around it."

Keir had flown more than 200 miles off track to avoid Jimmy's mug.

Keir was ordered to report to the Chief Pilot after the trip.

Life's Rich Tapestry

K eir and I played an away game for the Second XV
against Faringdon. Annie couldn't join us, but a
group of wives and girlfriends cheered us on from the side
lines. It was a cold, overcast dreary day, the pitch was uneven,
and the grass was patchy. I played badly and was sent off for
punching an opponent, but we won anyway. We celebrated
in the bar afterwards, singing smutty rugby songs and drinking
heavily. Soon we were all the worse for wear, including
Norman who was driving me home. Sofija, joined
wholeheartedly in the festivities and was tipsy too. She wore
muddy go-go boots and a miniscule white mini skirt,
underneath a pale suede sheepskin jacket. A purple knitted
scarf was wrapped around her neck and her hair was tucked
under a beret. We huddled in a tight group loudly discussing
our war stories when I felt her hand gently stroke my backside.
I shot her a glance, but she wasn't looking at me. Thankfully
Norman wasn't looking at me either, he was ordering yet
another round at the bar. She stroked me a few more times
before we staggered out to Norman's rusty white Ford
Cortina.

Keir got in the front seat beside Norman while I opened
the rear door for Sofija. She put one foot in the car and slid
her bum onto the seat. She looked straight at me and slowly

opened her legs; she wore no underwear. Nervously I glanced at Norman, closed the door and settled myself in the seat beside her.

Norman peered through the rain spattered windscreen and drove fast; much too fast. We left Faringdon on the way to Wantage and Sofija gently stroked my leg. She leant towards me and rested her head lightly on my shoulder with her legs pressed against mine. Alarmed, I noticed Norman looking at me in the rear-view mirror with a strange expression on his face.

We hit 70mph as Norman tried to negotiate two tightening curves in the road. With a screech of brakes, the tail of the car swung out on the first curve, the car juddered, and the tyres fought for grip. He lost control on the second, we jumped over the grass verge and slammed into a deep ditch on the edge of the road. The ditch was wider than the car, and with our momentum we followed it like a bobsleigh on the Cresta Run. We bounced along, branches, mud and grass were thrown in the air as the ditch narrowed. The wing mirrors were ripped off and we eventually came to a halt, with the engine steaming and the wipers clearing away the debris from the windscreen.

Trapped in the ditch we sat motionless listening to the hissing, ticking engine, and the impotent flapping of the wipers.

"Fuck!" Norman shouted, and hit the steering wheel with his enormous fist. "Are you all OK?"

We were.

"Let's get out of here," he snarled.

We couldn't open the doors. The only way out was through the windows and it was amusing to see Norman's huge bulk squeeze through the tiny window. I was treated to a panoramic view of Sofija's smooth, flawless backside as I helped her out of the window head first, before I escaped as well.

Keir drove me to Weybridge to look at his new pad. It was in a beautiful location on the River Thames and within easy reach of Heathrow. The builders had been hard at work, the foundations had been dug and the brickwork was complete to the top of the ground floor. Keir showed me the plans in the site office

"It's split-level and I've designed the whole house around a bar," he said, proudly, "the rest of it is immaterial and we should be finished by next autumn, with a bit of luck."

"Col, I'm going to call it Lakanooki."

I smiled and studied the plans spread out on the wooden bench, it was going to be large with four or five bedrooms.

"Just imagine," said Keir conspiratorially, "it'll be a right knocking shop! Best of all," he concluded, "I'll be covering most of my costs by charging you lot rent."

We had a couple of pints in 'The Crown' on the way home, and I felt green with envy.

The VC10 was designed for African operations. It performed well on hot and high-altitude airfields and as

Britain still had interests in most of the old colonial countries in east and southern Africa, I was a frequent visitor to Africa. We called ourselves 'The Africa Corps'.

The BOAC Flight Staff Recreational Club had membership of country clubs all over Africa where the vestiges of colonial life lingered precariously on. The sharp smell of floor polish and an air of faded, melancholic opulence pervaded the mahogany panelled rooms of those clubs. Empty tables with crisp, threadbare linen table cloths were set with tarnished silver cutlery, and chipped Staffordshire china. Bored black waiters in white uniforms served afternoon tea followed by gin and tonic sun-downers on the verandas.

South Africa was different, the old colonial lifestyle survived, and Apartheid was the law.

I played squash at the Wanderers Club in Johannesburg. At 6,000ft the ball bounced like crazy and I was knackered. I drank a Campbell's on the veranda overlooking the cricket pitch. It was a pity it wasn't the season for jacarandas, otherwise the horizon would be awash with purple. The smell of rich damp earth wafted towards me as the sun beat down mercilessly in the thin clear air.

I picked up a copy of the Rand Daily Mail.

The pound had at last been decimalised, so it was farewell to shillings, pence, ten bob notes, half-crowns, bobs, tanners, thrupenny bits and farthings.

An agreement was signed by OPEC in Tehran which forced an immediate 55% increase in the price of oil. I wondered how that would affect my career.

Annie was becoming more and more possessive and paranoid. She wouldn't let me out of her sight, it was claustrophobic, and I needed some space. Annie went to a funeral in Scotland and I bumped into Jenny in the Stag. I drove her home and she invited me in for a coffee. Her parents' house was a substantial Victorian pile with green painted windows and gables. Jenny made coffee and brought the cups into the living room. The room was draughty, cold and charmless. A thick, dark brown shag-pile carpet lay on the floor in front of the fireplace flanked by two uncomfortable-looking camelback sofas. The embers of a fire glowed in the wrought-iron fire basket, and a grandfather clock ticked loudly in the hall.

Jenny picked up a log from a wicker basket and threw it on the fire in a burst of crackling, fizzing sparks. She switched off the lights and picked up her coffee.

We sat on the rug, cross-legged, staring into the flames, carefully sipping our steaming coffee. Silhouetted by dancing shadows she placed her cup on the hearth, uncrossed her legs and turned to gently kiss me. I kissed her, cupping her face in my hands. Her freckles darkened in the flat light and her lipstick deepened to purple. I undid the buttons of her blouse as she explored my mouth with her tongue.

I thought of Annie. Why was this so exciting? Why was this so different? I should have felt guilty, but I didn't. Was it a power trip? Was it because I was cheating? I had no idea, I just wanted to continue.

Without saying a word, she pulled me down onto the carpet where we lay side by side. I teased the blouse from her belt and pulled it open. She wasn't wearing a bra, and I glimpsed her pale breasts in the fire light.

There was a mutual urgency, no awkwardness, no holding back. We caressed and united breathlessly on the carpet in front of the dying fire.

The fire glowed dull red as we turned over and lay on our backs, side by side, looking at the ceiling.

This was different, it was sex for sex's sake, no strings attached, no hard feelings. I didn't feel guilty, I felt elated.

The light in the hall switched on, and a befuddled voice shouted.

"Jen, for Christ sake, keep the noise down!"

I held my breath, but luckily, we were hidden behind the sofas. Jenny's father switched off the hall light and climbed wearily back up the stairs.

I let out a sigh of relief.

Ben and Alice were married, and I nearly didn't make it. Mount Etna in Sicily had been erupting for a couple of months, and we had been advised to avoid the ash if possible. We were late returning to London from Beirut and the stupid Captain decided to fly straight through the ash to save time.

We entered the edge of the ash cloud, and purple flashes of St Elmo's fire appeared on the front windscreen. An acrid, rotten-egg smell filled the cockpit. The two starboard engines surged. We switched on the engine and nacelle anti-ice and adjusted the throttles. The Captain flew the aeroplane away from the cloud as quickly as he could and a few seconds later we shot out from the cloud and the engines stabilised. It was a close shave.

Ben and Alice were married in the 13th century church of St Michael's in Bray, by the Thames. She looked very pretty in a mousey sort of way but, unsurprisingly, Ben's morning suit was too big for him. Ben knelt at the altar with Alice. We had painted the words 'HELP' and 'ME' on the soles of his shoes which caused much mirth among the assembled congregation. The church was packed, I didn't know Ben had so many friends and our gang skulked at the back, suppressing drunken sniggers. Norman towered over us all.

The reception was held at the Monkey Island Hotel, a couple of miles downstream from Bray. Battle scenes painted on the walls of the Marlborough Room provided a dramatic backdrop for the buffet. Swans glided serenely past the panoramic windows, bright bluebells and purple foxgloves lined the water's edge, and the first of the migrating swallows fluttered overhead. It was idyllic.

Until Keir's speech.

Why Ben asked Keir to be his best man I don't know, but it was a mistake.

Keir sat at the end of the newly-weds table, sandwiched between Ben's magnificently mammaried mother, and the multi-tiered wedding cake. A haze of fetid cigarette smoke hung in the air. The hubbub died down as Keir, plainly drunk, stood up to deliver his speech.

Swaying slightly, he slowly looked around and took a breath. The room fell silent expectantly. He started well enough with the usual platitudes, but then described the pre-wedding discussion with the vicar of Bray in the Sacristy.

"He asked me to look at the wedding ring, so I handed it to him."

Keir paused theatrically and continued

"Too small, the Vicar remarked. He said he wanted to stretch the bride's ring, so it could welcome the love of everyone."

Keir tried hard to suppress a giggle.

Ben's mother glared at him, her fascinator fluttered and her jubblies jiggled.

Keir composed himself and continued.

"Ben is always thinking of others, an attribute that Alice welcomes everywhere, except in the bedroom." He snorted trying not to laugh.

"Unlike most traditional best man speeches which are full of sexual innuendo, I have assured Ben and Alice that if there is anything which is even slightly risqué, I'll whip it out."

With that, Keir reached down towards his fly and, to cries of astonishment from the guests, started to unzip. Ben's Mum jumped back in shock, pulling the table cloth with her.

Crockery and glasses crashed to the floor with a shattering clatter, and a bottle of champagne toppled over and rolled towards Keir. Keir turned around in surprise and tripped over the bottle, falling gracefully into the wedding cake with a dull splosh. A blizzard of cream and icing showered Alice as the table fell off the dais with a splintering crash.

Keir slowly rolled over in the shambles, spat cream out of his mouth and quietly said to Ben

"An eight out of ten for style perhaps?"

After the uproar had died down and the remaining speeches were made, I left Annie talking to Sofija and wandered out onto the little wooden bridge which connects the island to the mainland.

I leant with my elbows on the hand rail looking down at the stars reflected in the lucid water, when Norman came over and stood by me and chatted idly about the evening's entertainment. He took out a joint and lit it with a match which he flicked, glowing, into the water below. He turned around with his back on the rail, took a toke and regarded me intently with a strange look on his face. He slowly exhaled a cloud of acrid white smoke.

"I'd like you to fuck my wife," he said quietly.

The long rains were heavy.

The Norfolk Hotel in Nairobi was an incongruous mock-Tudor building on Sadler Street, once the favourite watering hole of the infamous Happy Valley Set. It was pleasantly cool, cars splashed through puddles in the road and hawkers tried to sell their wares over the low wall separating the veranda from the road. A tall black waiter in a white uniform brought me coffee on a silver tray, he was strikingly handsome, and I wondered if he was Maasai.

I took a sip and settled back in my chair and watched the rain.

Norman wasn't joking. He pulled me to one side for a quiet word in the 'Stag.'

"Colin, I was serious about what I said at the wedding" he whispered. "Are you OK with that?"

I was surprised.

"What about Soph?"

"She's cool. Can you come over for dinner on Saturday?" He paused, "on your own."

After a moment, I answered that I could.

"Right," he sipped his beer, looking at me intently. "Colin, it's not something we do very often but there are a few rules. No falling in love, no drinking too much, no drugs and no telling anyone else. Is that clear? Is that OK?"

I quickly nodded and hid my astonishment by gulping down my beer.

The following week I flew to Beirut. French influence was in the architecture, the gastronomy and the *joie de vivre*. Beirut was a colourful vibrant dangerous city, no wonder it was called the Paris of the Middle East. Palestinian refugees poured into The Lebanon after The Six-day War of 1967 and caused trouble between the Christians and the Muslims. The PLO stirred the animosity and a sense of uncertainty hung over the otherwise effervescent town.

I sat on a sun lounger drinking a cold Laziza beer by the swimming pool, watching our crew play in the water. Their bikinis were skimpy, and I wondered what the waiters thought? I closed my eyes and thought about the weekend.

I arrived at Norman's Council house. He opened the door and ushered me in. He held a cocktail and was dressed in a long white kaftan. Sofija was laying the table wearing a black PVC bustier-corset with a tiny pleated skirt over a suspender belt and stockings. She wore high heels and her dark hair was tied back in a tight pony-tail.

My heart was in my throat, I was slightly embarrassed, and I didn't know where to look.

"Hi, Soph," I mumbled.

She ambled towards me with her pigtail swinging and kissed me on my cheek. She seemed different, she exuded confidence, in control. She was almost predatorial. She looked at me suggestively with her mouth in a pout.

Norman strolled over.

"Here, Colin, have a drink," and handed me a cocktail. "I'd like to introduce you to our neighbour." He steered me into the living room.

A pale, sultry woman with bobbed dark hair sat on the settee clutching a drink in one hand and a cigarette holder in the other. Her bright red lips were in stark contrast to her otherwise sombre features. She wore a short, grey see-through top with no bra. She had a bare midriff, a long pleated maroon peasant skirt and beads hung around her neck.

"Colin, this is Mo, from next door."

"She knows the rules," he whispered to me, and winked.

I stammered a hello.

"Let's eat."

He walked to the candlelit table and pulled out a chair for me and sat down opposite. Music softly spilled from the gramophone while Sofija served the food through a hatch between the kitchen and the dining room.

We made small talk as we ate. Norman was relaxed and leant back in his chair as he chatted to Mo. I wondered what the dynamics would be. I felt uncomfortable about Norman.

At the end of the meal Sofija stood up, cleared away my plate and placed it on the hatch. She slowly walked over to Mo at the far end of the table and stood behind her. She kissed Mo's neck and slid her hands under the see-through blouse to fondle her breasts. Mo closed her eyes and leant back reaching up to stroke Sofija's long arms.

It was getting very interesting.

Norman watched intently.

Sofija gently withdrew her hands, picked up the remaining plates and took them to the hatch without a word. Mo sat at the end of the table smoking a joint while Norman washed the dishes in the kitchen. Sofija leaned through the hatch talking to him with her back to me. She turned her head towards me, opened her legs slightly and beckoned me with a small nod. I stood behind her and she wiggled her backside against me. I undid my fly and slid into her from behind. I held her hips steadily as she set the rhythm while continuing to speak to Norman in the kitchen. Sofija suddenly sighed and fell forward on the hatch breathing heavily.

Mo exhaled a cloud of pungent smoke with a wry smile.

Sofija stood up and led me upstairs.

Mo and Norman disappeared into the spare bedroom and I followed Sofija into the main bedroom. Candles flickered on small tables flanking a large Victorian bedstead and a bottle of champagne stood in an ice bucket on the dressing table. Propped against the bucket was a little card which read, 'Compliments of the management.'

Sofija was on fire. The Kama Sutra positions were but a primer to her. We tried 'The Crouching Tiger', 'The Catherine Wheel' and, for all I know, 'The Mounting of a Tyrannosaurus Rex'. She twisted and stretched me into all sorts of impossible positions. At one point my big toe was jammed up my nostril, my left testicle was trapped in the wrought-iron bed head while my knob was being singed by a candle. She rode me on my knees like a horse, slapping me on the arse energetically as she rose up and down. I was exhausted.

She pulled open a drawer and lifted out a short, wicked looking riding crop.

The bedroom door slowly opened.

'Oh Shit!'. I thought, instinctively cupping my balls in my hands. 'I hope it's not Norman!'

'God! I hope he doesn't fancy me!' my bum flinched involuntarily.

Mo tip-toed silently into the room and slid into the bed between us. She was naked with her arms across her ample breasts. Her smooth skin was porcelain white. Sofija put down the crop and turned to kiss Mo. She kissed her neck and breasts, and slowly descended. Mo lay back on the pillow with her eyes closed and opened her legs. Sofija licked her gently while Mo played with me. We cavorted, stroked and giggled in the candlelight, we rolled on the bed in a sweaty jumble of arms and legs like a heaving nest of vipers.

Mo eventually went back to Norman and we thankfully fell asleep.

In the morning, Norman breezed into our room, drew the curtains and presented us both with breakfast on a tray.

"Enjoy," he said brightly.

Lakanooki

Christmas was such a depressing time of the year. My mother put on a brave face and went through the motions, but my father became increasingly cantankerous and awkward. Our house no longer felt like home, it was dated, grey and frail like my parents and I was looking forward to moving in with Keir to escape the banality.

I had a second shiny gold ring on each sleeve. I had been promoted to First Officer, I was officially second in command of the aircraft.

My first trip as First Officer was a baptism of fire.

The Captain was an irascible, blustering bully and a disagreeable, non-standard one-man band. We flew on an eight-day trip to Singapore via the Middle East and back. He didn't say much except to bark orders, he kept himself to himself and thankfully, we didn't see him on the layovers.

After take-off from Singapore on the way to Bahrain, he got out of his seat and wandered back to first-class. I didn't notice him return to the flight deck and disappear into the flight deck WC. An hour later I needed a pee, so I clambered out of my seat leaving the Second Officer in charge.

The Captain had forgotten to lock the door, I walked in and found him sitting on the seat drinking from a half bottle of gin. He gaped at me with stunned surprise, the bottle fell from his hand to the floor and his mouth opened and closed like a fish out of water. His shoulders sagged, he looked at me dejectedly and wiped his mouth on his sleeve. He muttered something unintelligible.

I had no idea how to deal with this. I glanced at him. No longer the bully, he looked like a lost child and I almost felt sorry for him. I picked up the half empty bottle, threw it in the waste bin and turned to him

"Captain, what do you think we should do?" I asked.

He said nothing. My mind raced.

"OK. I won't tell the others and I suggest that you remain out of your seat until just before we arrive, and I will do the landing. Is that OK?"

He nodded, eyes downcast.

The next day we flew back to London from Bahrain as passengers. He was polite and almost deferent on the way to the airport. I made him promise to see a doctor on our return, but I doubted that he would. Perhaps I should have reported him? I felt certain that my career would have been badly affected if I was regarded as a snitch.

Maybe I abrogated my responsibilities?

Norman called me to invite me to dinner again and I readily accepted.

Sofija answered the door dressed in a simple black mini dress which was unzipped to the waist. She had no makeup on and wore her hair down. She looked very sultry.

Norman placed an LP on the record player and the soft voice of Neil Diamond filled the room.

"Hi Norman"

He shook my hand enthusiastically. I looked around

"How are you?" he asked.

"Fine. Where's Mo?"

"I'm afraid she couldn't make it this time, but never mind, we can still have some fun," he said smiling.

I was disappointed, but never mind, Sofija was a real turn-on anyway.

After we had eaten and cleared the dishes away, Sofija took my hand and pulled me upstairs to the bedroom leaving Norman behind. She switched off the main lights and I lay on the bed watching her in the dim light as she seductively unzipped her dress. She slowly pulled the zip apart and shrugged the dress off her shoulders. She was naked underneath. Her eyes were as dark as chocolate, set in the pale tear drop of her face. Her skin was opaque ivory, her breasts small, her long gazelle-like legs converged in a fine dark fuzz.

I quickly undressed and sat on the edge of the bed. She pushed me back with her breasts pressed against my chest and entwined her legs with mine. Hungrily we pawed at each other kissing, licking and panting.

The door opened, and light from the hallway seeped into the room.

Norman walked in.

Sofija knelt over me on all fours. She reached between my legs, steered me into her and slowly sat back on her haunches. She placed her hands either side of my shoulders and started to move her hips up and down. Her breasts were in my face, she grunted softly and a fine film of sweat covered her body.

The mattress creaked and recoiled as Norman climbed onto the bed. He knelt astride her.

There was a pause.

Sofija abruptly let out a yelp and groaned wildly.

Norman bounced violently and I was slowly crushed into the mattress. It was difficult to breathe, and I could hardly move, there wasn't much room.

Suddenly, Sofija's eyes closed, she fell silent and threw her head back with an explosive sigh. Her body convulsed involuntarily, and with a final tremendous shove, Norman fell forward on top of her with a shout.

They both collapsed on top of me and my ribs bounced off my spine with the wind knocked out of me.

Sofija panted gently in my ear with her head buried in my shoulder. I smelled the alcohol on Norman's breath as his stubbled chin nuzzled my cheek.

I suddenly lost interest.

It was bloody cold, and a state of emergency had been declared. The power stations had no coal because of the miner's strike and the country almost ground to a halt.

What a time to move in with Keir.

I walked towards the house, there were no street lights and it was dark, windy and spooky. I rang the bell and dead leaves blew across the door step. The outside light flickered on and the door creaked open. A tall Eurasian girl in a white tight-fitting cheongsam stood in the doorway with her hands pressed together in front of her, and her long black hair tied in a pony-tail.

"Mister Colin?" she asked in a sing-song voice.

I looked about and then realised she was talking to me. I nodded.

"Follow me please," she said, and picked up my suitcase.

She placed my case by the stairs and opened the door to the living room.

"Mister Colin." She announced and shuffled away, her sandals clicked on the floor tiles.

Keir lounged on a light brown draylon sofa in a dressing gown, drinking scotch. His feet were propped on a pouffe and he smoked a smouldering cigarillo. He looked like a young, smug Hugh Heffner. The Stones blasted out from the Goodman's stereo, rattling the glass in the Thames-side sliding windows. The room was carpeted in chocolate brown shag-pile, and the walls were covered in pale orange textured wallpaper. Keir wasn't known for his interior design acumen.

"Hi, Col" he said vigorously pumping my hand, "how was the trip? Hey, do you want a drink before we lose power again? Take a seat."

"A beer would be great. Shitty night out there!"

I sat down.

Keir clapped his hands twice above his head. The door opened.

"A beer!" Keir demanded.

A few moments later the girl came back into the room and took off her sandals. She padded across the carpet and knelt in front of me with a beer on a small tray. She poured it carefully into a glass and bowed as she handed it to me.

'Bloody hell!' I thought as I glanced at Keir preening and looking very pleased with himself. 'How did that puffed up bog-trotter manage this?'

It was a setup of course.

Aiko was Keir's current squeeze who worked in the Chinese restaurant on the high street, although she was actually half Japanese.

It was good to put some distance between me and my tangled life in Bracknell. My relationship with Annie was strained, and I could do without the complication of Norman and Sofija. The much talked about London Orbital motorway was unlikely to be built for some time and I hoped the one-and-a-half-hour travel time would act as a deterrent.

Annie was unhappy.

We went to a raucous party before Christmas in Bracknell. It was packed, and there was a lot of booze. The music was loud, and Keir tried to impress the girls with his latest dance routine. His arms and legs flailed around like a gangly, lumbering tarantula on LSD.

Annie was drunk.

"You don't love me anymore," she slurred, looking up at me with a glass in one hand and a cigarette in the other.

I said nothing.

"Why don't you say anything Colin?" she said, raising her voice with tears in her eyes.

Heads turned in our direction.

"You don't care, you selfish bastard. You only care about yourself!"

The room fell silent. Everyone was looking at us.

I felt embarrassed and walked away to talk to Chase who was chatting to some friends in the corner. I tried to avoid Annie for the rest of the evening, but as the party was winding down, one of Annie's friends rushed up to me and blurted out.

"Quick, Colin, Annie's cut her wrists in the bathroom!"

I sprinted upstairs and burst into the bathroom. Annie was kneeling over the bath sawing away at her upturned wrist with a knife. Tears streamed down her face and mingled with the blood in the tub which flowed to the drain in a pink rivulet. I snatched the knife from her, it was a dinner knife. It was incapable of inflicting much damage and I threw it in the hall with a clatter. I looked at her wrists, they were bleeding slightly but nothing serious. I pulled her to me, and she sobbed hoarsely into my chest. It was a cry for attention. It was the beginning of the end.

I hoped I would be able to get the blood out of my new denim shirt.

Annie had often asked me to take her flying. So as a peace offering, I rented a Chipmunk at Blackbushe. It was a beautiful, clear winter's day as I strapped her in the rear seat. Her father had given me his wartime leather helmet and was watching us somewhere with a pair of binoculars making me feel positively uncomfortable.

We climbed over the massive cooling towers of the Didcot power station towards Oxford when Annie asked me to do some aerobatics. It had been some time since Hamble, but not much can go wrong with a loop, so I dived down and pulled up into the manoeuvre. Maybe I pulled a little hard, and we nearly stalled at the top, but otherwise it wasn't too bad.

"What did you think of that Annie?" I asked over the intercom as we levelled out, but there was no reply. I twisted my neck around and Annie was slumped back in her seat with her eyes closed and a smile on her face.

"Are you OK?"

"Annie!"

"Wow, yes" came the confused reply. "Incredible, I nearly got off on that. Can we do it again?"

I obliged.

More! More!

By the time we landed I was feeling decidedly dodgy, and Annie was grinning like the Cheshire Cat.

I hope her Dad's binoculars weren't too powerful.

I ended my relationship with Annie a month later. I felt sorry for her and I felt sorry for myself. I missed her more than I expected, but life must go on, and I wanted to experience all that it had to offer.

I flew to Dubai for the first time.

Dhows sailed on the muddy salt waters of Dubai Creek outside my hotel window. The temperature was already more than 100 degrees and it was only the beginning of May. It reminded me of Aden in many ways, there was no air-conditioning in my room, just a rusty old ceiling fan. Oil had recently been discovered off shore and accommodation units were being constructed across the creek for the oil workers. The noise was deafening, and dust was everywhere. There was talk of expanding Dubai into a cultural and banking centre, but I couldn't see it. Who would possibly want to live in this fly-blown, arid dust-bowl?

Chase moved in with us and Keir was right, Lakanooki was a fantastic party house. We had an open house every Saturday evening and we invited girls we met on the route to join us. Crews from PanAm, TWA, Caledonian and Laker regularly turned up. It cost us a fortune in booze, but what the hell, we had a blast and we had a succession of casual girlfriends.

Girls often stayed the night and we devised a system of signals to let each other know how we got on the night before.

If we spread both butter and jam on our toast at breakfast, we had had full-on sex. Toast with only butter was heavy petting, a spoon of jam on a plate was the wrong time of the month, and eating a banana or sausage was self-explanatory.

One Sunday the kitchen table was surrounded by unfamiliar faces as we sat down for breakfast. Keir was munching through a plate of buttered toast and jam, when Chase ambled downstairs with his Thai girlfriend in tow. He plonked himself in his chair, leaned forward and stuck his finger in the jar of chocolate spread.

One of the downsides of those excesses was the possibility of catching something unpleasant. I carefully inspected myself each morning, and horror of horrors, one day I saw that something wasn't quite right. I called the BOAC medical centre and they gave me the address of a clinic in Hillingdon.

Feeling exceptionally self-conscious, I walked into the Hillingdon pox clinic. I spoke in a low voice to the frumpy receptionist who asked me to speak up.

"I'm Colin Fairdale, I have an appointment at 11 o'clock." I replied a little louder.

"Right. Colin Fairdale!" She bellowed. "Address?"

The patients in the waiting room looked up, I wanted to shrivel up and disappear. She finished filling out her form and told me to wait in the waiting room. I didn't look at the other patients, hoping that if I didn't look at them, they wouldn't notice me. I picked up the largest newspaper I could find, sat down and opened it wide to hide behind. An orange goldfish in a tank by my left shoulder was gawping at me through fronds of green weed. 'I wonder if goldfish catch VD?' I pondered idly, 'I'd like to change places with you for an hour if I could.' I tapped the glass.

"Is that you, Colin?" someone asked.

'Oh, Shit! I should have brought my false beard and sunglasses' I thought. Sheepishly I peered round the edge of my paper. It was Chase, looking at me with a cherubic smile holding a copy of Penthouse.

"Chase!" I exclaimed. "What the hell?"

It seemed we both had the same symptoms. In hushed voices we tried to guess who we might have caught it from, and it never occurred to us that we may be the culprits. I was really pissed off when I discovered that he had slept with two of my girlfriends before me. It hurt even more because they had told me I was their first.

"We had better let them know." Chase suggested looking at me cheekily.

"You can let them know. I'm not." I replied huffily.

My name was called.

I sat down at the Doctor's desk in his dimly lit office. He was bald, with a thin face and wore a white coat with a stethoscope around his neck. A desk lamp was angled in my direction, casting sharp shadows and making him look very sinister. It felt like an interrogation room in a concentration camp.

"Right, let's have a look." He cackled. "Hmmm," he hummed, examining it through wire framed glasses and flopping it about like a sausage on a barbeque.

"Been to Bougis Street or Wan Chai, have we?"

"I most certainly haven't" I replied indignantly.

What me? Pay for it?

"Well. I'm sorry to say that I'm concerned that it may have infected your prostate, and we need to check it out."

I had no idea what he was talking about.

"Give me the pills and I'll be off then," I suggested, hopefully.

"Not that simple, I'm afraid. We need to put a finger in your anus and a take a sample from your penis."

My heart stopped and my mind raced.

"My nurse will do it now, down the corridor, second on the left."

He finished abruptly.

A nurse!

Images of Sophia Loren or Anita Ekberg with skimpy nurse's outfits flitted through my mind as I knocked on the second door on the left.

"Ooh Helloo love," said the effeminate mincing queen as he opened the door. "What can I do you for?"

Filled with foreboding, I gave him the doctor's note.

His eyes lit up.

"Let's hope you're not an incurable romantic." he chortled.

He pulled open a drawer and lifted out a box of rubber gloves. Theatrically, he slowly pulled on a pair and stretched each fingertip in turn. He dipped his finger in a jar of Vaseline and walked towards me with his finger in the air glistening menacingly.

"Drop 'em, turn around and bend over" he said camply, his eyes gleaming.

Before I did as he requested, I put my fist against his nose and squashed it flat against his face. I looked him in the eye and snapped.

"You do all you have to do and nothing else!"

He looked slightly hurt and, sounding as if he had a bad case of flu, replied.

"When you feel both of my hands on your shoulders that's when you need to worry."

After he had taken the sample, he stuffed a cocktail umbrella down the eye of my dick, opened it and dragged it out to take his second sample.

I avoided alcohol and sex for the next two weeks and took my pills carefully every day.

Out of Africa

The sun was shining, and the early morning mist had lifted from the Thames. Coots and swans floated by and 'Dark Side of the Moon' was on the record player. Keir had cut down one of the large willows on the river bank, but the substantial stump remained in place. We had half-heartedly tried to dig it out without success. Keir bought an old clinker dinghy which we were renovating, and we hoped to row it down to The Red Lion in Shepperton when it was finished.

I had been on a trip to Bombay, Hong Kong and Calcutta.

I liked India but most crew didn't. I loved the food, the history, the cultural diversity and the hotchpotch of sights, sounds and smells.

We spent the night in Bombay on the way to Hong Kong. It was illegal to drink alcohol in India and to my surprise, the BOAC Duty Officer issued us with medical certificates stating we were alcoholics Not far from the truth, I thought. The certificates allowed us to buy alcohol in the hotel bar.

A few days later, just before dawn, we made our approach to Calcutta, Dum Dum airport. The moon was full, but as was often the case, an early morning mist was forming on the ground. The monsoon hadn't arrived, but we could see one or two showers on the radar. About ten minutes from touchdown the tower ordered us to orbit as there was an obstruction on the runway. We were critically low on fuel when the tower finally gave us permission to land. We continued our approach and asked what the problem was.

"Sahib, there was an elephant on the runway, but we've chased it away," was his reply.

A few seconds before we touched down, the windscreen suddenly became opaque and the visibility was significantly reduced. We quickly switched on the wipers, only to realise we had flown into a vast cloud of insects.

The apron was completely covered by an ocean of hissing, fluttering, crawling beasts which we crunched and squashed underfoot as we walked from the aircraft to the airport terminal.

Calcutta is a teeming city sitting astride the Hooghly River in West Bengal. Once the centre of administration for the British Raj, it hosts several crumbling, imposing Victorian buildings. The streets are a confusion of dhotis, rickshaws, trams, sacred cows and beggars. The racket from horns, trams, scooters and street workshops is deafening. Rubbish piles up in the gutters clogging the foul-smelling drains and cow dung litters the streets.

I took a stroll near our hotel. 'The Grand' was a Colonial neoclassic oasis in a desert of destitution. It covered a whole block, at the centre of which, was a verdant tranquil garden. The contrast between within and without was obscene. I had a vast antiquated room with a live-in servant boy who was at my beck and call at all hours. It's a pity he wasn't a twenty-five-year-old buxom Bengali beauty.

The Monsoon had failed in Maharashtra the year before and caused a severe shortage of food throughout India, if it failed again it could lead to a full-scale famine. Emaciated children lay on mattresses of cardboard on the pavement, other cadaverous, grubby and wide-eyed youngsters knelt with hands outstretched begging for food.

The ragged little girl looked up at me imploringly from the pavement swatting away flies from her wide brown eyes. I'm not noted for my compassion, but I was moved to pull out a crinkled one hundred rupees note and place it in her grimy hand.

I was immediately mobbed, the clamorous rabble beseeched me with arms extended. Alarmed, I retreated backwards towards the safety of the hotel. I staggered through the revolving door and collapsed in a leather chair in the lobby. A teenage Indian boy wearing gold medallions, rings and cufflinks, was sitting in the seat next to me. Dressed in an immaculate suit he observed my inglorious arrival and said in perfect English.

"Excuse me sir, but why did you tip that girl?"

"Why?" I spluttered, "she's starving, she needs it for God's sake."

He took a sip of tea with his little finger raised.

"Well Sahib, all you are doing is encouraging begging. She won't keep the money. She will give it to her Maalik in his smart car around the corner. She will still be starving"

He finished his tea.

I wanted to punch his sanctimonious face in, but he's right of course, and that's the biggest problem of all in India; the huge chasm between the haves and have-nots.

The FSRC had membership of the Tollygunge Club in Calcutta. The three stewardesses wanted to go for a ride. I suggested that I could oblige, but unfortunately, they were talking about the equine variety, so we went to the Tollygunge Club instead.

The clubhouse of the Tollygunge Club was built nearly 200 years ago and stands in 100 acres of grounds in south Calcutta. A jaded anachronism, the white facade was streaked black with mold and green patches of mildew crept up the walls. The grounds were overgrown and poorly maintained. The stables had recently been bombed by Naxalite terrorists and part of the roof had collapsed.

The entrance hall had a dark mahogany floor and yellowing distempered walls. The tang of floor polish and damp hung in the air.

The manager approached us, he was the spitting image of David Niven. He was tall with an oval face and a deeply furrowed brow. His hair was slicked back, and he wore a thin black pencil moustache. He smelled of scented soap and eau-de-cologne. He was suave, sophisticated and impeccably dressed in jodhpurs, boots and white riding shirt. He introduced himself as Bob Wright in clear precise English.

"Delighted to meet you, I'll be taking you for a hack before the sun sets."

Two hours later as the long shadows teased mosquitos from under the leaves, we reined up in front of the club house.

"We're not exactly busy at the moment," said Bob, "and I could do with some company. Would you like to join me for dinner?"

We sat around a faded Indian rosewood dining table laid precisely with tarnished silver cutlery and chipped Spode china. Turbaned waiters in crisp white uniforms served a spicy vegetable curry.

Anonymous portraits lined the walls of the dining room. Damp dark drapes hung by the windows and the brass oil lamps suffused a pale-yellow light around the room.

Bob was a Kiplingesque big-hearted philanthropist. His predecessor was shot by a Maoist Naxalite terrorist, but that didn't deter him. He ran charities for the disadvantaged, the aged and street children. He threw open the club twice a year to Mother Teresa and her orphans. He hoped that when the political upheaval settled down, he would be able to restore the club to its former glory.

At midnight we climbed into our taxis and said our good-byes to this fascinating compassionate man.

There was only one thunderstorm within hundreds of miles when we left Calcutta the following evening, and yet the Captain managed to fly straight into the titanic tempest. He turned towards it after take-off and switched the radar off by mistake. It took two minutes for the radar to warm up, and blind, we flew straight into the storm. The aircraft pitched and rolled like a bucking bronco, the Engineers flight bag flew up to the cockpit roof and fell to the floor with a crash. The turbulence was so great that it was difficult to read the instruments, the airspeed fluctuated wildly, and the auto-throttle struggled to keep up. With a deafening clatter the windscreen was bombarded with a scatter-shot of hail. The cloud around us streaked with rapid flashes of lightning and the steady red pulse of our anti-collision beacon. Quivering purple tendrils of St Elmo's fire danced across the windscreen.

With an incandescent blaze of light and a loud crack we were hit by lightning. I was temporarily blinded. We were hit again, and my instruments flickered. We were pointing six degrees nose down, yet we were climbing at 6,000 feet per minute in an updraft. The pressurisation system was unable to keep up.

"Pressurisation failure!" Shouted the Engineer.

I reached for the check list.

Suddenly, we popped out of the side of the cloud like a cork, and the pressurisation system stabilised.

We sat in silence for a minute.

Many of the wartime Captains were 'one-man bands' and tended to operate the switches themselves at the same time as flying the aircraft. The VC10 was designed to be flown by a crew of at least three. He should have asked me to switch the radar on, but he didn't and look what happened.

It was indelibly imprinted in my brain to never go into a thunderstorm again.

For all his Australopithecine traits, Ben was making a name for himself as an affable prankster.

It was a requirement for us to attend a class on First Aid each year. The routine was always the same. After lunch, we reported to the lecture room where we practiced Cardiopulmonary Resuscitation on a manikin. 'Resussie Annie', as she was affectionally known, lay in anticipation on the floor covered by a blanket with just her plimsolls poking out.

Ben arrived early for his class and hid Annie behind the rear row of seats. He put on a pair of plimsolls and lay on the floor under the blanket with just his feet poking out. The bored Nurse arrived and started her auto-gabble. In mid diatribe, Ben moaned and slowly sat up.

The Nurse screamed and ran out of the door.

On a trip to Chicago, Ben's Captain was an ex-Wartime pilot. He was a blustering, pompous man with an enormous handle-bar moustache. Everything was 'Tally-Ho', 'Wizard prang' and 'Jolly good show!'

He had a shock of auburn hair which didn't match his sideburns, or his moustache and most people assumed it was a wig. No one was brave enough to find out.

In the middle of the Atlantic the Captain fell asleep in his seat with his head resting against the side window. Ben was navigating but found time to clip the Captain's hair to the oxygen mask securing line at the top of the window.

Ben reached up to the overhead instrument panel and pressed the 'Fire bell test' button.

The bell rang shrilly.

The startled Captain abruptly sat up leaving his resplendent rug dangling from the clip like a lynched cat.

Captain Humpty Dumpty fell off his wall in a big way.

There was uncertainty about our jobs owing to the Yom Kippur war and its effect on the price of oil. OPEC had doubled the oil price again and BOAC had had no option but to cancel some flights. Inflation was rising, the miners were on strike, and Britain was in a recession. Edward Heath ordered a nationwide three-day working week. Petrol prices rocketed and petrol stations ran dry.

I returned from a 10-day trip to The Seychelles and Mauritius. This was normally a popular trip reserved for senior crew, but because the trip spanned Christmas and New Year, we were all junior. The Captain was Chris Jenkinson, one of the youngest Captains on the fleet, and the only one I felt comfortable with.

The unapproachable nature of some captains was a safety issue which should have been addressed. I could quite happily have watched Jimmy the Fish fly into a mountain without saying a word just to have the satisfaction of seeing him realise that he wasn't as shit hot as he thought he was. If something wasn't done there would be an accident, all it would take would be a timid co-pilot too frightened to speak up at a critical moment.

Chris was in his late 30s, he was competent, reserved and a good pilot. The Engineer, Ron, was tall, thin and weaselly with thin slicked back hair. I didn't get on too well with him.

We left a cold, grey London behind and spent Christmas at the recently opened 'Reef Hotel' near the airport in The Seychelles. The hotel had a private sandy beach and was surrounded by coconut palms. There were only two flights a week to the Seychelles, so we had plenty of recreation time before taking the next flight to Mauritius and back. The hotel organised Christmas lunch for the crew and the festivities continued around the swimming pool in the afternoon.

The crew was disappointed not being home for Christmas, but we were determined to make the best of it and have a good time. The three stewards joined the flight deck crew for football on the beach while the girls cheered us on with rum punches. Libby was great fun, she was short, blonde, bubbly, and could drink most of us under the table.

A cyclone briefly threatened Mauritius, but otherwise the trip went smoothly. We held room parties most nights and we gelled well together as a crew, that is apart from myself and Ron. He was one of those annoying people who was always right. He thought he knew everything and felt superior. We had a few niggling moments on the flight deck and by the end of the trip he was definitely irritating me.

I held a room party on our last night of the trip. I ordered rum punches and beers from room service, and we had a riotous party. Before long everybody was roaring drunk. Two of the stewards played strip jack naked, Libby was telling crude jokes and Chris helped to throw one of the girls into the bath. The evening wore on and one by one people wandered off to bed. Eventually I was alone with Libby, she crawled into my bed and I joined her.

I couldn't wait to crow to Ron.

The following night I navigated the sector back to London.

I flicked through the Almanac doing the calculations for the first fix while Ron logged instrument readings and adjusted knobs and switches. His sallow face was highlighted by the glow from his instrument panel.

"Hey, Ron. You know that girl down the back, the small blonde one?" I said without looking at him.

I couldn't wait to tell him and to rub his nose in it.

He turned towards me in the dark.

"You mean Libby?"

"Yeah," I said casually, and hit him with the punch line.

"She stayed in my room last night. We had a great time"

"Really Colin?" he said turning back to his instruments.

I was really enjoying it.

A few moments later he added.

"I'm not surprised."

I looked at him.

"What do you mean?"

"I shagged her the night before last. She told me she wanted to shag everybody on the crew!" he snickered, "everybody! There's seven of us, and you were the last."

His shoulders shook as he chuckled into his instruments.

I was arrested by a Colonel in the Ugandan Army when we arrived in Entebbe from Cyprus.

General Idi Amin seized power from President Milton Obote in 1971, and shortly after, expelled all Asians from Uganda. The result was the collapse of the economy. Commerce ground to a halt, shops were empty, and most had been looted. My favourite tool shop on Shimoni Road near the Speke Hotel was burnt to the ground and the affable grey bearded Sikh owner murdered. Drapers, the only department store in Kampala, had been sacked, the windows smashed, and squatters moved in. The roadside stalls selling samosas, the smell of spices and booths hawking brightly coloured bolts of cloth had disappeared. Amin was from the north and was systematically killing other ethnic groups. Rumours were rife of bodies floating down the Nile into Lake Victoria. Armed gangs roamed the streets and fear and apprehension lurked at every corner. The Barman in the hotel was dragged out and shot in the garden because he came from the wrong tribe.

Amin had been stirring up trouble with the British government. 'The Last King of Scotland' severed ties with the UK and nationalised British businesses in Uganda.

I was completing the shut-down checklist on the apron at Entebbe when a Colonel and two armed soldiers burst onto the flight deck. The sweating Colonel pointed his pistol at the Captain and accused him of smuggling weapons into Uganda. We were carrying mortar barrels in the hold destined for the next stop, Lusaka in Zambia. They were properly manifested, and we carried them legally. The two soldiers fidgeted nervously with their rifles at the back of the flight deck.

The Captain argued with the Colonel profusely, but it was obvious he wasn't getting anywhere, and eventually we were marched off the aeroplane and bundled into a waiting army lorry. It was two o'clock in the morning, and the two mean-looking guards kept us quiet for the ninety-minute drive to Kampala. We were prodded at rifle-point through the entrance of the multi storied concrete Police Headquarters and frogmarched into a small dark cell. It was hot and stuffy and smelt of sweat and fear. Other prisoners, wide-eyed, looked at us with surprise. No food or water was offered, I was tired and thirsty.

The mouth-watering smell of fried bacon drifted into our cramped cell as the pale dawn filtered through the tiny barred window high in the wall. The door opened with a crash and the guard ushered in a dishevelled white man in a crumpled beige linen suit. He walked up to the Captain, shook his hand and said in an almost imperceptible American twang.

"I'm Hennessy, the British High Commissioner. I've come to sort this lot out." He waved his hands around, "sorry about my appearance." He tried to straighten his tangled black hair.

"This is a bit of a surprise. Been dashing around like a blue arsed fly trying to make Idi see reason. He's making mischief you know, but HMG persuaded him to release the two junior crew members. That's you I assume?" He pointed his finger at me.

I nodded.

"And?"

The Engineer put his hand up.

"Splendid," he went on, "they'll take you under house arrest to 'the Apolo'. Is that understood?"

We nodded.

He turned back to the Captain and the Senior First Officer.

"Look, I'm sorry, that's the best I can do. You'll have to stay here for a while. Don't antagonise them and try not to admit to anything you didn't do."

He wiped flecks of imaginary dandruff off his shoulders.

"Um, I don't suppose you managed to bring the latest copy of 'The Times' with you, did you?"

The Engineer and I were taken to the hotel. Nobody guarded us or restricted our movements around the hotel, but we weren't allowed to visit the Captain at Police HQ.

I received a call from Hennessy. BOAC had managed to get permission for us to inspect the aircraft at Entebbe. An army Land Rover and two guards took us to the airport. We sat in the back and I felt very vulnerable as we drove down the airport road through the banana plantations. Obote supporters could have hidden a whole army without being noticed. There was no shade, the sun beat down and we were covered in red dust by the time we arrived at the aircraft.

Two machinegun emplacements had been setup under the wings. Perhaps they expected us to storm the aircraft and hit them with our flying manuals? Or eviscerate them with our navigation compasses?

An overpowering sickly stench hit us as we neared the aircraft. We had been carrying 20,000-day-old chicks bound for Lusaka when we arrived a week before. They had died and rotted in the heat. We climbed the stairs to the cabin. The flight deck was untouched but the food in the galleys had gone off adding to the overall stink. The bars had been looted and most of the blankets were missing but otherwise the aircraft seemed to be in good shape. It would take weeks to get rid of the smell.

We inspected the exterior of the aircraft. The Engineer carefully looked at the tyres and noticed that they weren't round. The tyres were flattened where they contacted the tarmac and they would need to be all changed before the aeroplane could leave.

I doubted if there were ten tyres in all of Africa.

A week later the Captain and Senior First Officer were released from prison and brought to the hotel. They were gaunt and dishevelled but otherwise OK. We flew back to Heathrow as passengers later that evening. The aircraft with brand spanking new tyres was flown home a few days later by a management crew.

BOAC merged with BEA to form British Airways. The date I joined BOAC affected my career from that moment on. Command courses, postings and leave all depended on seniority. I was concerned how the merger would affect my situation. How would the two seniority lists be recalculated? I was sure it would not be to my advantage as there were many more pilots in BEA. I was certain that my time to command would be increased exponentially. It was a take-over by the 'Flat-Earth Wankers.

Jimmy Futcher was the bravest and kindest Captain that I ever had the privilege of flying with. He was old school in many ways, with short hair and a greying bushy moustache, but he was approachable, kind and competent. He was a good pilot and a good Captain.

The flight from Brunei to London landed in Dubai for a refuelling stop and Jimmy was scheduled to fly the final leg from Dubai to London. The inbound Captain briefed Jimmy in the briefing room while the VC10 was being refuelled on the apron. Four terrorists stormed the aircraft and shot a stewardess in the back. They reached the flight deck and realised there wasn't a Captain on board, they demanded one immediately or they would shoot the First Officer. Without a second thought Jimmy calmly picked up his briefcase and walked out to join them.

They were forced to fly to Beirut, Tripoli and eventually landed in Tunis where the hijackers decided to make a stand. The hijackers demanded and secured the release of jailed terrorists in Holland. They shot and killed a German passenger and wired a large bomb to the centre console on the flight deck. During negotiations the hijackers pretended to touch the centre console with a wire which would complete the explosive circuit.

The psychological pressure was immense.

Jimmy never lost his cool and fortunately the hijackers surrendered without further loss of life.

He was quoted by the press after the event.

"I'm not a brave man. Anyone would have gone out."

I could think of quite a few who certainly wouldn't have.

Royal Flight and Brigitte Bardot

I politely refused a bowl of sheep's eyes offered by a smiling, wizened, bearded old man in the banqueting hall of a black granitic fortress in the middle of Sana'a. The cavernous hall was gloomy and little light came from small slits high on the walls. White silk sheets with Arabic inscriptions hung from brass rods fixed to the arches. An octagonal marble fountain stood in the centre of the hall, the cascading water drowned the distant sounds of the city and gave some welcome relief from the desert heat.

I took a handful of saffron rice with my left hand and dropped it onto a brass plate. I scooped some saltah with a piece of flat bread which I slowly ate while looking around the table. Four Yemeni government officials and a translator sat at one end of the table. They wore dark jackets over their flowing white thoobs, and tightly wrapped, patterned turbans on their heads. Each had an intricately carved, curved Yemeni dagger sticking out from a wide red satin belt.

The Captain and the Engineer sat opposite me and next to me were the Second Officer and the cabin crew.

The interpreter told us the history of Sana'a.

The city lies at 7,500ft and is one of the oldest continuously inhabited cities in the world. It developed into a wealthy trading centre as it is situated at the juncture of two important trading routes. The Ottomans occupied the city for centuries, and after the fall of the Ottoman Empire at the end of the First World War, The Yemen was divided into North and South. The North was now Democratic, and the South became communist after the withdrawal of Britain in 1967.

Lt Colonel Ibrahim al-Hamdi took control of the North recently in a military coup. The young, progressive President had radical, ambitious plans for his country. He wanted to calm fractious tribes, end bribery and corruption and implement a sweeping modernising infrastructure plan. Most of all he wanted to see a reunification of North and South. He needed money for that, lots of it.

That is why we were there, on a State Visit.

The Sheikh of one of the Gulf States owned a private VC10 which was crewed on rotation by flight crews from BA. The six-month secondments were very popular as HRH was well known for his largesse. Our cabin crew were from Middle East Airlines based in Beirut. The Purser, Haasim, was a tall polite fellow and was utterly indispensable as a translator and go between. The five girls were from wealthy Beirut families and wore heavy makeup and strong perfumes. The youngest, Samya, was not like the others, she was Christian and was not there to make money. She was flirty, adventurous and liked a drink.

It wasn't long before we ended up in bed together.

Sana'a airport is in a valley surrounded by mountains. We had no charts for navigation, so we made it up as we went along. We arrived overhead at 20,000ft and spiralled down in the valley through the haze and thermals. We landed on a short rough runway and taxied to the crumbling terminal.

President al-Hamdi met the Sheikh on the red carpet at the bottom of the steps and they disappeared in a motorcade of flashing lights and sirens. We were scheduled to leave with HRH later that night, so we were escorted away by officials to be entertained for the day.

There was only one paved road in Sana'a, which led from the airport to the city. Dust devils danced in the shimmering heat haze and kite hawks circled overhead as we drove through the ancient Yemen Gate. A labyrinth of tiny streets meandered between a jumble of gingerbread white-edged adobe houses perched on rocky crags. The noise, heat and flies were overbearing. The guards stood to attention as we drove through the entrance gate to the fortress. One of the guards was very young and, as he stood to attention, his oversized helmet rotated slightly on his head. Later, I walked in and out of the gate a few times to see if I could get it to complete a full circle.

This was our final trip of our chauffeuring tour for HRH.

The Sheikh was a tall, majestic figure with a large aquiline nose and jet-black beard. He rarely smiled, and his beady black eyes seemed to bore straight through me. His crisp white keffiyeh was kept in place by a black cord tied at a jaunty angle. He treated the aircraft like a taxi and had little concept of flight time limitations. We were continuously on standby and we were often on duty for 16 hours a day.

We were accommodated in pleasant private bungalows close to the city while the cabin crew shared one large villa.

Our first flight was to Karachi to hunt bustard with his prized falcons. The hooded birds were brought to the aircraft perched on a pole which was a little too long to fit through the door. The pole was tipped, pushed and poked in a vain effort to board the bothersome birds. The valuable falcons clung grimly to the perch with some hanging upside down flapping frantically when someone had the bright idea to saw the end of the pole off. They were placed in the economy section and promptly shat all over the cabin.

Three days later after a successful hunt, we flew home. The Sheikh's personal assistant came on the flight deck with an envelope for each of us. The PA was a tall, darkly handsome man with an immaculately groomed, short boxed beard. He had a large hooked nose and clear sparkling eyes. He spoke good English and at the end of each trip he asked Haasim for a half bottle of brandy which he surreptitiously secreted in his dishdasha.

My envelope contained a *pourboire* of £1,000! It was almost enough to by a car! The Captain decided not to open his as flight crew orders stated that we were not allowed to receive tips. I politely reminded him that it would cause great offence to both the Sheikh and myself if he declined.

It was stressful and tiring being on call all the time, but we visited some very interesting places such as Casablanca, Kabul, Tunis and Djibouti. The hours were long, but the allowances were excellent, and besides, I had a playmate.

Samya came from a small town to the north of Beirut called Jounieh. She was younger than the other girls and I suspected she was not as privileged. She had straight auburn hair with a long nose and wide mouth. She smoked, but unlike the others, liked a drink or two. The political situation in The Lebanon worried the cabin crew considerably, and they often huddled round radio sets listening to the news. Palestinian refugee militia and the PLO had been fighting the Kataeb Christian Militia on the outskirts of Beirut and large parts of the downtown area had been destroyed.

We returned from a trip to Lahore and the PA approached me in the galley. He took me to one side and smiled.

"You are finishing your tour soon, I believe?"

"Yes sir."

"I would like you to arrange a party tomorrow night. How about 'The Hilton'? It would be nice to say goodbye to the crew in an informal way and I would especially like the girls to be there. I would make it worth your while."

"Of course, sir," I replied obsequiously and added, "the BA crew stay in the Hilton and I might be able to get some of the crew to join us as well. Would that be OK?" I simpered.

He nodded, smiled broadly and left the galley in a flurry of robes.

An offer of free food and drink is impossible for cabin crew to turn down, so all it took was a quick call to the BA crew.

The Hilton had reserved a large conference room for us. In one corner a small jazz band played next to a long buffet table overflowing with food. White jacketed waiters hovered, refilling our glasses with champagne and offering hors d'oeuvres of all shapes and sizes. A gaggle of skimpily dressed BA girls arrived and made for the champagne. Soon the room was filled with loud voices and laughter. The Lebanese girls sat quietly in the corner smoking heavily while looking at the BA crew with distain.

'The PA will be happy with this lot' I thought jovially, imagining the sack of gold I was going to receive.

Samya joined me and looked at me with her dark almond eyes.

"Are your girls always like this?"

"Yes, mostly."

"How lucky to have that freedom, without fear of criticism."

As we spoke, one of the BA girls wandered over to me.

"How did you manage this?" she asked admiringly, waving her arm around.

"Ineffable charm of course. It took a lot of persuasion, but after some delicate negotiation he agreed," I replied smugly.

The double doors opened, and the PA strode in. He looked magnificent. He wore purple robes with gold edgings, a red and white keffiyeh, and his beard had been dyed and trimmed. He beamed at me when he saw all the girls.

"Well done" he said.

'King Croesus eat your heart out,' I thought

The evening went very well. The BA crew played games, sang songs and danced provocatively to the music. The PA pirouetted expertly with the girls and looked exceedingly satisfied. At the end of the evening he strolled out arm in arm with one of the BA girls with a big grin on his face. He winked at me as he passed.

I rubbed my hands with glee. A vision of me pulling up at Keir's in a Rolls Royce flashed before my eyes.

The PA didn't acknowledge me again, not even on my last trip and I came to the reluctant conclusion that my first attempt at being a pimp ended in abject failure.

No matter where I looked, I couldn't find Brigitte Bardot. I searched everywhere, high and low, bars, back streets and beaches for the sex-kitten to no avail. She must have been avoiding me.

A whisper of muggy air wafted through the tiny grimy window of my miserable garret. My sad collection of clothes hung from a rail in a tattered, patinaed armoire, and an ancient seersucker mattress lay forlornly on a rusty wrought iron bedstead. Cobwebs festooned the ceiling beams and dull grey balls of fluff rolled silently across the bare floorboards in the draught. The stale shabby room had been my home for six weeks.

My trip to Sana'a with the Royal Flight turned out to be my last trip on the VC10. I was posted to the new Boeing 747 on my return with immediate effect. The next day I was informed my conversion course would be delayed for up to six months because of the recession. I was released on basic pay with the requirement to telephone Operations once a week in case the situation changed.

Keir and Chase immediately flew to Lisbon and boarded a yacht to sail across the Atlantic; there would be no way they could phone home.

I decided to try to find the girl of my dreams, the girl of everyone's dreams, the French blonde bombshell film star, Brigitte Bardot. Her fame and notoriety turned the sleepy little fishing village of St Tropez into a trendy Mecca for the super-rich jet-set and I set off on my *pèlerinage.*

I packed a rucksack and started to hitch-hike to the South of France. I was on the A27 on the way to Portsmouth when the heavens opened. The rain cascaded from the hood of my anorak and my jeans were soaking wet from passing traffic when at last, a bronze coloured Rover 2000 drew up beside me. The driver wound the window down and leant over.

"Where are you going mate?" He asked, smiling.

"Portsmouth" I replied, hopefully.

"That's' funny, so am I!"

And with that, he drove off laughing, the bastard.

Nobody else stopped that night, so I trudged into Bosham and spent the night in 'The Anchor'. The landlord mentioned a job vacancy at the Sailing Club, and I spent a very pleasant two weeks washing up in the kitchens. I had great fun frolicking with the waitresses, but I was sacked for improper behaviour. The Commodore was only jealous, the old fart.

Eventually I arrived in St Tropez.

It was surprisingly quiet. The season didn't start until the end of June but there was plenty of part time work available as the cafes and restaurants prepared for the summer onslaught.

The restaurant had seen better days. It was on one of the shady *allées* which meandered randomly behind the Avenue Foch. Set back slightly from the street, the pale rosé plaster was stained, and the azure shutters were faded and cracked. A portly unshaven man with tufts of short black hair, sipped pastis in the warm sun in front of the restaurant wearing a string vest. He lounged on a rusting cast iron chair under the shade of a sun-bleached awning. I waved away the acrid smelling smoke from his Gitaine and walked into the resto. It took a moment for my eyes to adjust to the dark, and to my amazement I saw Brigitte! Well, not exactly, it was a beautiful blonde mirage. She was drying glasses behind the bar, and her ample breasts jiggled under her loose white chemise with each wipe of the cloth. She was about my age, with long blonde bouffant hair which fell to her shoulders. A flawless long nose divided her perfectly symmetrical face. Her wide mouth was in a seductive pout and her alluring grey eyes were accentuated by dark eye-liner. A Gauloise smouldered between her long fingers.

"Bonjour madame. Je cherche du travail." I stammered.

She looked at me with her watery grey eyes, and sensing my discomfort, raised an eyebrow.

"Monsieur, I'm sure there is a *lot* you can do for me, but you better ask my 'usband."

She nodded in the direction of the mangy *clochard* finishing his pastis outside.

'Oh shit!' I thought.

I walked into the sunlight.

He was ancient. He was swarthy with weak lips and a heavy stubbled chin. His tiny eyes examined me as we spoke. With the aid of a dictionary and a smattering of French and English, he agreed to hire me for 25 Francs a day including board and lodging.

Amélie led me to my garret. I was hypnotised by the swaying of her mini-skirted bottom as we climbed the steep spiral stairs.

And so, began a happy few weeks. I repaired and repainted the *volets*, scrubbed floors, moved furniture and washed up in the kitchens. There was a palpable excitement as the season approached. A fine dust of mimosa pollen coated the streets, leaves sprouted from the plane trees and early tourists explored the alleys.

Amélie flirted with me and I didn't know how to respond. I was afraid of her Mafia-boss husband, so I kept my distance. I fantasied about her in the lonely dark of my attic each night, holding my pillow tenderly in my arms until I fell asleep.

It was always the same routine. After the last patron had left, I finished the washing up in the grubby kitchen while Amélie cleared up the bar and rearranged the tables and chairs. She would squeeze past me and brush her breasts against my back or pat my bottom to move me aside. Gerrard sat with his three cronies playing cards, drinking and smoking heavily until the early hours. By the time I went to bed they were huddled in the corner, almost invisible in a *brouillard* of cigar smoke.

I crawled onto the spongy bed. There was a gentle knock at the door. I wrapped a towel around me and opened the door. Amélie pushed me towards the bed and closed the door behind her. She didn't say a word as she urgently kissed me, her tongue darting in between my lips. She smelled of Guerlain, Gauloise and Galliano as we tumbled onto the bed. She tore off my towel and grasped me firmly as I fumbled with her blouse. We were soon naked. She rode me as I lay on my back, her magnificent boobs above me visible in the pale glow from the dirty attic window. She moaned loudly, the bed springs creaked, and the bed bounced across the floor as we thrashed about.

I was terrified that Gerrard would hear us.

Panting and bathed in sweat, we lay side by side looking at each other.

"You must go, Amélie" I said, gasping, "what if he comes looking for you?"

"Pfaff! Le connard!" she spat. "He never comes up before three o'clock, and when he does, he's too drunk to notice anything."

We lay together for a few minutes before she slowly got dressed and tiptoed out.

Our dangerous liaisons continued, as did the risk of being discovered, and it was with some relief that during my weekly call to BA I was asked to return immediately to start my course.

I bade au revoir to my Brigitte Bardot.

It is said that the best way to learn a language is from pillow talk.

It didn't work for me.

The only use I had for the pillow was to *stop* Amélie from talking too loudly.

I took the train back to London and returned to Lakannoki.

I was worried about Chathura.

My father had one of the biggest private butterfly collections in the world and when he was based in Singapore, we joined him on his weekend forays in the jungles of Malaya in search of lurking lepidoptera.

We drove deep into the jungle along dusty logging trails in a clapped-out Land Rover. Iron wood, blackwood and Kempas trees towered over us festooned with creepers, large-leafed banana, ferns and shrubs filled the understory.

Once we stopped by a fast-flowing muddy stream. The humid gloom enveloped us like a suffocating damp blanket while six-inch buffalo leeches fell from leaves and silently attached themselves to our legs. On the forest floor, a giant centipede tried to crawl away from a swarm of soldier ants which were eating it alive from behind. As the ants ate, circular segments of the centipede detached themselves and rolled down the slope into the water.

The jungle was a riot of sound. Frogs croaked, insects rasped, and monkeys whooped in the tops of the trees. They pissed on us or threw turds in our direction if given half the chance.

My father opened the back of the car and unpacked his collecting kit. He gave us a butterfly net each and told us to catch whatever we could. We set off down a trail and almost immediately came face to face with a tiger. It stopped in its tracks and so did we. It crouched, bared its teeth, hissed and disappeared into the undergrowth. It had killed and eaten a villager in nearby Ulu Sedili, so it probably wasn't hungry.

It certainly would have lost its appetite if it had tried to eat me.

We despatched the fluttering butterflies in a chloroform killing jar and stored them in neatly folded butterfly papers.

Sometimes my father set up moth traps, so we spent the night in the Land Rover surrounded by the sounds and smells of the jungle. The raucous chirping of insects and croaking of tree frogs continued until day break occasionally interrupted by grunts from Malayan wild boar.

I flew to Ceylon frequently on the VC10. My father gave me a collecting kit and asked me to catch him some Ceylonese specimens. Collecting butterflies was time consuming, hard work and it interfered with my socialising, so I enlisted the help of a boy from the beach. The Pegasus hotel was on the west coast near Columbo and I befriended 10-year-old Chathura as he played on the dirty sand. I showed him how to catch, kill and preserve the butterflies and promised him 1 rupee for every good specimen.

This arrangement worked well, and my father was pleased. The 747 was unlikely to fly to Columbo for some time and I wasn't able to warn Chathura that I wouldn't be back.

Poor Chathura, he would probably have a hanger full of butterflies the next time I saw him.

The Hot Summer of '76

K eir and Chase did join me on the 747-conversion course after all as they were thrown off the yacht in Las Palmas for too much frigging in the rigging.

We slogged, cheated and blagged out way through the course and eventually flew to Prestwick for circuits and bumps.

The instructor demonstrated 'pilot incapacitation' immediately after take-off at Prestwick. At 500ft he shrieked, slumped forward against the controls theatrically, and pushed the left rudder. How we didn't crash I don't know; the Engineer saved the day. He leapt up and released the Instructor's seat, which slid back and released the controls.

I was in a 50-degree left bank and approaching the stall before I finally regained control.

My first flight was to Barbados.

The masts of the yachts were uncomfortably close and disappeared under the nose in a blur. On the left-wing tip, the crowded beaches of Barbados were a smear of white against a backdrop of green baobabs. The cameras of the BA Film Unit whirred in the cabin as we soared past at 200ft above the sapphirine sea.

"We'll give them a bloody good view." The Captain said during the briefing.

The Film Unit were on board making a promotional film for BA about the Caribbean. For continuity they wanted to film us flying past from the same beaches on our departure for Trinidad the next day.

It was my turn to fly to Trinidad and I asked the Captain what height he wanted me to fly.

"It's your bloody sector! Do what you want!" he replied.

I took-off, retracted the flaps to 10, accelerated to 180 knots and levelled off at 500ft. I turned right towards Paradise Beach, to the north of Bridgetown, and started a slow descent. I shot over the crew at 100ft and opened the throttles fully to climb away.

I kicked sand in their faces.

I was only 26.

I flew to Singapore and the Captain's wife came along for the trip. She was friendly, full of fun and much younger than him.

We ate at Fatty's and then went to Bougis Street for a drink.

Fatty was a round, bald Chinese man who owned a small Chinese restaurant on Albert Street which was popular with forces personnel before the War. The Japanese invaded Singapore in early 1942 and threw their prisoners in the infamous Changi jail. Fatty risked life and limb smuggling food into the jail for the starving inmates. Fatty's heroism was not forgotten and after the end of the War almost everyone who had been in the military made a pilgrimage to his restaurant.

The grubby shop houses lining Bougis Street traded their wares during the day but at night, when the street was closed, a different trade flourished.

It was the haunt of transvestites who tried to entice tourists to buy drinks from street vendors at exorbitant prices. Their goal was to save enough money for 'the operation'.

The street became an outrageous parade of *basse-couture*, tottering high heels and excessive make up; an exaggeration of curves and colour.

The trannies were undeniably beautiful and by mistake they were sometimes taken to hotels by drunken visitors.

Imagine the surprise!

The street was packed, the babble of voices echoed in the shadowy shop houses and punctured the clammy night. Rats scurried down malodourous storm drains where the stall holders washed the glasses. The 'Queen' of Bougis Street trotted to our table and chatted to the Captain's wife. She was extraordinarily beautiful with dark hair, swallowtail eyes and long elegant legs. Her breasts peeked cheekily from her long blue décolleté dress. She was flawlessly feminine, apart from her Adam's apple.

She informed us that she had had 'the operation' and Mrs Captain was fascinated. She bought her another drink and demanded that she tell her all about it.

They whispered together at the end of the table.

Mrs C. put her hand against her mouth and gasped.

"I don't believe you!"

193

"I'll show you if you want, for another drink," the 'girl' said loudly in a lisping sing-song.

The table fell silent and everyone stared at the Captain.

Mrs C looked at her husband.

There was a momentary pause.

"Well, OK I suppose. Colin, escort my wife will you, old boy?"

Everyone looked at me.

The 'girl' took Mrs C. by the hand and led her towards a nearby shop. She opened the door and walked towards a dusty counter. She hoisted herself onto it, pulled her dress up and lay back with her legs apart.

Mrs C. leant forward for a closer look and gasped.

I moved over to have a look. I can't say that I was much of an expert, but it looked very realistic to me.

I flew to Rio de Janerio which was one of our more popular destinations.

Rio was an exciting but very dangerous city. Brazil had been run by a military Junta for six years and they were slowly losing their grip. Corruption was rife, law and order was almost non-existent, and it was necessary to be extremely vigilant. Rio was a city of contrast, teeming Favelas sprawled in the city centre and ragged children begged from finely dressed Brazilians. Street urchins played football on rubbish dumps while tourists sunned themselves on the pristine beaches.

We arrived in Rio and checked into the 'Sheraton Hotel'. The Captain was Tarquin Stuart-Foley, a tubby, jolly character with a posh accent. He was one of the more affable Captains and had an oval ruddy face with wild hair and round twinkling eyes. He was scruffy and a little out of touch, in a mad professor sort of way.

The crew met at 'The Lord Jim,' a small mock-Tudor pub, close to Ipanema beach. The evening wore on and Tarquin and I were left propping up the bar. The smoke-filled bar was full of cheap plastic furniture and cheap looking clients.

Tarquin peered over the froth of his beer and turned to me.

"Boy. Take me to 'The New Munich'."

I gulped.

'The New Munich' was a dodgy live sex bar in Copacabana. I felt certain it wasn't the sort of place the seemingly straight-laced Tarquin would want to visit.

"I think it would be better if we went to the Japanese next door. I wouldn't recommend 'The Munich,'" I mumbled, looking at the floor.

"Not what I've heard," he retorted, taking a gulp of beer.

"I don't think it's in a very safe area" I ventured.

"Nonsense boy. Let's go."

He finished his beer and walked out to find a taxi.

Tarquin flagged down a canary yellow Volkswagen Beetle taxi. Night had fallen, few street lights were working, and the closeness of the air felt heavy and menacing. We hopped in the back of the cab and Tarquin said to the sullen dark-skinned driver in clipped English.

"'New Munich', old boy."

The driver peered quizzically at Tarquin in the rear-view mirror and we set off. The bars along the beach in Ipanema were packed, revellers spilled onto the pavements laughing and shouting as we swept past. The heavy rollers from the South Atlantic crashed loudly onto the deserted sandy beaches.

The journey should have taken half an hour, but we were still driving after forty-five minutes. I could make out the bright lights of Copacabana in the distance to our right.

I turned to Tarquin.

"Sir, I think we're being taken for a ride, literally. That's where 'The New Munich' is."

"What!" spluttered Tarquin. He tapped the driver forcefully on the shoulder. "Stop now!"

"Stop! We'll walk!"

Before I could intervene, the taxi slowed, we got out and Tarquin paid the driver.

It was eerily silent as the sound of the departing taxi faded in the distance. A dog barked somewhere, the sound echoing softly off the shuttered shops. A siren wailed in the direction of the beach and a scrap of paper slid across the road in the breeze. We started to walk towards the bright lights half a mile away. The street was dark, utterly pitch black, except for one lonely pale street lamp a hundred yards ahead. As we approached, I could make out a man lounging under the light looking at us.

"Senhor. Luz Por favour." The man said, holding out an unlit cigarette.

I tried to steer Tarquin towards the far side of the road, but Tarquin, ever the gentleman, took out his lighter and walked towards him.

"No!"

Tarquin approached the man. The man suddenly produced an evil looking knife and pointed it at Tarquin.

"Run!" I shouted, scared fartless.

I sprinted away. I could have easily out run Tarquin, so the chances of my survival were stacked in my favour. What's more, I might have risen one place higher on the seniority list.

I turned around expecting to see Tarquin being stuck like a pig, but to my amazement he was running towards me, still very much alive.

Tarquin's chest was thrust out, his eyes bulged, and his face was flushed bright red. His arms and legs were going like the clappers as he slowly drew away from his assailant. Close behind, the would-be mugger held a knife at arm's length and shouted something at Tarquin in Portuguese. He dragged one leg behind him in a lumbering gait.

He only had one leg!

That's why the corpulent Captain was able to get away, the knife-man had a wooden leg! I put my hands on my knees and burst into a fit of hysterical laughter.

Our hearts were beating wildly as we were ushered to our seats in the cold dark theatre by an attractive hostess. We sat at a small table close enough to touch the small low-level stage.

In the gloom spectators huddled around tables drinking quietly.

The room fell silent and the curtain slowly rose to a smatter of applause. A buxom, olive-skinned Brazilian woman strutted onto the stage in high heels and nothing else. Tarquin was transfixed. She danced for a while and then lay down on her back with her head over the edge of the stage by Tarquin.

A crackly fanfare announced the arrival of a second performer. A tall, lean, naked man strode onto the stage and stood facing the audience. His oiled, pale-yellow skin shimmered. His long slim nose and high cheek bones were accentuated by the overhead spot lights. He wore a feathered headdress and two gold torqs on his arms. Mayan hieroglyph were tattooed on his shoulders. His weapon was outstanding, and like him, it was long, thin and purposeful.

He walked towards the woman on the stage and lifted her legs.

The show began.

Tarquin fidgeted uncomfortably in his seat with the woman's head almost in his lap. She opened her eyes, looked up and winked at him.

He almost had a heart attack.

I joined the mile-high club.

Technically it should have been called the six-and-a-half-mile club, as my investiture occurred at 35,000ft.

April had been an on and off girlfriend for some time. She was a beautiful long-haired brunette who enjoyed a drink and was always up for a good time. She was one of the boys. We had talked about the mile-high club and she suggested that we should join on a trip we did together to Lusaka.

On the night flight back to Heathrow she waited for me in the toilet at the top of the spiral stairs. I opened the door and slipped inside. The cubicle was very small, she had her back to me with one leg on the toilet seat facing the mirror. Unfortunately, I could hardly move. I stood behind her, but there wasn't enough room to position myself, so I opened the door fractionally, found the correct angle, and closed the door behind me.

It was perfect, she couldn't move, I used the door as a buttress, and we could watch ourselves in the mirror.

A few hours later, shortly before the top of descent, one of the stewards presented me with a signed certificate. It was a modified passenger route map with our route drawn on it.

'Hear Ye! Hear Ye!' was written on the front in flowery letters.

'In recognition of a record-breaking shag of 462 miles across Lake Chad, Colin and April are hereby elected to the venerable, the most august 'Mile-High Club.''

The heat wave continued.

It was a record, temperatures had been above 80 F every day for five weeks. We were fortunate living by the river where it was cooler, but England wasn't prepared for such extremes of weather.

I finished renovating the little dinghy. The clinker joints were caulked, the wood stripped and varnished. It looked immaculate and I was proud of my handywork even though it had taken nearly two years of hard labour. We had all but given up trying to dig out the old willow root. We used scaffold poles and steel bars as levers but to no avail, it moved a little each time we tried, but not enough. It was too hot to work.

The River Police became regular visitors at weekends. They moored their launch on our makeshift pier and joined us for a beer or two. They lived in police cottages above Sunbury lock, about 20 minutes downstream.

We held our usual weekend party, it was hot, and the garden was packed with merrymakers. Girls wandered around semi naked and some even swam in the murky river. The beer flowed and Keir's HiFi system took a pasting. It wasn't long before the policemen joined us for the barbeque. Alan, the sergeant, was vaguely handsome and found himself the centre of attraction. His tales became taller and increasingly lurid the more he drank. Ron, his partner, was lanky and spotty with short red hair. The girls were less interested in him, so turned his attention to the booze.

The sun dipped behind the trees casting long shadows across the river, swans paddled silently by and swarms of midges drifted in from the river. Alan leant against the makeshift bar with a glass in hand and looked at the tree stump.

"'ere, Keir. What's with the stump? You've been pecking away at it for weeks!"

"It's in the Bloody way, taking up half the garden. We can't shift the sodding thing," replied Keir.

Alan knocked back his rum and coke in one and looked at the stump in silence.

"Recon' we'll be able to pull 'er out with the launch. Give us another drink," he slurred.

Keir rushed off to find him one, with a huge smile on his face.

"I'll tell you what," Alan continued, looking at the stump quizzically, "you lot grab 'old of the poles and we'll use the boat to pull it out."

It seemed reasonable to me in my befuddled state.

Alan and Ron jumped on the launch, and the twin Volvos burst into life as we traipsed towards the offending stump. The launch burbled noisily as it backed upstream towards us. Alan stood in the stern holding out a heavy steel hawser attached to the transom. The launch backed towards the root and churned up the mud on the river bed.

"Wrap this round it. When I drop my hand, pull those poles like hell!" he yelled.

We secured the braided steel cable around the root and took our positions by the scaffold poles. The launch moved slowly forward downstream taking up the slack in the hawser. It stopped with the engines ticking over.

Alan dropped his hand and shouted.

"Go for it you bastards!"

Ron slammed the throttles forward, and with a deafening growl, the water at the back of the boat erupted in an explosion of froth. The cable twanged ominously as it tightened, and two moorhens flapped frantically past. The prow of the launch rose into the air and the root moved slightly. We pulled with all our might on the poles. Chase's pole nearly bent in two, and the stubborn stem groaned, but then stopped moving.

The engines were overheating, and the root was stuck fast. Ron closed the throttles and backed the launch once again towards us.

"Fuck me that's in tight. We'll have to take a run at it. Get me another drink." Said Alan.

Warning bells were ringing somewhere in the foggy recesses of my mind.

Keir's girlfriend, Sandy threw him a bottle of beer.

Ron gingerly backed up to the stump as Alan swigged his beer. We curled the hawser in the grass by the bank of the river. Alan threw his empty bottle in the river and shouted.

"Ready?"

"Yes!" we yelled.

"Here we go!"

Ron opened the throttles again and the launch shot down river like a scalded cat. The cable rapidly uncoiled throwing clods of earth into the air. We levered the rebellious rhizome desperately as the loose cable uncoiled and thrashed in the water like a crocodile. With a resounding twang the cable reached the end of its travel. The ground shook and the root moved. The prow of the launch juddered high in the air and the engines screamed.

Something had to give.

Unfortunately, it wasn't the root.

With a splintering crack, the transom was wrenched off the back of the boat, and sounding like a crashing helicopter, whistled over our heads into the bushes behind.

Ron cut the motors.

There was a stunned silence. Suddenly the onlookers cheered and burst into a deafening applause.

I'd like to say that the launch sank, but regrettably it didn't and Ron and Alan slowly limped home down the river.

The landlord of the 'White Horse' in Sunbury phoned us the next day to tell us of their fate.

Alan and Ron arrived at their cottages but failed to secure the launch properly and it slipped its moorings during the night. It was washed over Sunbury Lock weir and smashed to pieces.

I didn't think we would see them again for a while.

We tried to visit the crash site in my beautiful dinghy. Eight people piled into the pocket-sized skiff and we set off down the river. Almost immediately we took on water, and in the middle of the river, we sank. I never imagined that a wooden boat would sink, but it did, straight to the bottom.

All that work gone to waste.

I never really understood why most ex-RAF pilots liked to wear white leather gloves when flying the aircraft. They were to protect hands in crashing fighter jets, but they were totally irrelevant in a passenger aircraft. I thought them pretentious.

I flew to Rio with an ex-BEA Captain. He was quiet and unfriendly and flew the first three legs of the trip wearing white gloves. He told me I could fly the last leg home.

I went shopping.

As we taxied out to the runway, I reached down into my flight bag and pulled out a pair of gloves.

Theatrically, I made a grand show of pulling on my sequin covered elbow length cocktail gloves which sparkled brightly in the cockpit lights.

I put one hand on the thrust levers, the other on the control column and smiled cheekily.

The Engineer smirked.

The Captain glowered.

"Are you taking the piss?" he growled.

Watershed

Elvis was dead and so was Annie.

Elvis died in Memphis and Annie died in Santa Monica.

Annie had been dating an American cameraman who lived in the City of Angels. She followed him to the States only to discover that he was married and had two children. She put the barrel of a shot gun in her mouth and blew her head off. How she managed that I have no idea, but she did. No blunt dinner knife this time, it was the real deal.

Poor depressed, confused Annie deserved more from life than that.

My life was approaching a watershed. I had a few grey hairs and I'd put on weight. Something was missing.

Maybe I needed to find a steady girlfriend and settle down? Most of my friends were married, our wild nights were few and far between and life just wasn't fun anymore. Perhaps I needed to move on? I couldn't imagine what it would be like to be monogamous and responsible, but I supposed it was the inevitable next step. Biologically I was on the earth to procreate and help the species to survive. I liked the procreational bit, but I wasn't sure I could survive without it.

Chase moved in with his Armenian girlfriend and Sandy was playing an increasingly important role in Keir's life. Keir had become much more responsible and even talked about getting married. I don't think Sandy liked me very much, she probably knew I was trying to dissuade Keir from getting married. I couldn't imagine why, but she treated my suggestion to continue living with them after their marriage with utmost contempt.

I was promoted to Senior First Officer. I had three gold stripes on my sleeves. The next step would be Captain.

Iran was in a state of turmoil.

The Shah, one of the most powerful and respected leaders in the world, had persuaded OPEC to increase the price of oil. The cost of a barrel of crude increased fivefold in less than two years. Iran had vast oil reserves and the Shah intended use this newfound wealth on a massive program of modernisation. He wanted to reduce the influence of Islam in Iran and restore the glory of the old Persian Empire. The Shah celebrated the 2,500-year anniversary of Cyrus The Great with an expensive and lavish display at the ancient Persian city of Perseopolis.

The Shah planned to modernise commerce and introduce free trade. The clergy, conservatives and the Bazaari, were concerned and became increasingly vociferous in their opposition.

Mostafa Khomeini died in Najaf in Iraq and his exiled father, Ruholla Khomeini, was seen as the spiritual leader of

Iran. Rumours suggested that the Shah's secret police were involved in Mostafa's death which precipitated a wave of riots and protests in Tehran. SAVAK was ruthless and thousands of political prisoners were jailed without trial.

The Grand Bazaar is one of the largest souks in the world, it covers eight square miles and comprises roughly 200,000 shops. Although the market has been in existence for over a thousand years, most of the buildings are less than 400 years old. It is a cavernous cornucopia of colour and sounds. Brightly coloured bolts of cloth, intricately woven Persian carpets and brown hessian bags of aromatic herbs are for sale. Gaudy plastic toys, brass and silverware balance precariously on rickety tables and shelves. Traders shout, shoppers haggle, and calls to prayer from a nearby minaret echo along the endless alleyways.

We booked taxis to go to the bazaar.

Flight crew orders indicated that stewardesses should dress conservatively in public, but two of the new girls paid no heed. They hadn't covered their hair and they climbed into the taxi wearing short skirts.

The mournful sounds of the early evening call to prayer mingled with the city hubbub as we entered the bazaar through one of the many side gates. It was almost deserted, and we weren't hassled as we sauntered past the loaded stalls. The sun set and the maze of passageways became gloomier and more foreboding.

I assumed everyone was at the mosque.

The crew liked to buy soapstone chess sets, brass plates and leather camel-saddle stools which could be sold at a tidy profit back home. They wandered in and out of the shops and we walked further into the market.

We were completely alone.

Suddenly, a youth darted towards us from behind a stall and thrust a dead chicken in the face of one of the girls without a headscarf. She screamed shrilly and we recoiled in horror as the boy scampered off into the darkness.

I attempted to calm her without success. A small pebble hit me on the head. I looked behind, a chanting crowd of men and boys approached throwing small stones and rubbish.

"What should we do?" the trembling girl asked.

I was the senior crew and the others looked to me to lead. I had no idea, I was scared to death, but I was more scared that the crew might notice my fear and ineptitude. I told them to form a tight group and I would face our assailants at the rear.

"Which way?"

I didn't have a clue, we were completely lost in the catacombs.

"That way" I replied purposefully, pointing in the opposite direction of the crowd. It was all I could do to stop myself sprinting away, leaving them to fend for themselves.

We set off with me walking backwards at the tail.

More people joined the jeering rabble.

I was hit on the head again by something quite heavy and a thin line of blood trickled down my cheek. I was shocked and slightly stunned.

"Faster!" I shouted urgently, hoping no one would notice the panic in my voice.

Our motley band broke into a jog and, running backwards, I had difficulty keeping up.

The baying mob drew close and threw their missiles with increasing accuracy as we tumbled out of a side door of the bazaar onto the street. A line of taxis waited by the pavement and we gratefully fell into them and sped off back to the hotel.

I had no intention of returning to Tehran if I could help it, and I sensed that the Shah's time was up.

It was going to end in tears.

No life for a single man

I bought a small mews house in London and I intended to move from Lakanooki before Keir married Sandy.

Keir held his stag party in Jersey the weekend before his wedding.

I'm not sure that Jersey knew what hit it when twenty pilots and rugby players descended on 'The Old Court Inn' in St Aubins. I didn't arrive at the hotel until late Friday evening and I walked into the bar to find Keir sitting on a chair pissed as a parrot, soaking wet and covered with sand and seaweed. Half an hour earlier he had been thrown in a dinghy in the harbour and pushed out to sea. He somehow managed to swim ashore in the dark and staggered back to the bar.

Keir booked a restaurant in the centre of St Hellier for lunch on Saturday and we arrived after consuming copious quantities of beer in the 'Court'. The meal started civilly enough but soon degenerated into a bun fight. Keir bought a cheap guitar from the shop next door which I strummed disconsolately. The guitar lasted twenty seconds before I was hit over the head with it. My head went clean through the back of the guitar and came to rest against the strings. It was like a carnival hat with the strings bent over my head, the body wrapped around my chin, and the fretted neck jutting out from one side. Every time I moved, I clouted Keir across the back of his head with the tuning keys.

Two women were sitting at an adjacent table. They hadn't been frightened off by our antics and I persuaded them to join us for a drink. They were plain and blousy, but they looked more and more beautiful with each drink. I sat them next to Sam Napier, the pugnacious, stunted prop from the rugby club. He was almost bald with a shaved head, cauliflower ears and broken nose. He wasn't exactly an Adonis, but he had a great sense of humour and we both thought we were in with a chance.

The last of our party went back to the hotel in the early evening leaving Sam and I with the ladies. He invited them to dinner and they readily agreed. They took us to an extremely expensive seafood restaurant where they ordered lobster and drank champagne all evening. I was seriously worried about the cost, but I felt sure that it was all going to be worthwhile.

We sipped our coffee at the end of the meal. I had been playing footsie with the prettier of the two girls, so things were looking rosy.

The girls went to the ladies together to 'freshen up'.

Sam said they were preparing themselves for an evening of fun and frolics. We ribbed each other as we tried to work out who fancied who.

We waited
and waited
and waited.

They never returned. We had been stitched up

It slowly dawned on us that we were not going to have much fun that evening and it was time to go back to the hotel. I had just enough money to pay my share of the bill, and we wandered out in the rain to find a way back home. It was too far to walk, it was too late for the bus, and we didn't have enough money to pay for a taxi. So, we started to hitch hike. Nobody stopped. Who on earth would want to pick up two soaking drunken slobs staggering down the road in the dead of night?

We had no choice and started to walk in the direction of the hotel. Soon we ambled past St Hellier Police Constabulary.

Sam stopped and turned towards the Police station.

"Hey, Colin" he slurred, "I read that jails in Jersey treat prisoners well. They even serve a proper breakfast in the morning."

"Bollocks, Sam! No way," I scoffed.

"No, it's true, I swear. Come on, let's get arrested."

And with that, he started to trot towards the Police Station.

I was tired, wet, miserable, and just wanted to lie down. There didn't seem to be much of an alternative.

We lurched into the Police station with our hands above our heads. The lone sergeant on duty looked up at us, totally unimpressed.

"We've come to give ourselves up!" exclaimed Sam waving his arms in the air.

The sergeant drummed his sausage-like fingers on the desk and looked at us with distain.

An image of a warm, cosy cell and a busty policewoman serving me a full English breakfast floated before my eyes.

"We give ourselves up!" said Sam again impatiently, lowering his hands.

The sergeant sighed.

"What for?"

"Drunk and disorderly."

The sergeant looked at us with narrowed eyes. A pulse beat in his temple and the muscles of his bull-like neck twitched.

"Listen here, sonny!" the sergeant growled, slowly getting up from his chair and prodding Sam in the chest with his fearsome finger. He gradually uncoiled as he stood up. He was huge, his head nearly touched the ceiling.

"I suggest you fuck off and stop bothering me, you turds!" He slammed his fist on the desk with a crash to emphasise the point and glared down at us.

"OK sir" I replied meekly and grabbed Sam by the arm and dragged him out.

Sam was in fighting form, he swore at the sergeant and waved his fists in the air as I pushed him past a squad car in the car park. Sam kicked the car door and tried to rip the rotating light off the roof. I managed to calm him down, and we continued towards the hotel.

It rained heavily in the night and we arrived at the hotel as the dawn broke a few hours later.

We were saturated, knackered, bruised and sober.

We had lunch in the 'Court' on the last day. We were slightly better behaved, but even so we hauled Keir into the stock room in the middle of the meal. We laid him on a table and pulled down his trousers and underpants. Chase produced a tin of dark oak furniture stain and poured it liberally over Keir's parts. He squealed and thrashed about, particularly when it trickled into his bum hole.

I loved it!

A couple of hours later we arrived at the airport. Chase found an empty supermarket trolley and squeezed a barely conscious Keir into it with his spindly arms and legs sticking out like prickles on a hedgehog. The road from the carpark sloped down towards the airport apron. We lined him up with the security barrier and let the trolley go. The wobbling trolley gained speed and slowly rotated down the slope as Keir's arms and legs waved frantically about. Chased by a couple of disgruntled policemen he shot sideways under the barrier and came to rest on the apron between a Dan Air 748 and a BEA Trident.

We scarpered as Keir was escorted off the airport.

The seamen were on strike, there were no ferries and all the flights to London were full. Chase, Keir and I were on standby tickets and the only flight available was the Dan Air. I'm not sure why they let us on, but they did, and we chuntered along in the small 748 to Southampton.

By the time we arrived we were bursting for a pee, so we clambered down the steps and peed against the wheels of the aeroplane.

Amid sighs of relief, clouds of acrid smoke billowed from the wheels.

The Captain marched up.

"What the fuck are you lot doing?" he spluttered.

That was a very good question.

Eventful Times

Sixty-seven Victorian coach houses huddle shoulder to shoulder either side of the uneven grey cobbled lane which runs the length of Holland Park Mews. At the far end an imposing balustraded stone arch backs onto Holland Park road. My flat was above one of the stables and was accessed by a brick staircase which climbed the side of the building to a wrought iron balcony above the wide wooden stable doors.

Picture the bustling industry of this little back-alley towards the end of the nineteenth century. Listen to the clatter of hooves on the uneven stones, the shouts of the 'Cabbies' and the rumble of Hansom and Clarence cabs as they lurched on their way. Inhale the sweet smell of dung and horse sweat mingling with the fog and the black, acrid choking smoke from the chimney pots.

The horses were long gone, replaced by a different form of horse power, and the Cabbie's once squalid, cramped flats were now fashionable and sought after. Luvvies moved in and stamped their mark on the street with brightly coloured garage doors, cheerful curtains and floral extravaganzas flowing over the balconies. The 'Gee Up!' of the Cabbies was displaced by effete cries of 'Oh Dahling!' Cheerful music hall tunes superseded by 'Bohemian Rhapsody' belted out at a million decibels on someone's obscenely expensive HiFi.

My flat had seen better times. The roof leaked, there was rising damp and the stable doors were rotten. The magnolia woodchip wallpaper was peeling off and the windows were impossible to open.

The Public Sector workers were on strike and overflowing dustbins in the street tempered my urban idyll. It was about time politicians had enough guts to stand up to the unions who held us to ransom.

It was expensive to live in London and I had a large mortgage, so I let the garage space to an exclusive car dealer who stored his priceless cars there. Sometimes I wandered round the exotic sportscars and wondered who drove them. What made the owners different from me? Where did I go wrong? I suppose I was jealous, I worked hard all of my life but there was no way that I would ever be able to afford one.

I let the box-room to a girl called Dee and the small bedroom in the attic to a BA stewardess called Rosemary.

Dee was a plain, serious girl of about 25 who worked in the men's department of C&A and spent much of her time cooped up in her tiny little room. She was a Queen's Park Rangers fan.

A few years older than me, Rosemary was a freckled, effervescent 'BA personality girl'. She was dark haired, warm and gentle. She came from east Anglia and her father was a farmer who seemed to own most of Essex.

One day, Dee called us to join her for a drink in Bayswater to celebrate Ranger's success in the UEFA cup. Rosemary and I roared off in my canary yellow Morgan Plus 8 open-topped roadster. The Morgan was an anachronism, it was uncomfortable, cold, and like everything else in Merrie England, wooden framed. Full-of-fun-Rosemary spiked my drinks for a laugh and before I knew it, I was roaring drunk.

The steering of the Morgan was a bit loose at the best of times, but on the way home it seemed to have a mind of its own. I became aware of a mournful wailing sound and a pretty flashing blue light in my rear-view mirror. I pulled to the side of the road and rode up onto the kerb. Two policemen disgorged themselves from the white Triumph 2000 squad car and strode purposefully towards me.

Unfortunately, I failed the breath test.

"I only just had a drink." I slurred, lamely.

"Right" said the police officer, rolling his eyes, "you'll have to come to the station and do another test in 30 minutes."

He steered me towards the back seat of the Triumph.

The second policeman jumped into my car and started the engine.

"Wait!" shouted Rosemary, "you can't go without me!" She hoisted up her dress and leapt into the seat beside the bemused plod.

We arrived at Kensington Grove police station and the Morgan drew up behind us. Rosemary was giggling and the copper guffawed as they jumped out. They led me to a brown and green tiled waiting room and closed the door.

I was alone, the walls closed in on me. I started to panic. Shit! What if BA found out? Frantically I breathed heavily, puffing madly to try to expel the alcohol from my lungs. I ran on the spot, I even prayed. In the background, I could hear roars of laughter from the two policemen punctuated with Rosemary's shrill laugh.

The minutes ticked away and eventually one of the policemen walked in.

"You've got one hell of a girlfriend," he said wiping tears from his eyes.

'She's not my girlfriend' I thought.

"She told us what happened, and we've decided you've learnt your lesson."

He looked at me and smiled.

"We need the bag as evidence, so I'll tell you when to stop."

I couldn't believe it, I was going to get away with it. I had no idea what Rosemary got up to with the boys in blue, but whatever it was, it worked.

I was driven home in the squad car while the younger policeman joined Rosemary in the Morgan. They came upstairs for a drink and I went straight to bed.

I put a pillow over my head to drown the sounds of their carousing and fell into a fitful sleep.

A swirl of feathery snowflakes fell noiselessly outside the window, tumbling and twinkling in the light from the street lamps. A pure white blanket of glaze smothered the dirty snow and bent the branches of the fir trees lining the empty road. A sense of excitement was in the air.

Keir snored and dribbled in a bed on the other side of the room. Our wood-panelled bedroom was in the eaves of a chalet not far from the slopes in Val d'Isère.

His hair was receding and grey at the temples, but he hadn't changed that much since I first met him. He snorted softly, he sounded like a snuffling asthmatic aardvark frantically ferreting in a termite mound.

How I missed the old days. The wild, carefree times we had were but a distant memory. Most of my friends were married and some even had kids. Everyone was so grown up and responsible.

I tried to socialise in Holland Park, but everyone seemed vacuous, self-interested and dull. I had nothing in common with any of them.

The population of London was more than six million, but it could be a very lonely place.

I persuaded Keir and some of the gang to come on a boys-only ski holiday. It took a lot of organising as everyone had to ask permission!

It started off well enough, but we managed to upset one guest in our chalet who had the temerity to call our loud, heavy-rock music 'a disease.'

After a boozy dinner in the chalet, I hoodwinked Keir into trying out the latest craze; 'plastic-bagganing.'

We stuffed him into an outsized plastic bin bag and pulled the draw-string tight around his neck. Only his bobble-hatted head was poking out of the top. We dragged him to the top of the slope by our chalet, turned him upside down and prepared to send him on his way. We spun him hard as we let him go and the look in his eyes was priceless as he whirled down the slope. He shouted frantically as he flew off a snow drift, and with a satisfying crunch collided with a tree. We stood and listened to the pleasing sounds of crashes and screams fading in the distance before returning to the chalet for another drink.

One day it snowed heavily, and we spent the day in a small bar in the village. Val d'Isère was very popular with the English and the hostelry was filled with loud, posy Hooray-Henrys. We wanted to warm ourselves by the open fire in the middle of the room, but they elbowed us out of the way. After a few drinks Keir had an idea.

The snow banks made it easy for us to climb onto the roof. We made two large snowballs and pitched them down the chimney. A sudden cloud of smoke belched from the open door and a couple of OK-Yahs staggered out coughing and spluttering.

We scarpered.

At the end of the week they were all eager to get home. We'd had a lot of fun, but they had other, more important things to go home to.

I didn't.

It just sort of happened, Dee moved out and I eased into a comfortable and unspectacular relationship with Rosemary. She was gentle, kind, romantic and bubbly. I wanted to be in love and be loved, but I was sleepwalking in a starry-eyed romantic dream. I have been told that it is dangerous to wake a sleepwalker. No one woke me up, and we married a year later.

We flew to Delhi and took the train to Srinagar for our honeymoon. We were delayed for three hours in London because of a go-slow by the BA baggage handlers. There was widespread dissatisfaction with the management in BA, and the chairman, Miles Hardy, was particularly unpopular. He fought the unions, and slogans proclaiming **'Hardy must go'** appeared everywhere. The words were scrawled on hangar doors, on walls and even in aircraft toilets. It was splashed in large red letters on the BA billboard at the entrance to the airport.

Britain granted independence to the Indian Empire in 1947, and Kashmir was divided by the partition. It became one of the most militarised areas in the world as China, Pakistan and India tried to exert their territorial claims. Srinagar was in the Indian controlled area of Jammu and Kashmir.

We were greeted by Noor at the gangway to our houseboat, 'The Golden Bell', which was permanently moored on Lake Dal. Noor was middle aged with pale eyes and dark hair. He was dressed in a deep blue dhoti, white pantaloons and open sandals. Lake Dal is at 5,200ft on the outskirts of Srinagar in the foothills of the Karakorum mountain range.

The polished, carved walnut panelling and intricate marquetry of the 'The Golden Bell' smouldered in the late afternoon sun. Patterned Kashmiri carpets lay on the floor, the sofas were covered in a bright red polka-dot fabric, and heavy Edwardian furniture lined the walls.

We had a drink on the veranda and watched the shikaras of the floating market glide by piled with vegetables and flowers. The houseboat rocked gently as the water lapped against the hull. The reflection of the Karakorums shimmered in the still water of the lake as the sun slowly set, and the last rays of the sun dabbed the snow-capped Himalayas with a dash of rouge. Frogs croaked gently among the reeds and the buzz of cicadas grew louder as the shadows lengthened.

It was so romantic.

The stars appeared, and so did the mosquitos. At first it was solitary dive-bombers, but it soon became an aerial armada. We danced around on that little veranda, trying to swat the pernicious little bastards with our arms flailing around like Whirling Dervishes on speed. The boat rocked, churning up the mud by the stern, and a delicate aroma of sewage and marsh gas wafted towards us on the light breeze. The sound of a record player cannoned off the lake like a shock wave from the houseboat next to us.

I suddenly doubled up with stomach ache. I only just made it to the sordid little loo and exploded in relief.

I awoke in the morning and scuttled to the bathroom, with my cheeks clenched and my stomach churning like a cement mixer. My face looked like a spotty, scrophulous elephant's testicle, my ears felt they were bleeding and my backside resembled the red arse of a rutting baboon.

We didn't get up to anything that night, I can't imagine that there was anything faintly alluring about me on my knees, cuddling the cracked porcelain toilet in the fetid bathroom. I was poorly for two days, after which, I felt well enough to go on our pony trek to the Thajiwas glacier.

We drove by the fast-flowing Jehlum river to the south east in a battered, mud-brown Toyota Landcruiser. The river meandered down a wide rock-strewn valley, between two mountain ridges. At Anantnag we turned north and followed the Lidder tributary to Pahalgam.

Pahalgam is an old hill station at an elevation of 9,000ft in the lush green Lidder valley. Far to the north, the jetstream blew plumes of snow from the peaks of the majestic Himalayas. Tendrils of cloud wound sinuously down the steep gullies of the valley and forests of pine, poplar and deodar covered the lower slopes. Fisherman cast their rods into the troubled stream fishing for brown trout.

Our ponies and porters waited patiently for us in a meadow by the river. Six sturdy little ponies grazed on the grass swishing away the flies with their wiry tails.

I stared in disbelief.

Wicker picnic baskets filled with chipped china and silver cutlery stood on top of an upturned brass bathtub. Two full-sized single beds were loaded onto one of the poor ponies, and an enormous, ancient, campaign tent was strapped to another. A black feathered chicken clucked angrily in a small wooden cage tied to the back of the last pony.

We were embarking on a four-day junket around a benign little valley, not on a Royal Geographical Society expedition to the source of the Indus river, for goodness sake.

Abdel, our guide was a gnarled, bandy-legged old man with greying hair and long black beard. He shouldered his ancient looking jezail and leapt onto his saddle-less pony in one bound. I tried to look cool by doing the same. With a yell of 'Allahu Akbar,' I put my foot in the stirrup of the startled pony and launched myself into the air. I flew over the top of the miniscule mount, nearly emasculated myself on the pommel, and fell in a crumpled heap on the far side. The porters hooted and roared with laughter and produced a step ladder for me to clamber, ignominiously onto the thin saddle.

Our caravan meandered slowly up the damp mountain trail in the fresh mountain air. The going was uneven, and it wasn't long before my already sore backside was killing me. Thankfully, after a few hours, we came to a meadow in a high-altitude clearing. Abdel said we would camp for the night close to a small stream. The jabbering porters scrambled to erect our big-top, into which they carried our two camp beds, a dining table and the brass bathtub. Abdel set a fire and it wasn't long before the wood was blazing away merrily.

Dinner was prepared, and Abdel triumphantly produced two fresh eggs. Rosemary wandered over to the cage, put her fingers through the bars and tried to pet the little black chicken. I walked behind, doing my best impression of a bow-legged John Wayne.

"She's so pretty, how nice to have fresh eggs"

The chicken strutted around the tiny cage, pecking at the dirt on the floor.

'How nice it will be to have fresh roast chicken at the end of this trip,' I thought.

The temperature dropped rapidly as the sun set behind the mountains and we decided to go to bed. There was no ground sheet but plenty of ground shit. We picked our way through the piles of evil smelling goat manure towards our tiny cots at the far end of the smoke-filled tent. We undressed and quickly climbed into bed. There were no sheets, only smelly, coarse, horse-hair blankets. We could hear the voices of the porters clearly through the thin canvas as they huddled round the camp fire.

'No chance of honeymoon hanky-panky', I thought wistfully as I drifted off to sleep.

We didn't break camp in the morning, and Abdel took Rosemary and I sightseeing. We climbed above the tree line, our ponies expertly finding a route on the barren, rock-strewn slope. We arrived at a small, stone goatherd's hut and dismounted. I could hardly stand. It was magnificent desolation. The air was clear and thin, the snow line was just above us and the imposing Himalayas stretched as far as the eye could see.

Abdel led us into the hut. A deeply wrinkled man dressed in furs squatted by a small smouldering fire. Abdel spoke to him and the goatherd nodded his head towards us. The goatherd offered us a bowl of pink, milky tea. Abdel informed us that it was made from special tea and goat's milk. We politely accepted it and took a sip. It was revolting. The old man smiled.

I went for a pee in a cubicle at the back of the hut and when my eyes to became used to the gloom, I noticed **'Hardy must go'** scrawled on the wall.

We returned to England with the first unconsummated marriage since Henry VIII and Anne of Cleves.

We brought back a memento of our hapless honeymoon, we were infested with crabs from the dirty horse-hair blankets.

Rosemary soon fell pregnant and was overjoyed. I was surprised, I hadn't expected it so soon.

Rosemary started nesting. She threw the bed out from Dee's room and bought a cot. She stripped the wall paper and painted the walls a pastel pink. She went to neo natal classes and spent hours in the library reading books on childbirth. She brimmed with happiness and excitement, she was fulfilled.

One Sunday morning we lay in bed looking at Rosemary's tummy. She nestled her head on my shoulder as she tenderly stroked the non-existent bump.

"I'm going to grow her toes this week." She said lightly and turned to kiss me on my cheek.

"Each week I'll grow a different part of her until she's whole."

I smiled, we didn't know what sex it was, but she desperately wanted a girl.

The next week Rosemary grew her arms and then her fingers.

The doctor frowned and put down the stethoscope. He touched Rosemary gently on the arm.

"I'm going to book an ultrasound scan at the Hammersmith. It's a new technique, but it should give us a good look at your baby. It's just a precaution."

He didn't offer any further information and we walked out in silence.

Rosemary lay on the inclined couch and pulled up her blouse, she was 14 weeks pregnant and there was a sizeable bulge in her belly. She held my hand as the doctor smeared her with gel and ran the scanner over her skin. The monitor flickered into life and a fuzzy outline appeared on the screen.

"Hmm," said the doctor as she moved the scanner around, "it's definitely not a boy."

Rosemary grinned at me.

The doctor scanned the same small area repeatedly, I could make out the inert grainy, shape of our baby curled up on her side. She seemed to be sucking her thumb.

The doctor peered closely at the screen and sighed.

"I'm really sorry," she said putting down the scanner, "I'm sorry, but there is no heart beat."

Rosemary gripped my hand and looked at me with wide imploring eyes.

"I forgot to keep her heart beating." She whispered.

Poor Rosemary sank into the slough of despond. Her sparkle faded, her fizz evaporated, and she became withdrawn and emotional. She didn't set foot in the nursery for a long time and it put a tremendous strain on our relationship.

Two long years later we had a baby boy. Matt was a boisterous little lad, but Rosemary was obsessively protective, and I felt excluded. I was relegated to somewhere between wood lice and cockroaches in the family pecking order. The stress, fatigue and demands of raising a child weighed heavily on us, we had little time together and we often bickered over nothing.

The life style of an airline pilot put enormous strain on relationships and marriages. I spent more than half of my life away from home in five-star hotels socialising with young, frolicsome stewardesses. Rosemary, on the other hand had to deal with the everyday management of home and family. She learnt to become practicable and independent and dealt with the inevitable mini-crises on her own without support from me.

It was difficult to contact me; phone calls were unreliable and expensive. She had to consider the time change and knew not to disturb me before a flight. Conversely, a drunken phone call saying how much fun I was having in Bangkok, didn't go down well at 7.30 in the morning as Rosemary was getting Matt ready for nursery. She stopped trying to contact me. She handled the problems on her own and I was left very much to my own devices when I was away. I liked it that way.

She made her own world and I made mine.

When I came home, she resented me interfering with her routine and cracks started to appear in the foundations of our relationship.

My world was not real, I could escape the drudgery and banality of home life the moment I stepped into my car to drive to the airport. It was easy to live parallel lives and most crew accepted the status quo without question. The mantra was, 'what goes on down-route stays down-route.' There was some flexibility in the rostering system, and crew could arrange to fly together regularly. Affairs were commonplace, some of which lasted for years.

Berlin was a divided city surrounded by Communist states. BA was one of a few airlines permitted to operate the highly lucrative routes in and out of West Berlin. Ten flight crews were based in Berlin for three weeks every month and some of the very senior crew bid to be based there most months of the year. Berlin had a reputation for being a wild and vibrant city. Women vastly outnumbered men, and siege mentality led to some unlikely relationships.

At the height of the Cold War when BEA operated the flights along the Berlin corridor, one of their older Captains became involved with a vivacious blonde twenty-five years his junior. He spent more time with her in Berlin than with his wife in England.

Captain John Smith packed his bags as usual and put on his uniform. He pecked his wife on the cheek and departed for Berlin.

A week later John's mother had a stroke and was critically ill in hospital.

John's wife called the scheduling office and asked to be connected to her husband.

A few moments later a baffled voice replied. "I'm sorry to tell you, Mrs Smith, but Captain Smith retired six months ago."

Two bald men and a comb

The damaged pink and grey camouflaged Argentine Pucara stood forlornly by a stream in the valley between Mount Longdon and Mount Tumbledown. The nosewheel had collapsed, the nose was half buried in the soft peat, the propellers were bent back, and the sleet laden wind whistled through a jagged, gaping hole in one wing. Snagged tufts of wool fluttered on the barbed wire fence surrounding a minefield which ran under one wing. Bomb craters were filled with dark brackish water, brass shell cases littered the valley and miles of tangled telephone wire lay on the ground. Discarded plimsolls and empty packets of foot rot powder were piled in the shallow trenches.

The detritus of war.

The Falklands war ended in 1982. It was a pointless war over a scrap of useless land the size of Wales. A thousand people had died for a principle. Jorge Borges described the war as two bald men fighting over a comb.

I pulled my collar up and tried to warm my hands. The Captain was looking intently at a minefield map. We had been briefed that some mines were plastic and could be washed down streams. We were standing on the edge of a brook and I felt decidedly uncomfortable. The Captain wiped his large nose with his sleeve, squinted and pointed towards the east.

"Maybe we should go home?"

The Captain and I spent our time exploring the island on foot, visiting battlegrounds with such familiar names; Wireless Ridge, Sapper Hill and Mount Kent. It was a beautiful, wild, windswept country so reminiscent of the Yorkshire moors.

We ferried troops from RAF Brize Norton in Oxfordshire to Ascension Island in the South Atlantic were we had a five-day layover before we continued to the Falkland Islands. Ascension is a tiny British volcanic island just south of the equator in the middle of nowhere. It has a solitary cloud covered peak surrounded by a rocky, barren lunar landscape.

There wasn't much to do in Ascension apart from visiting the volcano or watching turtles hatch. One night we made our way down to the beach with a six pack of beer and perched on a rock. Waves lapped gently on the shore, the sea sparkled blue with bioluminescence and shimmering reflections of the full moon danced on the sea. Soon, the sand all over the beach started to move. Thousands of little turtles hatched and began their perilous journey to the ocean. They frantically scampered towards the sea, the night-time minimised the threat from Frigate birds and Black Triggerfish. The last stragglers reached the comparative safety of the ocean as the sun rose. We picked up our empty beer bottles and staggered off to the dormitory.

We were invited to celebrate Ascension Day at Government house in Georgetown and were ushered into the dining room of the unprepossessing pink and white two-storey building.

The Governor was splendidly dressed in a white tunic with gold and red trimmings. He wore an ostrich feather plumed pith-helmet, and a ceremonial sword in an ornate scabbard hung from his belt. He looked like a character from a Gilbert and Sullivan comic opera. He made speeches and presented awards, after which, an aide played The National Anthem on a record player. We were singing merrily along when the record player suddenly stopped mid chorus. Perplexed, the Governor turned towards the record player, and his scabbard knocked the sherry decanter off the table with a crash. He turned back rapidly and his befeathered bonnet fell off his smooth bald head onto the table and demolished the china tea set. Valiantly, his aide tried to save the day by continuing to sing the anthem without the accompaniment. Unfortunately, he had a squeaky, high-pitched voice and was utterly tone deaf.

I stuffed my napkin in my mouth to stop myself roaring with laughter.

The next day the Captain and I climbed Green Mountain which rises to 3,000ft above sea level. The island was completely barren until 150 years ago, when a British botanist introduced plants and grasses. The southern trades spawn persistent clouds on the volcanic peak which provides moisture for vegetation. We climbed from the Officers Mess at Traveller's Hill and the countryside slowly changed from desert to dry grassland, to sub-tropical forest near the summit. Land crabs scuttled noisily along the trails, birds trilled, and insects rasped in the trees. It was an extraordinary contrast from the arid heat at sea level. We passed the Red Lion military barracks, and stopped by the Dew Pond, where we signed the visitor's book in a letterbox, and stamped our passports as proof of our visit.

The fighting in The Falklands ended on the 12th June 1982 after more than two bloody months of combat. The airport at Stanley was too small for large transport planes and a larger one was built at Mount Pleasant. BA was contracted to fly troops to and from the island.

The first rays of dawn appeared in the east as we approached The Falklands. Two Phantom F4 fighters suddenly appeared at our wing tips as we descended in the milky early morning sun. At 10,000ft they peeled off in formation and climbed. They crossed upside down over us and descended vertically abeam our nose with their afterburners flashing and crackling.

We were still at war with Argentina, the island was bristling with testosterone filled soldiers and it was decided that it would be safer with an all-male crew. We were paid danger money of £1,000 each which was the equivalent of two and a half months pay for a squaddie. The only dangers we were likely to face was from rutting rams, crapping seagulls or flocks of homicidal penguins.

I shared a room with the Engineer in the Uplands Goose Hotel. The hotel was a white brick building with a red corrugated iron roof. The furnishings in our room were sparse, and two iron framed beds, covered by grubby candlewick bedspreads, stood on a threadbare carpet. The distemper walls were faded, and the air was musty and damp. It was snowing heavily, and a draft of cold air seeped from the ill-fitting window. The Engineer had short, tight curly hair and a turned-up nose. Ben chewed his lip as he dabbed paint on a small canvas resting on the faux escritoire. It appeared to be an aeroplane, it was rather good, but an aeroplane for goodness sake? I would have much preferred a portrait of Kim Basinger in the nude.

"He's turned the bloody heating off again!" Ben grumbled.

I touched the radiator, it was cold.

Des King was the owner of The Upland Goose Hotel. He was tall, slim, long faced with thin lips and prominent chin. He was notoriously spiky and was unfairly accused of collaborating with the Argentines during the war. He didn't seem to like us, but I don't think it was personal. His pretty, blonde daughter brightened the dreary restaurant with her radiant smile when she served breakfast in the mornings.

We invited a couple of young RAF officers from the officer's mess to join us at the Upland Goose for a pre-dinner drink. We were quietly drinking a glass of Everards Penguin ale, when Des suddenly said.

"Right you lot. Out!"

The RAF officers looked at us in surprise and put down their glasses. Embarrassed, the Captain tried to reason with Des, but he continued.

"Come on. Out!"

We downed our drinks, put on our parkas and trudged out into the snow towards the officer's mess.

We were entertained very well in the mess, and we staggered back to the hotel a couple of hours later. We gently pushed open the creaky front door and stepped into the hall.

"Bloody hell! It's cold" exclaimed Ben, blowing on his hands.

Des often switched off the central heating at night while his guests shivered in their draughty rooms.

"I'm going to switch the damn heating back on," said Ben full of beery bravado.

He opened a side door and descended into the boiler room. A monstrous ancient steel boiler with a tangle of pipes and valves greeted us.

"Ah yes, let me see," said Ben, opening a few valves and flipping on a switch.

"Are you sure you know what you're doing?" I asked lamely.

"No problem".

With a woomph, the boiler burst into life, the pipes clicked, and hot water started to circulate. We closed the door and tiptoed upstairs. The radiator in our room began to give off some welcome heat when a mighty clunk rang out from downstairs.

I looked at Ben.

"Oh shit! The boiler's cavitating. I forgot to open the return valve!"

There was another clang, followed by repeated loud metallic knocking sounds. The noise was deafening, but not loud enough to drown out the sound of Des bellowing in the hallway.

"Which of you bastards have been messing about with my heating? Who was it? Come on!"

I cowered under my bed covers.

I flew to Los Angeles for a three-day layover.

There was concern among the citizens of Los Angeles about the militarisation of the Police Department. The formation of SWAT units and the adoption of military tactics were a result of the Watts riots in 1965. The concern was aggravated by rumours of fanatical splinter groups of policemen sporting names such as 'Men Against Women,' and 'White Anglo-Saxon Police'. The LAPD was sometimes referred to as an occupying army, and as a public relations exercise, the Mayor of Santa Monica invited members of the public to accompany police on duty, to experience at first hand their difficult working conditions.

I read about the 'Ride-Along' scheme in 'The Argonaut' at breakfast. I called the City Hall and explained that I wasn't an American citizen. Perhaps their attendance figures were low because, much to my surprise, they told me to report at 6pm that evening.

I signed the usual waivers at reception and was escorted into the briefing room. I sat at a desk, surrounded by about twenty policemen listening to an older sergeant standing at a lectern. It was like a scene from 'Hill Street Blues'. The briefing continued for ten minutes.

The sergeant put his hands either side of the lectern and peered over his half-moon glasses.

"We're down on numbers so most of you'll drive alone tonight."

"Foster!" he called.

"Yes sir!" A pudgy red-faced looking patrolman put his hand up.

"Your assessment ride will be with Sergeant Schneider here. OK?" He indicated a man standing in the corner in plain clothes.

The flustered patrolman nodded in acknowledgement.

He shuffled the papers on his desk.

"Be careful out there," he said laconically," some kook has phoned in to say he is going to kill a cop tonight".

The policemen stood up and chatted amongst themselves. I was completely ignored.

The duty sergeant wandered over to me holding a piece of paper.

"Fairdale?"

"That's me."

"You'll be riding with Earl." He pointed towards a tall muscular policeman with blond hair, standing on his own writing in a small black notebook.

The sergeant looked at the paper in his hand and turned it over.

"He's gotta renew his handgun proficiency. You'll be patrolling the beach and Wilshire Montana. Listen to what he says for your own safety. Good luck"

Earl didn't shake my hand or even acknowledge my existence as he strode off down the corridor. I followed him to the underground range where I was relieved to see each of his bullets hit the target dead centre.

We climbed into a Dodge police cruiser and drove off. He screeched to a halt just outside the precinct gates and jabbed me in the chest with a stubby finger.

"I don't know why the fuck you're here!" He growled with his lips curled back, glaring at me. "I don't like being spied on. I can't stand Coons and I hate Spics!" he spat.

"If you don't like that you can fuck off!"

So much for public relations!

"No. I, um" I stammered as he accelerated toward Ocean Avenue.

The sun was low in the sky illuminating a shimmering path in the Pacific Ocean, as we cruised along Ocean Avenue. Earl warmed himself up by bullying an old lady and giving her a parking ticket. The next call was to a domestic dispute. He barged into the flat, manhandled the Hispanic husband roughly to the floor and bent his arm painfully behind his back. His wife tried to defend him, but Earl yelled aggressively and pushed her away. She backed off in tears.

Earl lectured them and let them off with a verbal warning.

Five police cruisers were on duty, and every two hours, we met in a diner for coffee and a sandwich. I sat next to Sergeant Schneider. He was an approachable crew-cut man with a large moustache and tanned face. Patrolman Foster was on probation, and this was his final chance. I had the impression that Schneider had already made his mind up to fail him.

We cruised along one of the many small alleyways off Pico. Earl was sweeping driveways with his spotlight when he saw something and stopped. A group of blacks stood around a large rusty Chevvy.

One of the men looked away.

"I recognise him." said Earl pulling on the handbrake. "He's wanted for attempted murder and aggravated assault."

He pulled out his pistol and opened the door.

"Follow me!" he barked.

No bloody way! I thought, there were at least eight of them. I locked the door and slunk down in my seat.

Give him his due, he fearlessly waded into the pack and dragged a large, loudly protesting black dude along with him. He handcuffed him and threw him on the back seat just behind me. We were separated by a thin wire grille, he was breathing heavily, and his breath smelled of alcohol and weed.

We sped back to the City Hall and our prisoner started to wind Earl up. He called him a white honky and suggested that Earl had had immoral relations with his mother, amongst other things. Earl lost his cool, jammed on the brakes, pointed his gun through the grille at the suspect and shouted.

"How'd you like a bullet in the knee, Nigger?"

I wished I had a sign to hold up explaining I wasn't a cop, and that I mistakenly thought I was on a trip from Universal Studios.

Thankfully we delivered our captive without further incident and we were back out on patrol an hour later.

Just before midnight the radio crackled into life reporting a burglary in progress at a gas station.

"We'll surprise them." said Earl gleefully.

We buckled our 5-point seatbelts, he switched on his siren and we shot off like a rocket, wailing like a banshee. He drove like a demon possessed, mounting the pavement, swerving around cars and missing bystanders by inches. It was incredibly exciting, and it wasn't long before we caught up with the others.

So much for stealth, we could be heard all the way to San Francisco.

As we approached, the sirens and lights were finally switched off and the cars quietly coasted to a halt surrounding the gas station. That is except for Foster who backed into a pile of dustbins, which fell over with a clatter and rolled noisily down the street. Foster got out of his car, slammed the door and promptly dropped his pistol.

Schneider covered his eyes with the palm of his hand and moaned.

The robbers were long gone.

The shift finished at two in the morning. Police were not allowed to buy alcohol in uniform, so I was asked to go out and buy a couple of six packs.

We sat around a table in a brightly lit canteen drinking what Americans laughingly call beer.

Foster wasn't there.

Command

The popular image of an airline Captain as a dashing, chisel-jawed, steely-eyed Biggles-type character is seriously flawed.

This perception is a legacy from a bygone era, when aircraft were unreliable, weather forecasting was inaccurate, and navigation was in its infancy. Pilots were real pilots, often having to fly by 'the seat of their pants'. Modern aircraft rarely have serious problems, weather forecasting is relatively accurate, bad weather can be avoided with the use of radar, and the navigator has been replaced by inertial navigation systems. Some self-important pilots like to perpetuate this myth, but pilots have become no more than glorified bus drivers.

Most of our passengers, I sensed, were uncomfortable trapped in a claustrophobic aluminium tube hurtling through the sky at great speed, miles above the ground. They had no control over events, little knowledge of what was occurring, and lurid stories of aircraft accidents filled their minds. Hundreds of anxious people had their lives in my hands, but I didn't feel any great responsibility. If I didn't kill myself, the chances were, that I was unlikely to kill anyone else.

The Command Course was intense. We spent two months in the classroom learning about legal responsibilities, decision making, crew co-ordination and a host of other subjects. We flew six diabolical simulator sessions and finally flew four scheduled flights under training.

I had four gold stripes on my sleeve.

At last.

The Manager Special Services called me to tell me that I would be taking Prince Edward on an unofficial visit to Toronto. He would be accompanied by a Metropolitan Police Sergeant, and they were travelling under the names of Smith and Jones. How original, I thought.

Apart from the Queen, I have never been a fan of the Royal Family, and I am hard pressed to know which Monarchical minion is which.

When I boarded the aircraft, I was annoyed to discover that they had been upgraded to first-class. After lunch, I put on my jacket and hat, and made my way downstairs to talk to the Prince.

A spiral staircase behind the flight deck descends to the galley at the back of first-class. The first-class cabin was in the nose of the 747 with all seats facing forward. The chief steward excitedly pointed them out to me in the two front seats on the left side. The backs of their heads were just visible over the large armchair style seats. I knew the Prince was young, so he had to be the one with a full head of dark hair; the other was sparse and balding.

With some trepidation, I walked towards them. No one had told me what the protocol was. Should I call him 'Your Holiness'? 'Your Beatitude?' 'Your Oneness'? Should I bow? or what? I turned to face them in a quandary. I managed a sort of bow which looked like a mincing, genuflective half curtsy. Stuttering, I addressed the hirsute passenger in the most obsequious fashion. Halfway through my lubricious litany he interrupted me.

"Excuse me Captain, but this is the Prince"

The Sergeant pointed to the follicly challenged young man sitting next to him.

I said goodbye to my MBE.

I might have been able to find a job with the Met though.

I flew to Johannesburg with a First Officer who was on his first trip to Africa. Alan had completed a long-term commission with the RAF and joined BA. He was bearded, tall and serious. He turned down my offer to eat at the 'Forestica Magnetica' in Nairobi and I was joined by two stewardesses and a tall, barrel-chested, gay steward nicknamed Dutch Johan.

The makeshift band finished the first stint in the crowded smoky restaurant, and we had a chance to talk without shouting. Johan sat opposite me, and the girls faced each other at our table on the edge of the dance floor. The waiters cleared away the plates and refilled our wineglasses. Rosie was an impish, short, freckly redhead while Claire was a tall thin blonde.

"It's so boring compared with Tristars." cooed Rosie, her eyes focussed on me.

Claire nodded in agreement.

They had been transferred to the 747 from the Lockheed L1011 Tristar fleet when the fleet was disbanded.

I took a sip of wine, looked at Rosie and replied.

"Why was it better on the Tristars?"

Rosie paused.

"Well we had great room parties"

"So, do we."

"We always jumped into the pool with our uniforms on in the Caribbean."

"Nothing new there."

"We'd get naked at room parties," she said defiantly.

I paused.

"OK Rosie, you win. Doesn't happen on the 747." I conceded.

The wine flowed and the band finished its second stint. We were a bit tipsy and I felt a foot stroking mine under the table.

I looked at Rosie and Claire. I surreptitiously peeked under the table, and there was Johan's size 11s on top of my foot.

Johan grinned at me impudently.

I glowered at him.

I hatched a plan.

"If you lot are so wild, I dare you to serve the First Officer his breakfast in the nude on the way to Joburg."

It was a four-hour daylight sector between Nairobi and Johannesburg and the timing was going to be tight.

The girls thought about it for a moment and both agreed.

'Fat chance' I thought.

"I'll stand guard and use the Polaroid to prove it," Johan chipped in.

A Polaroid camera was included in the amenity stores for the passengers to take snaps of themselves having a wonderful time with BA.

Pickup was at 0700 the next morning and the two girls looked decidedly worse for wear as we climbed onto the crew bus.

An hour south of Nairobi, Alan cupped his hands over his headset as he struggled to understand Dar es Salaam on HF radio. The static was caused by a thin layer of cloud we were flying through. We adjusted the sun visors to shade us from the sunlight reflected from the cloud.

The curtain drew back. Rosie walked with a breakfast tray dressed only in suspenders and stockings. Claire followed wearing just an apron.

Johan stood in the doorway, standing guard with the Polaroid in his hand, grinning.

The Engineer turned around and slumped in his seat with his mouth open in surprise. Claire stood behind my seat with her glorious naked backside facing the camera.

Rosie tapped Alan on the shoulder, and he swatted her hand away in irritation, still trying to understand Dar-es-Salaam. Eventually he turned around.

The look on his face was priceless.

The look on my face was lecherous.

I know, I have the photographs to prove it.

Flying proffered a unique perspective of the world. We crossed folded mountain ranges with impunity, we followed mighty rivers to the sea, and we witnessed the celestial ballet in the immensity of space. We were humbled by the power of immense thunderstorms, of inexorable glaciers inching to the sea and the primal force of erupting volcanos. We danced with northern lights, surfed stratospheric jet-streams and chased the sun.

In the same way I am at home in the mountains. I delight in the wide-open spaces, the humbling majesty and the stark beauty.

I learnt to ski from an early age and became proficient. I loved to show off on precipitous slopes, trek inaccessible peaks or pose at fashionable ski resorts.

I met Greg on a two-week ski holiday in Courcheval.

He flew Hunters for the Royal Navy based at RNAS Yeovilton. He was socially inadequate and at times seemed remarkably thick, yet he was a finalist on Mastermind. He was impulsive, clumsy and blunt. His table manners were appalling, and he was loud and boastful. No one wanted to ski with him although he was a good skier. I felt sorry for him and skied with him for the rest of the holiday.

On the last day of the holiday he asked me if I would like a flight in a Hunter. Most pilots would jump at such an opportunity, but I had my reservations. He had firmly attached himself to me on holiday and I wanted to distance myself.

Not wanting to offend him, I agreed.

RNAS Yeovilton is in the west of England and is the Royal Navy's largest airbase. Greg told me I had to wear uniform and my four gold stripes commanded interest wherever I went. I was saluted incessantly, but I had no idea how to return the compliment. My best efforts resembled a sort of limp-wristed Regal wave.

Two hours later carrying a bulky parachute, I staggered towards the apron, wearing rubber underwear and a G suit. My helmet had a large white cross painted on top, and an oxygen mask was clipped to one side. It was too small and dug painfully into my temples. I felt like Darth Vader.

Greg was by the Hunter doing the walkaround check. The Hunter was tiny, and I made a big mistake.

"Christ, Greg, it's like a Cessna with a jet engine!" I joked.

He didn't see the funny side of it and ignored me.

The Hawker Sidley Hunter T8 was a 1960's two seat, side by side fighter trainer used for ship radar tracking exercises. I sat in the right seat while Greg busied himself with the checklist. I carefully placed a BA sick bag in the stowage by my right knee. I clipped on my oxygen mask, adjusted my throat microphone and armed my ejector seat.

We taxied onto the runway and Greg opened the throttle. The acceleration was impressive as we short down the runway and lifted off. Greg overcontrolled the aircraft as we climbed away, and he yanked the joystick around as if he was stirring a bowl of porridge. It was most uncomfortable.

"I suppose you'd like a go, Colin?" His voice crackled in my ear phones.

'Have a go?' I Thought, 'Have a go?' it was the only reason I was there.

"Be careful. Don't over control. It's not like your 747."

It was easy-peasy and feather-light. We gracefully climbed towards the south. Passing 25,000 ft Yeovilton Control informed us our mission had been cancelled, and we could return when we wished.

"Aerobatics, Colin?" asked Greg looking at me, his visor and mask completely hid his face. The bright sun reflected off the scratches on the windshield and it was uncomfortably warm.

"Want to try a loop?"

A loop is the simplest aerobatic manoeuvre, I hadn't done one for years, but Greg talked me through it.

I dived down and pulled up too hard. At the top of the loop the wings shuddered in a stall, and we tumbled out of the sky.

"I have control, I'll show you," Greg chuckled.

The next ten minutes was a blur of G forces and a kaleidoscope of whirling colours and shadows.

I felt decidedly uncomfortable.

"What now?" he asked.

'Anything but bloody aerobatics', I thought.

"Low flying perhaps?" I ventured, knowing that he couldn't do aerobatics close to the ground.

We tumbled out of the sky like a falling leaf until we levelled out over Exmoor at 200ft upside down. The umbilicus of my oxygen mask waved in front of my eyes in the turbulence as we bounced along. It was hot, very hot and I was perspiring. Sweat was trickling on the inside of my immersion suit. Suddenly I realised that I was going to be sick. I ripped off my oxygen mask and reached up for the sick bag by my feet. It's amazing how projectile vomit is. With one loud retch I puked into the upside-down bag. The sound was amplified by my throat mic and the smell percolated the cramped cockpit.

Aghast, Greg glanced at me and quickly rolled the Hunter the right way up. The sudden movement surprised me, and I let go of the bag which floated gently towards Greg and impinged itself on his left window. It exploded, and for a moment of zero gravity, the contents of the bag hovered over

Greg in a gelatinous cloud. Normal gravity returned and the pervasive puke plonked onto Greg.

"We should return to base," he spluttered, wiping diced carrot from his visor.

That was surprising, I hadn't eaten carrots for days.

I just wanted to get out and walk.

On the approach to land, a Sea Harrier backed across the runway and we were forced to go around. Fighters are fuel critical and they need to land as soon as possible after a go around. Greg pulled up into a gut-wrenching 4G left turn, and one minute later, we were once again on the approach. I needed to vomit again. The problem was that my sick bag was still stuck on the left window. I picked up Greg's hat and was violently sick once again into it.

Greg wound back the canopy and he leaned out of the cockpit as we taxied onto dispersal. The mechanics laughed their heads off at the sight of a very highly paid blob of BA green jelly slumped in the right seat.

I gave them £10 each to clean up the mess.

Northwest Frontier

With an audible crack, the bolt of lightning struck. My instruments briefly flickered, I glanced quickly around but everything looked normal. There were no comments from the other two, so I announced.

"Gear Up! Continuing!" and we climbed slowly into the leaden, turbulent evening skies above Manchester towards Islamabad.

We were at our maximum take-off weight, and the airspeed was fluctuating wildly in the turbulence, so I had to be careful not to overstress the flaps. The last section of flap retracted and suddenly a warning sounded. The landing gear wasn't fully up.

'That's not possible' I thought, there's no vibration or any other indications. The lightning must have fried the electronics. Reluctantly I called for the 'gear not locked up' checklist.

My heart sank, my brother John was sitting in the observer seat behind me, and we were on our way to find our Grandfather's grave.

We had a problem.

My ancestors served in the Royal Artillery for generations. My Grandfather was one of the first soldiers to arrive in France in the Great War, and one of the last to leave. He was posted to the North West Frontier of India where he died in 1928 near the Khyber Pass in one of the many small tribal wars which sprung up in the lawless border zone between the Pathans and the Afghanis.

John had a black and white photo of the headstone and on the bottom of the plinth was the inscription 'Kadar Bux, Nowshera'. Nowshera is a garrison town not far from Peshawar, the capital of the Province of Khyber. We had a five-day layover in Islamabad and my brother, and I intended to find his grave, and perhaps visit the Khyber Pass. The Khyber Pass has an infamous place in British military history. The road between Afghanistan and India passes through a narrow, treacherous, ravine in the mountains straddling the border. It is easy to defend, and many soldiers and tribesmen have died trying to cross it.

The Russians had invaded Afghanistan and the border was closed.

The Engineer read out the checklist while Alan, the First Officer, flipped switches and pulled circuit breakers. To no avail, the gear still showed unlocked. I had no choice, we couldn't continue, and we had to return to Manchester. We were above our maximum landing weight and we needed to dump fuel. I obtained clearance from air traffic control and called for the 'Fuel Jettison' checklist. Soon we were dumping kerosene at a rate of two tonnes per minute into the sky above the sleepy town of Leicester. A couple of minutes later the gear warning light extinguished, and we immediately stopped dumping. We had dumped five tonnes of fuel. I rapidly calculated that if we used long range cruise and took a few short cuts we should be able to make it to Islamabad.

I heaved a sigh of relief.

The solitary first-class passenger was dressed in an immaculate suit and tie and sipped a cup of tea. He was slight, with grey flecked hair, pale olive skin and a bushy black moustache. He asked what had happened out of Manchester and I explained. He seemed convinced that I had saved his life.

"I understand you have five days in Islamabad Captain? Is that correct?" he asked in perfect English, peering at me with his dark gentle eyes. "What do you intend to do?"

I explained my proposed search.

"Nowshera is a long way from Islamabad. You must take my driver. It's a dangerous road. I insist"

I politely declined.

He changed tack.

"Which hotel do you stay at in Islamabad, Captain?"

"'The Holiday Inn'."

"I own the Holiday Inn."

"I'll take the car then" I said without hesitation.

The chief steward had informed me his daughter was travelling with him in economy, so I asked him to upgrade his daughter to first-class after the meal service.

The staff at the 'Holiday Inn' literally rolled out the red carpet for us. The early morning filtered through the large arched windows of the lobby as the manager presented me with a large bouquet of flowers.

"If there's anything we can do for you, please let us know?" he said politely.

"There is, I would like to visit the Khyber Pass. Is that possible?" I asked.

He thought about it for a minute and replied.

"The border area is closed because of the Russians. You will need a pass. The only way is to ask the Chief of Police in Islamabad." He looked at me. "If you can find him."

The next morning our driver picked us up at the hotel in a grey Hindustan Ambassador car. Iqbal was slight with a small black moustache and a drawn-out face. He opened the door for John and me.

"Nowshera Sahib?" he asked as we drove away from the hotel.

The road soon became pot-holed and uneven. A few scrawny bushes struggled valiantly in the strip of parched and rocky earth alongside the rail track which followed the Grand Trunk Road west. Clouds of dust and flies filled the air as gaudily painted, high sided lorries trundled past loaded with goods. We overtook smoky, crammed busses with luggage precariously perched on the roofs and avoided skittish pony carts trotting in the centre of the road. At Attock we drove slowly across the fast-flowing Indus on the steel bridge built almost a century before. A steam train puffed and clattered across the bridge above us. A few minutes later we passed the confluence of the Kabul and Indus rivers, where the murky, silt laden waters collided in a froth of turbulent eddies.

We arrived at the gates of the Nowshera Cantonment. An arched sign over the entrance proudly proclaimed, 'GUNNERS' 'School of Artillery'. Britain handed the camp to Pakistan after partition in 1947 and little had changed.

Iqbal spoke rapidly to the guard and showed him the photograph of the headstone. The guard scratched his head and picked up a cracked Bakelite telephone. A few moments later a sergeant arrived and escorted us to the Commandant's office.

A creaky ceiling fan whirred in the roof beams of the Victorian office ruffling charts and papers scattered on the Colonel's large oak desk. The sergeant sat down at a small desk in the corner of the room and picked up a file. The Colonel stroked his chin and looked up from the photo.

"I'm sorry, I don't think I can help."

He opened a drawer, pulled out a magnifying glass and examined the photo closely.

The sergeant started to type on an ancient type writer. The irritating, mechanical clack clack of the keys filled the room

"There's a building in the background which looks familiar. I'll ask my bearer." Muttered the Colonel

He shouted something towards the door and it slowly opened. A timorous grey bearded old man stood to attention.

The Colonel showed him the photo and spoke to him. Grasping the photo in his crooked hands, the wizened old man peered intently at it. He slowly nodded in recognition.

We followed the shuffling old man across an empty dusty parade ground surrounded by crumbling barracks. We crossed a road and arrived at a walled patch of overgrown land. He pushed aside a rusty iron gate and it was apparent that we were in an old cemetery. A few headstones stood above the scrub and grass, while others lay flat beneath the undergrowth. It seemed that they had been deliberately broken. A sea of wild grass covered the cemetery, and befittingly, the field was covered in a carpet of red poppies.

It was very strange, I knew he was there.

I was certain

We lined up the photo with an old tree and started lifting the stones. We found a dirty headstone in two pieces lying face down on the ground and cleared away the grass and earth. We turned the heavy pieces of stone over and fitted them together.

In Memory Of
1048887
BSM Fairdale PE
Died 20ᵗʰ July 1928
Aged 35 years
Erected by his comrades

I felt a surge of emotion standing six feet above a person I never knew, but without whom I wouldn't be there.

We stood quietly with the old man next to us.

John pulled a small phial out of his pocket. He sombrely sprinkled a few drops of water from the river Thames over the grave and buried a silver sixpence, minted the year of Grandfather's birth, in the stony soil.

He had obviously been much more optimistic about finding the grave than me.

Iqbal stood in silence watching us.

"We must mend the headstone, Colin" said John with a halting voice.

I pointed out the name 'Kadar Bux' on the headstone to the old man and Iqbal soon learnt that the stonemason still had a workshop in the village.

Iqbal led the way into the small workshop which was lined with marble monuments adorned with Arabic writing and brightly coloured motifs. Dust wafted in from passing cars and pony traps.

The two grandsons of Kadar looked at the photo with amusement. They didn't look like brothers, the chubby one had a round grey stubbled face and wore a flat Pashtun pakol hat. The thinner had a heavy black beard and a white linen sindi cap perched on his shaven head. They agreed to look at the headstone.

We huddled around the grave as passing soldiers looked on. I haggled the price down from the equivalent of £1 to 70 pence, we shook hands and departed for the hotel.

We arrived back at the hotel mid-afternoon and Alan met us in the lobby. We decided to try to visit the Khyber Pass the next day and Alan said that one of the stewardesses wanted to join us.

Alan came to the Police Headquarters with me. He looked like a local, his thick black beard and dark skin was very Pashtun. I had flown with him to Joburg the previous year, and we laughed as he recounted the tale of being served breakfast by naked cabin crew.

We arrived at the entrance gate of the white five-storey Police Headquarters and asked the surly looking sentry if we could see the Chief of Police. The guard looked puzzled and picked up the telephone. He spoke quietly into the phone and replaced it in the cradle.

"Not possible. Mr Khan is busy for now." he said abruptly.

"OK, in that case we'll wait in the garden."

We sat on a bench. The warmth of the early evening sun and the scent from the flowers made us feel drowsy. Sparrows chirped in the bushes, traffic hummed in the distance and motes of dust floated in sunshine. I was in no hurry.

After a long wait, the guard slid open a side window and said that Mr Khan would see us after all.

I asked Alan to see what it was all about.

A few minutes later Alan returned.

"He wants to see us, Colin" he exclaimed. "He's on our flight on Thursday, and guess what? He's in economy!"

The guard led us to an oversized office. Mr Khan was a larger than life, theatrical character with black hair and moustache. He wore a blue shirt covered in medals and was addressing a group of journalists. He was in an expansive mood, gesticulating grandly at maps and charts pinned to a message board and talking loudly in Urdu. Eventually the reporters picked up their papers and pencils and filed out of the room. Mr Khan closed the door, turned to face us and motioned us towards some chairs by a large desk.

We introduced ourselves.

"Please, sit down. What can I do for you?" he asked in slightly accented English.

I explained.

He sat back in his seat and put his hands behind his head.

"The border is closed. It's very dangerous. The Russians launched a missile attack only a few days ago. I'm sorry but I can't permit you to go."

Undeterred, I turned to him and said.

"I believe you are flying to England with us on Thursday Mr Khan, and you are in economy? Is that correct?"

He nodded.

"Well I'm sure that I could arrange a more comfortable seat for you if you wish. Our new first-class seats are the best in the world, or so I'm told."

He put his elbows on the table, intertwined his fingers and peered at me with his dark eyes.

A few moments later he said.

"I see. I could make an exception, I suppose".

He unlocked his fingers and scribbled on a piece of paper which he handed to me.

"My brother is the Chief of Police in Peshawar. I will call him. Report tomorrow morning at 0800 at the Police station in Peshawar and he will have the passes for you"

With that he stood up, shook my hand and said.

"See you on Thursday."

At five o'clock in the morning we clambered into the car. We planned to drive through Nowshera to Peshawar and I hoped to check on the repairs to the headstone. Julie, a cheerful curvaceous blonde, sat next to me. I had warned her we would be visiting tribal areas and told her not to wear anything provocative. She met us in the lobby wearing a diaphanous jump suit.

John had dinner the night before with a school friend who was the Naval Attaché at the British Consul. His friend mentioned that the Pakistan Army was about to test the latest version of the Chinese silk-worm missile in Nowshera.

"If you see anything, would you mind taking a few photos old boy?" he asked him.

I threatened to confiscate John's camera if he so much as took it out anywhere near Nowshera.

Peshawar is a medieval fortified town. The centre is a warren of mud brick alleyways and buildings in various states of disrepair.

We were ushered into Police Chief Khan's office with a minimum of fuss. We handed him the piece of paper from his brother which he studied for a few moments. He called for tea and sponge cake which we politely ate as he asked us about our trip. He sat with his feet on his desk and said he never flew Pakistan Airlines as they didn't serve alcohol. He then extolled the virtues of Glenlivet whisky.

He put his feet on the floor and turned to us.

"Mr Fairdale, you must realise that the border area is very dangerous. I will provide a five-man armed guard and you must always follow their orders. They will take you to the Political Agent in Landi Kotal at the top of the Khyber Pass. He is the senior government official in the Khyber Tribal area. I have also arranged for you to visit the village of Darra where replica weapons are made. You will find it very interesting."

He stood up and shook our hands.

"I don't know how you've managed to persuade my brother" he said without taking his eyes off Julie, "but be careful."

Our guard was waiting for us in an open-backed black lorry as we drove out from the police compound in Peshawar. They were a mean looking bunch dressed in dark blue military fatigues, wearing red-badged black berets and toting Kalashnikov AK-47s.

The road to Jalalabad snakes through precipitous mountains towards Landi Kotal at the top of the Khyber Pass. Abandoned forts line the route, some from British times, others from hundreds of years earlier. Each is a mute testament to the strategic importance of the pass. On the right, the now disused railway doggedly follows the road, half buried in sand.

We drove into a compound in Landi Kotal and were met by a middle-aged white-haired man wearing white baggy trousers, white linen kurta and dark grey waistcoat. He warmly shook my hand and we followed him into a walled garden in front of a flat roofed, red brick bungalow with large arched windows. It was an oasis of colour. Flowers bloomed everywhere. Foxgloves, lupins, marigolds and roses grew in the shade of almond trees, olives and pines. We sat on chairs arranged around a small table in front of the bungalow. A waiter placed food and drinks on the low table. A door opened and a large man in long white kurta and pyjama trousers strode towards us and introduced himself as the Political Agent. He seemed quite confused as to who we were. We must be important as we had such a large escort. Poor Iqbal looked quite overwhelmed, surrounded by such important political bigwigs.

He sat down and helped himself to some figs.

The Agent took a shine to Julie's breasts. He couldn't take his eyes off them as he explained how important he was. I think he was trying to impress her.

A waiter served him a large slice of sponge cake which he shovelled into his mouth.

Julie asked him if we could go into Afghanistan.

"It's normally not be possible my dear," he said, as he leered at her, "but I'm sure I can make an exception."

Crumbs fell from his mouth as he spoke.

After lunch we drove down the snaking road towards Kabul with our guard in tow.

The Agent beamed at Julie.

Two small castellated stone towers and a large iron gate marked the border into Afghanistan at Torkum. The gate was symbolic as there was no fence either side of the towers. We jumped out of the minibus and stood on the edge of the sandy road. Julie's voluptuous figure was accentuated by a strong cool wind.

The Agent purred in delight.

A gaggle of armed Mujahedeen milled around the gate, one without legs sat in a wheelchair. The Agent pushed through and heaved open the gate while our guards stood in a line with their guns at the ready. I felt most uncomfortable.

We filed through the gate into Afghanistan, and that was it. We turned around and walked back into Pakistan. For good measure, the Agent took an AK47 from one of the Mujahedeen and gave it to me to have our photograph taken.

The gun-less Mujahedeen stood behind me muttering and growling. I thought he was going to rip my head off.

Back at the bungalow, the Agent asked me to sign the visitor's book as we said our farewells. The most recent entry was Princess Anne, 15 years earlier.

Our convoy trundled down the Khyber Pass and turned towards the south. Half an hour later our escort was relieved by one from Darra. We were now outside the jurisdiction of Peshawar. Our five strapping commandos were replaced by two octogenarian policemen in mismatched light blue uniforms, brown berets, and armed with what looked like antiquated matchlock rifles.

Darra is 40 miles south of Peshawar on the road to Kohat. The unkempt village is famous for fabricating weapons from the most rudimentary materials and it is said gunsmiths can make an exact replica of an unseen gun in less than ten days. The weapons range from simple pen-pistols to anti-aircraft guns. Nearly all the shops in this miserable wood and adobe village are small arms factories.

The village elders were courteous and greeted us warmly. A young boy, with striking pale blue eyes, was our translator. We sat at a low table among bright carpets and leather pouffes and ate Dud Patti, fruit and sponge cake. The young boy's English was very good, and he explained that he wanted to go to England to become a doctor. I looked around at the squalor and thought his chances were slim.

After tea we were taken on a tour of the arms factories and shops. The young lad led the way as we walked between the shops, and we soon attracted a crowd of curious onlookers. The shops were small, dark and cramped. Men and boys filed cheap steel concrete reinforcement rods with hand rasps or worked at lathes. The crowd tried to follow us into each shop we visited, and we could barely move. In one of the larger 'showrooms' Julie was handed a pristine AK47 and our translator asked her if she would like to try it out. Apparently, she could test fire it in an alley next to the shop, and after a little coercion, we persuaded her to give it a go. Holding the gun Julie was steered outside by the excited crowd.

Our Home Guard looked a little uneasy.

Julie stood in the alley with her feet apart and pointed the AK-47 slightly up in the air. Flat roofed shops with faded shop signs lined the dusty back alley which terminated in a large mound of earth. The store owner put his arms around Julie to steady the gun and explained what to do.

He lingered a little longer than perhaps he needed to. He backed away and the crowd fell silent

Julie took a deep breath and closed her eyes. The gun wobbled. She squeezed the trigger and started firing in a deafening staccato. With each round her boobs jiggled dramatically, and the crowd roared encouragement. She gradually lost her balance with each recoil; the barrel rose alarmingly in the air and Julie fell flat on her back without releasing the trigger. Bullets sprayed everywhere, ricocheting of the buildings and kicking up puffs of dust in the alley. The crowd hooted with laughter as they dived to the ground or scurried for cover.

It was late evening and we prepared to depart for the hotel. An old man presented me with an intricately designed pen-gun and a box of bullets. It was an oversized, damascene, gun-metal Montblanc pen. The blue -eyed young translator asked if I would like to try it out. It looked bloody dangerous to me, so I politely asked if someone could demonstrate it for me. We walked out towards the car.

The old man removed the nib, unscrewed the cap and inserted a .25 bullet into the tube. He replaced the cap, held the pen at arm's length and pointed it down the street. He pulled the clip back and released it. There was a loud detonation and a brick on the corner of a building disintegrated in a cloud of dust.

I thanked them, took the gun and got into the car. The blue-eyed boy waved energetically as we departed in a cloud of dust.

I threw the bullets away as soon as we left the village, but I took a long time to decide what to do with the gun. It was a beautifully made memento of an extraordinary trip, but what would happen if it was discovered by security at the airport?

I dreaded to think.

I tossed it out of the window into the moonless night.

The Wrath of God

I was frightened to death.

I was sure I had it and I wished I had been more careful. It got to the stage where I didn't let Matt share my towel, use my toothpaste or even take a sip from my glass.

It was World AIDS day.

There was so much ignorance, hysteria and fear. The disease seemed to be fatally incurable and easy to catch. The Sunday Times suggested that half the planet would be dead by the year 2000 and headlines such as 'Is this the wrath of God?' or 'Plague brings new havoc' appeared in the tabloids.

Initially it was thought to be a 'gay disease'. A disproportionate number of the male cabin crew were gay and some swung both ways which is why I was concerned. A few of the more promiscuous crew described gay bath houses in San Francisco where it was possible to have as many as 20 encounters in one night. It was not surprising that the disease was out of control.

The virus had a long incubation period and symptoms might not be apparent for months or even years, so an unwitting carrier could infect many people. Rumours had it that a few stewards had already died from AIDS and others were gravely ill.

Long-haul crew were required to be inoculated against yellow fever every 10 years. The inoculation can activate AIDS, and many male cabin crew transferred to short-haul to avoid the jab.

Maybe it was my imagination but life down the route became more reserved and I wondered if wild room parties would become a thing of the past.

I flew a trip to Dhahran and back just before Christmas and I heard on the radio on the way to the airport for that a PanAm 747 had crashed in Scotland killing all on board. How tragic, 259 people had died returning to the USA for the Christmas holidays.

There was speculation it might have been a terrorist attack.

How anyone could do such a thing was totally beyond me.

I departed Dhahran for a night flight back to London on Christmas Eve. Most of our passengers were oilmen coming home for Christmas. Saudi Arabia is dry and BA, in their wisdom, loaded twice the normal amount of alcohol for the flight.

It was a dark moonless night as we cruised at 35,000ft over Turkey. I decided to do a walk-about and talk to the passengers. I put on my jacket and straightened my tie in the mirror. 'Very much the steely-eyed jet Captain' I thought.

The first-class passengers were asleep, I chatted to a few club class passengers and then pushed aside the curtains into economy. A fug of cigarette smoke and alcohol hit me. The lights were out but most of the passengers were awake. Some passengers were walking aimlessly around stretching their legs.

Two rows of toilets separated by a narrow corridor are at the back of the aircraft. A group of rough looking men crowded the entrance to Death's dark vale with drinks in hand. Resplendent in my uniform I squeezed past to return to the flight deck.

Somebody grabbed me by the balls!

I was completely flummoxed, I had no idea what to do! I wasn't taught how to deal with this sort of situation on my command course.

I went bright red, spluttered and pushed my way past.

A few seconds later, a man caught up with me and tapped me on the shoulder.

"I'm really sorry, Captain, my friend thought you were a steward."

A steward!

I looked at my impressive gold rings. How could I possibly look like a steward?

"Well tell your friend," I snapped, "I can have him arrested for interfering with the Captain if he's not careful!"

It just didn't sound right.

The man smirked.

I went bright red again and sloped back to the flight deck looking like Rudolph the Red nosed reindeer.

We landed early on Christmas Day. It was cloudy all the way and we didn't see the Star of Bethlehem. There certainly weren't three wise men on the flight deck either.

The weather was bleak, grey and mournful but Rosemary had made a cheery fire and the lights on the Christmas tree winked colourfully. Matt was excited but had to wait until after the Queen's Speech before he could open his presents. I wasn't sure why the Queen made a speech on Christmas Day, I thought it irrelevant, but it was a tradition and Rosemary liked a traditional Christmas.

I watched Rosemary playing with Matt on the carpet. She tickled him and his giggles filled the room. I wasn't sure if I was in love with her any more. I think I fell in love with the idea of being in love, I thought love was going to be a fairy tale, but I chased rainbows instead.

Our neighbours invited us for Christmas drinks and Rosemary insisted went. I knew some of the guests, but I didn't feel comfortable and I didn't want to be there. We sipped champagne, ate canapes and indulged in small-talk. We were envied, we were a handsome couple with a beautiful child, a romantic job and a lovely home. Rosemary kept up the pretences as we mingled but it was a well-practiced charade and we walked home in silence.

Blender

I was posted to the Beach Fleet.

BA based five old 747s at Gatwick to operate flights to the Caribbean, Miami, Los Angeles, Seychelles and Mauritius. It was affectionately known as The Beach Fleet. The aircraft were 747 variants, the allowances were poor, and the trips could be long, but there was a tremendous *esprit de corps* among crew.

BA was heavily unionised and industrial relations with the closed shop unions was at an all time low. In the eighties there had been at least one industrial dispute every year. Some unions were more militant than others and the pilots were far less belligerent than the cabin crew. Pilots were seen as pro-management and by association, anti-cabin crew.

On my last trip from Heathrow I flew with a chief steward who was one of the more extreme cabin crew union representatives. He had been advocating that the senior cabin crew member should be the second-in-command of the aircraft.

I handed him the weather forecast and flight plan and asked him for his advice on which airfield we should nominate for a diversion alternate.

He stormed from the flight deck.

The Gatwick cabin crew were more interested in having a good time than politics and us-and-them' barely existed.

My first flight on the Beach Fleet was from Antigua to Trinidad and back. We were only scheduled to be away for a few hours, so we left our suitcases in the hotel in Antigua. We landed at Piarco as the sun set.

At 10pm we ran through the pre-flight checks for our return to Antigua. Faint flashes of lightning illuminated a line of thunderstorms in the distance and silhouetted the hills surrounding the airport. The warm, humid trade wind blew across the brightly lit apron as the last passengers boarded the aircraft and the doors were finally closed.

The overhead air louvre blew hot air onto my face, sweat ran down my back and my damp collar stuck to my neck. The ait-conditioning fans whirred, struggling in vain to control the heat from the instrument panel.

"Before start checklist." I called

The engineer motored his seat forward and leant between the front seats and read the checklist in a slow monotone. Craig was tanned and wiry with a mop of dark brown hair. He wore an almost perpetual mischievous grin.

The First officer turned systems on and flicked switches in response to the checklist. Ian was reserved with curly short black hair. He was a Phantom F4 pilot and had recently joined BA from the RAF.

One by one we started our agricultural Prat and Whitney JT9D jet engines and taxied towards the departure runway.

"Before take-off checklist." I called.

A rusty perimeter fence was visible in the taxy lights as we slowly taxied past.

"Speedbird 257 Piarco, hold your position!" The tower called urgently, "there's someone below your aircraft."

"Speedbird 257 Roger, hold position" Ian replied.

I slowed to a halt and applied the parking brake. I looked at Ian, he shrugged.

The whir of the air conditioning fans circulated some welcome cool air in our cramped cockpit.

We waited for further information.

I turned to the engineer.

"Craig, would you mind going outside and having a look?"

"Don't leave me behind," he answered as he left the flight deck and descended to first-class. He lifted the carpet at the rear of the cabin and pulled open the trap door to the electronics bay. He opened the small hatch in the floor of the bay and slid out a retractable ladder.

Craig returned to the flight deck.

"I've been down to the tarmac and had a good look around, I can't see anything."

Clearly agitated, the tower called.

"Speedbird 257 security have arrested the man, continue taxying, you are cleared to line up and wait runway one-zero."

"257, continue taxying. Cleared to line up and wait one-zero." Repeated Ian.

I opened the throttles and steered the lumbering 280 tonne aircraft onto the runway.

An hour earlier, in a run-down room in an insignificant hotel near the airport a fight broke out. It started as a lover's tiff but rapidly deteriorated into something much more serious. Two naked men, high on drugs, shouted and punched each other viciously, smashing the furniture as they rolled about the room. One, a US Marine, picked up a heavy brass lamp and smashed it on the skull of his smaller partner. His skull caved in and he slumped lifeless to the floor. The marine shook his partner, and realising the enormity of what he had done, ran naked into the corridor in a panic. He grabbed a fire extinguisher from the wall, put the nozzle in his mouth and pulled the trigger. The extinguishant shot into his mouth and he fell backwards onto the floor coughing and spluttering. He stumbled out of the hotel, crawled through a hole in the airport fence and ran towards a large aeroplane taxying towards the runway.

He ran under the slowly moving behemoth in a daze as it came to a halt. A pickup truck appeared, and three large black security guards jumped out, they bundled him inside and drove off. The big man sat in the back and shivered as the two guards laughed and taunted him. Still high on adrenaline, he attacked the guards, knocked one unconscious and broke the neck of the other. The driver stopped the truck, ran off into the dark and the grim-faced marine took his place.

The tower called us once again

"Speedbird 257, Hold your position. He's escaped and hijacked a truck. Standby."

"257, Roger, standby."

Baffled, I applied the brakes and looked out of the windscreen for the truck. The runway carpet lights surrounded us, and the runway edge lights stretched into the distance. Two or three vehicles with yellow flashing beacons moved frantically about in the distance on the right but there was nothing close by.

It was so crazy and slapstick, it was like an episode from Keystone Cops. I told the passengers there was nothing to be alarmed about.

How wrong I was.

The controller answered our calls with "Standby!" and I sensed he was struggling to cope.

We were blocking the only runway and two aircraft circled overhead waiting to land. The PanAm flight suggested that someone should 'shoot the guy.'

A yellow flashing light appeared off to the right and sped up the blue taxiway lights parallel to our runway. It stopped and turned to face across the runway half-way down.

"Speedbird 257, the truck's behind you. You are cleared for immediate take-off!" The controller said urgently.

I looked at Ian and we both shook our heads.

"257, Negative!"

"257, Take off now!"

"257, Negative, negative" I shouted back.

The truck moved onto the runway and accelerated towards us. A figure hunched over the steering wheel of the yellow truck materialised in the landing lights. It shot past the right of the nose and hit us hard. The aircraft shook.

I'm convinced that he was waiting to crash into us during our take-off roll.

It would have been catastrophic.

The engine fire bell rang loudly, and red lights flashed.

"Fire engine 3 checklist!" I called.

We shut the engine down with well-practiced actions, and the engine spluttered to a halt, the fire extinguished.

"Bloody hell!"

"Craig, have a look." I pointed towards the flight deck door.

Craig unclipped his seat belt and strode from the flight deck.

"257, we've been hit by the truck!" Exclaimed Ian on the radio, "the runway is blocked. Standby."

There was no reply.

The two waiting flights diverted.

Craig came back to the flight deck from the upper deck.

"Captain, the engine's a mess, there's something smouldering on top of the wing, but it's OK. I think the cab must have gone straight through."

The marine had hit engine the engine head on. The bottom of the engine cowl is five feet from the ground, and it had smashed the windshield and ingested the cab. He ducked at the last moment and scraped under the length of the engine.

Bleeding heavily, he drove away in his now convertible truck. A few hundred meters later the Toyota ground to a halt with a pierced radiator.

BA had only two staff in Trinidad, they were both passenger handling agents with little technical knowledge. I called the office on company frequency.

"Arjun, can you come out to the aircraft and have a look at the engine?"

Five minutes later, tubby, turbaned Arjun Singh walked towards us in the landing lights.

My headset crackled as he plugged in.

"Captain, Arjun here."

"Hi, Arjun."

There was a brief pause.

"Captain! I have to go. He's running at me!"

"Run. Quick!" I yelled.

Arjun ran away with arms and legs flailing in the bright landing lights.

We heard a strange noise, it was a subtle change of engine pitch. I looked at the gauges, nothing looked out of order.

Arjun turned around, ran back to the aircraft and plugged in.

"Captain, you're not going to believe this, but he's just jumped into engine 2!"

"What! Arjun, are you sure?"

"I'm afraid so."

I took my headset off, put it on the coaming, buried my head in my hands and called for the engine shut down checklist.

The chief steward came onto the flight deck and I explained what had happened. He explained that the stewardess sitting by door 2 left had seen him jump into the engine and had collapsed with shock.

I reassured the passengers, we taxied back to the apron on two engines and disembarked them through the front right-hand door. The stewardess was taken to hospital.

I contacted Speedbird London on HF radio and asked to be connected to the Chief Pilot.

A sleepy voice answered, and he soon woke up when I explained what had happened. He couldn't believe it, neither could I.

We discussed a plan of action. A team of engineers and experts would be sent from Heathrow to New York on Concorde, and then by chartered jet to Trinidad. They should arrive in less than 24 hours. They asked me to assess the damage, secure the aeroplane and await further instructions.

Down time of our aircraft was extremely expensive, and BA wanted the aircraft repaired as soon as possible and returned to service.

We secured the aircraft and I walked down the steps to the apron to inspect the engines. The damage to the engine he had hit with the truck looked serious, the cowling was badly dented, the blades were bent and there were some wrinkles in the pylon.

The intake of the other engine was covered in blood, it was red, very red. I suppose blood is that colour when oxygenated by an engine rotating at thousands of revolutions per minute. Chunks of meat, entrails and teeth were jammed into every crevice, and a line of what looked like pale brown ribs were stuck on the inside of the cowling.

I jumped. Two eyes, in half a face stared lifelessly at me from behind an inlet guide vane.

'What could have driven him to do this?' I wondered, feeling decidedly sick.

Apart from a few bent blades, the engine looked in remarkably good condition.

The crew nicknamed the aeroplane 'The Blender.'

We went to a shabby hotel near the airport. It was 0330 in the morning.

I couldn't sleep and I was awake when my phone rang at 0800. The receptionist told me that the police were in the lobby and wanted a statement. I called Craig and Ian and asked them to join me.

We sat around a table in a small stuffy conference room. A large black police woman was laboriously writing in a note pad while a sweating black police sergeant asked questions. We told him our story, and the sergeant told us what he knew. The two men lived in Brownsville, Texas and were on holiday in Trinidad. The police found cocaine in their room and evidence to suggest that they were gay. He told us about the murder in the hotel, how the man got onto the airport, and how he escaped from security.

The police woman closed her note book.

"I'm afraid we can't release the aeroplane until we have the body." The sergeant stated, "we need it for evidence."

I tried to explain that it would be difficult to retrieve the remains, and that it was imperative that the aircraft was repaired as soon as possible.

The air conditioner wheezed, and the room smelled of damp. The sergeant drummed his fingers on the table and looked at me with his large brown eyes.

"Can't you just open the engine and let the parts fall out?" he asked helpfully.

Craig sarcastically explained that there were quite a few whirly things in the engine, and it wasn't just an empty tube.

I kicked him under the table.

"Any ideas?" I asked Craig.

He shrugged and after a moment replied.

"Perhaps we could hose them out, Colin? Most airfields have a water bowser, I'm sure the Fire Department would have one."

"That might work."

The police sergeant looked satisfied, his chair scraped on the floor and he stood up.

"OK, that sounds good to me. Collect what you can, and you can have your aircraft back."

They put their hats on and strode out of the room.

I volunteered to deal with body parts, I asked Craig to find a bowser, and Ian said he would coordinate. The police had told us that the couple were probably gay, and I was extremely worried about AIDS.

I decided to find an undertaker to help.

I flipped through the yellow pages, and "Burns crematorium and funeral services" caught my eye. I called, explained the situation and arranged for an undertaker to meet us at the airport at midday.

The crew reported in the lobby at 0930. We were dressed in our day-old uniforms as our bags were still in Antigua. I authorised $100 for each crew member to buy some clean clothes. Unfortunately, I didn't realise that $100 Trinidadian was not worth very much and they would only be able to afford cheap shorts, T shirts and beach wraps.

The cabin crew returned to our usual crew hotel and we took a taxi to the airport.

Buzzards circled lazily in the thermals over our stricken aircraft which stood in the bright sunlight on the apron. They looked like vultures to me. The breeze was in our direction and the pungent, sickly smell from the engine was nauseatingly overpowering in the 32-degree heat.

An olive-green water bowser truck stood by the aircraft and a gaggle of muttering firemen lounged around with their backs to the engine. Craig asked them to start hosing the engine, but they refused. Maybe they were superstitious, but no amount of cajoling would coax them to start.

"It's a Bedford, just like the RAF," said Craig, squinting at the truck, "I'm sure I could fire it up."

"Great, Craig. Go on then." I walked towards a pile of fire hoses.

I picked up one of the deflated hosepipes and pointed the nozzle at the engine. Craig opened a panel on the bowser, started the engine and turned on the pump. The kick-back from the hose caught me by surprise and I managed to spray the firemen before I brought it to bear on the engine.

The firemen protested.

Craig grabbed the hose to steady it and we directed the stream of water into the engine. Unmentionable stringy body parts tumbled from the rear of the jet-pipe into a heap on the tarmac.

Perhaps it was a loss of face, but thankfully the youngest looking fireman strode over and took the pipe and continued to spray. The others joined in. A large puddle of water covered in a foul-smelling film started to form and I had to dance about to avoid stepping in it.

A large crimson coloured vehicle lolloped across the apron towards us. It seemed to be a 1950s Chevrolet hearse conversion. It stopped next to us and the tinted electric window wound down with a hum. An enormous black man with a bristly shaved head looked at me through his dark Aviator sunglasses. He was wearing a string vest and had no neck, his head seemed to merge seamlessly with his torso. If he had been wearing a bowler hat, I would have sworn he was Odd Job from Goldfinger.

"Hello, Skip." he said with a broad Caribbean accent.

"I'm de undertaker."

"Hello."

"It's hot. Can I park under de nose of the airplane in de shade?"

"I'm sorry, you'll have to park over there." I pointed towards the bowser.

"Dat's in de sun, Boss. How about under de wing?"

"Look." I spluttered. "I've had enough of vehicles being near my plane. Please park over there."

Odd Job looked hurt, pointed to the back of the hearse and replied.

"Dat's a pity. I've got a stiff in de back and he's already beginning to smell!"

He wound up the window and drove over to the bowser.

This is not real, I thought. This isn't happening to me.

I decided to warn Odd Job about the possibility of AIDS. Like a kangaroo, I hopped on the remaining dry patches of tarmac towards the hearse.

"You should know this guy might have had AIDS."

He took his shades off, and with a puzzled look, stared at me with his dark piercing eyes.

"What's dat?" he asked frowning.

I'd just about had enough. The stress, the lack of sleep and the theatrical quality of this whole episode was getting to me.

"He was gay! He might have had AIDS! Do you understand?"

Odd Job looked up at me.

"Ah. No problem. I have de protection," he said with a wide grin.

Two gold teeth flashed in the sunlight.

I stood with my mouth open in surprise.

The pile of body bits was about eighteen inches high, Odd Job emerged from the hearse carrying a large plastic shopping bag.

"OK. You can stop now, I'll deal with dat."

The firemen shut down the Bedford and an eerie silence descended.

Odd Job strode purposefully towards the engine straight through the scummy puddle. I couldn't believe it, he was wearing flip flops and eating an apple. The cruddy water flicked over his back as he walked.

He put the plastic bag down and reached inside. I was surprised his AIDS kit could be so small, I imagined he needed at least a bio-hazard suit and a full-face oxygen mask.

The bag was filled with smaller plastic bags. He put his hand inside one of the bags and picked up the pieces, which he threw in a large bin bag.

So much for AIDS protection!

It took Odd Job an hour to fill four large bin bags which he safely stowed in the hearse, but few stubborn scraps remained jammed in place. I climbed the steps into the aircraft and found a wire coat hanger in the wardrobe which I fashioned into an eighteen-inch-long, non-CAA-approved, body extraction hook.

The sun was setting behind the hills as I completed the paperwork with the police. Still wearing our blood-stained, filthy uniforms, we piled into a van and set off for the 'upside-down' Hilton.

The Hilton is built into the side of a hill. The reception is on the top floor and the guest rooms are below. The Aviary bar has a panoramic view of Queen's Park, the Botanical gardens and the mountains beyond. It is one of the most famous bars on the island, it is very chic and very popular with the wealthy locals.

Looking like a trio of chimney sweeps we arrived at the hotel. Before we could go to our rooms, we were intercepted by the chief steward holding three large, eminently quaffable beers. Foolishly he steered us to the Aviary bar. It was packed with people wearing very posh tuxedos, very posh frocks and drinking very posh martinis with very posh raised pinkies. The look of horror on their faces as we traipsed in was priceless. The cabin crew were ensconced around a large table wearing very un-posh T shirts, el-cheapo shorts and beach wraps. They were very loud and boisterous, even more so when we walked in.

Everyone talked at once, drinks flowed, and the crew became more rowdy.

One of the stewardesses said to an overtly gay steward.

"Show me your willy and I'll show you my tits!"

The table fell silent, and to the rising chants of 'Show it. Show it,' he undid his fly, reached inside and flopped his todger onto the table. It lurked, coiled up on the table, and regarded me with malicious intent. The stewardess did a striptease, lifted her T-shirt and showed off her magnificent boobs.

In the middle of a vulgar rendition of 'Old MacDonald's Farm', a dapper white man in a suit and tie approached our table.

"Captain Fairdale?" he asked in a soft Geordie accent.

I looked around and then realised he was talking to me.

"I wonder, could have a statement?" he continued politely.

The BA team had arrived at the hotel, and the man in the suit was either CAA or BA crisis management wanting a statement!

There we were; rowdy as a soccer fan club, half dressed, completely bladdered with the island's Glitterati looking on in shocked distain.

And he wanted a statement?

I think I was a bit rude to him and told him to come back in the morning.

The next day, I phoned the Chief Pilot and said we were suffering from shock and we needed to get away from Trinidad. He agreed to send us to Barbados for a few days and then position us home.

I have a sneaky feeling that we weren't suffering from shock at all, we just wanted to continue the party.

I have often been asked what I could see in the engine. I don't like to think about it too much, so I tell them that I found his willy stuck to the cowling. It had been greatly elongated by centrifugal force, so I put it in an ice bucket and took it to the BA doctor to ask for a transplant. The doctor politely refused on two accounts. First, it was misappropriation of BA property, and second, he was sorry to tell me, he couldn't find anything to graft it on to!

That normally shuts them up.

Beach Fleet

We sometimes played a game on the PA. The cabin crew gave us a word which we had to include at some point in our passenger address. If we didn't include the word, we had to buy the cabin crew a drink each. However, if we did, they had to buy us one. The stakes were high as there are 15 of them and just 3 of us. It required a great deal of ingenuity to include words such as 'salmon,' or 'dreadlocks' seamlessly into a passenger briefing.

We flew from Gatwick to Montego Bay in the north of Jamaica, and then across the island to Kingston.

We were about to start the engines when the chief stewardess came onto the flight deck to announce that boarding and security checks were complete. She was a bubbly, extroverted blonde with a wicked sense of humour.

"Right boys," she sniggered, "your word for today is 'bollocks'."

She clambered on her broomstick and flew out of the flight-deck.

The First Officer was responsible for the announcements on the first leg. I looked at him in despair, trying to calculate how much 15 rum punches would cost in Kingston. Pale and grim he looked at me. At the top of climb he did his introductory speech to the passengers. Sweating slightly, I listened in, but no 'Bollocks!' I put my head in my hands.

Similarly, there was no 'Bollocks' anywhere in his remaining briefings. We were scuppered!

I considered going sick in Montego Bay.

We landed and glumly taxied towards the apron. The docking guidance system was lined up with my seat, so I took control to park. As we approached, I asked the First Officer to call for the doors to be switched to manual and cross checked.

He switched on the PA and announced.

"Cabin Crew, doors to bollocks and cross check!"

I was stunned.

The chief stewardess rushed onto the flight deck and said we had cheated.

I replied smugly that we had followed the rules, and we were looking forward to five, frosted Red Stripes each when we arrived in Kingston.

She stormed out in a rage.

Feeling very pleased with ourselves we taxied out for the short hop to Kingston. The chief re-entered the flight deck.

"Right, I've got you now," she said with a malicious glint in her eye.

"Your word, Colin is 'Chlamydia'."

My jaw dropped.

Cackling, she left the flight deck with a flourish.

My vision of free beer all night quickly evaporated. How on earth could I use that word on the PA? It was impossible.

The 747 wasn't designed for short flights and I didn't have time to think, completing checklists, doing calculations and weaving through the thunderstorms over the Blue Mountains took all my time and concentration.

Finally, on the approach my interest in history came to my rescue.

I pressed the button and spoke to the passengers.

"Ladies and gentlemen. We are now making our approach to Port Royal airport, and we should be landing in 5 minutes time. Port Royal was a notorious pirate town which sank after a disastrous earthquake in 1692.

It is rumoured that Captain *Clam hid here* when chased by the Royal Navy in 1685."

I had a bit of a hangover the next day.

There was little affection any more between Rosemary and me. We were drifting apart, and I felt trapped.

Rosemary said I was stifling her, and she had lost her identity and her independence. Everyone said she was so lucky to be married to me. She was always the wife of Colin rather than Rosemary in her own right.

She said I was too arrogant to notice.

She was right.

I was cornered.

Gary Clough was tall, handsome and rugged. He was a prankster who was adored by all the girls. Like me, he was a long-time member of the 'Africa Corps' and he used to paint a large white outline of Africa on the cabin crew bags during African trips. The bags of favoured girls had the map of Africa sprayed in gold.

On baggage carousels all over the world it was clearly obvious who had flown with Gary.

He had a party trick.

He would ask stewardesses who visited the flight deck if they wanted to see his cock. He would then unzip his fly and pull out a rubber chicken he had stuffed down his trousers.

Gary was my Engineer on a trip to St Lucia.

We had a trainee stewardess with us, and I suspect the chief stewardess must have warned the young girl about Gary. She came up to the flight deck to introduce herself and Gary asked her if she wanted to see his cock. To his surprise she readily said yes.

Gary unzipped his fly, put in his hand and pulled out his real cock.

The girl fled screaming from the flight-deck.

A few moments later the chief stewardess strode onto the flight deck. Gary was strutting around with his hands on his hips, proudly displaying himself.

"Put that horrible thing away, you nasty man!" she exclaimed and stabbed his cock savagely with a cocktail stick she had hidden behind her back.

I doubted if Gary would play that trick again.

Long flights could be incredibly boring. To pass the time I allowed visits to the flight deck and I often invited passengers to watch the landing from the cockpit.

It was the middle of the school holidays, and the queue for flight deck visits stretched almost to the back of the aeroplane. A Down Syndrome boy in his late teens and his father were the last to come up. He was a delightful, inquisitive young man who beamed and giggled with delight at everything. I was acutely aware of how fortunate I was. This fizzy young man had been dealt some cruel cards in the lottery of life.

I invited them both up for the landing into Miami.

During the descent the chief brought the passengers onto the flight deck, and the boy sat in the seat directly behind me. His seat was in the fully forward position to give him a better view and his father sat behind him at the back.

We flew over Miami beach on the approach and I pointed out the swimming pools and houses. He became very excited and was sitting so close behind me that I could feel the breath from his excited gasps on the back of my neck. He became more and more animated, and at 1,500ft, he threw his arms around my neck and smothered the back of my head with kisses. His father frantically tried to get out of his seat but struggled with the harness. I could hardly breathe, he was a strong boy, and I couldn't shake him off.

'Shit!' I thought, 'what can I do?' I could bite his arm or poke him in the eyes, but I didn't have the heart.

"You have control." I croaked to the First Officer on the intercom.

The First Officer took over control of the aeroplane and executed a perfect landing while the boy, in tears, continued to stroke and kiss me.

The boy's father eventually managed to release himself and gently pulled the confused lad away. His father was acutely apologetic, but I told him that it wasn't important, and not to worry.

It was one of the most moving moments of my life.

Training

I left home.

I packed my suitcase as the pale insipid sun glimmered in the mournful sky. I slowly descended the stairs. Rosemary stood with arms crossed, glaring at me defiantly. I reached the bottom step. Poor Matt ran towards me and threw his arms around my legs pleading with me not to go. I gently prised his arms apart and edged towards the door.

The sounds muffled as I shut the door behind me.

Walking away from them was heart rending. I felt so guilty and selfish, I was sick to my stomach and wondered how long I would feel like that?

Poor Rosemary didn't understand, and I suppose neither did I. It wasn't really her fault, perhaps it wasn't mine. We just couldn't live together.

I rented a small cottage beside the River Thames at Goring. It was calming to watch swans and coots gliding serenely past my window, it was the antithesis of the destructive turmoil in my life. I felt scared and lonely. What if I had made a monumental mistake? Would I ever be forgiven?

I wondered if I should call BA to ask for compassionate leave? Maybe I was obliged to let them know about my situation as it could affect my performance on the aeroplane? I was professional enough to ignore my personal problems and anyway, I needed to get away.

I was posted back to Heathrow and I had been selected to become a trainer. It came with a 20% increase in salary, and I could certainly do with that.

I was broke.

Simulators are an indispensable part of pilot training. Extreme manoeuvres can be practiced in a simulated environment without risk. Procedures and teamwork can be honed, and pilot assessments made without burning precious fuel. The more realistic the simulators are, the more relevant they become.

The BA 747 simulator was a small, room-sized box, perched on five spindly hydraulic rams. The rams moved the simulator in all three dimensions, and when fully extended it could reach a height of more than ten metres above the floor. The cockpit of the 747 was faithfully replicated in the box, and computer-generated images of the simulated world were projected onto the front windscreens. It was remarkably realistic.

It hadn't always been like that.

At Hamble, we were subjected to the loathsome Link D4 trainer. It was an enclosed plywood cockpit sitting on top of a set of large pneumatic bellows which wheezed asthmatically trying to keep in step with the movement of the joystick. The instructor sat by a pantograph recording the movements of the Link in red ink on a large piece of paper. It could be very disorientating, particularly as there was a time lag between joy stick inputs and movement of the Link. Once, I became completely unsynchronised with the infernal machine and panicked. I frantically whirled the joystick around and with a humongous fart, the bellows split, and the box crashed to the floor on its side, with the last of the air escaping in an exasperated sigh.

By the time I joined BA, the technology had advanced by leaps and bounds. Rudimentary hydraulic motion systems had been introduced, but computer-generated images had not. The VC10 visuals were provided by a small camera, linked to the movement of the controls, which moved over a large three-dimensional model of an airfield and its surrounding countryside. Little villages with churches, roads and fields were faithfully reproduced on a board nearly sixty feet long, fixed to a wall. The runway on the model was 10 feet long, simulating a 10,000 ft runway in real life, so everything viewed by the camera was magnified about 1,000 times. The board was illuminated with very powerful lamps to increase the depth of field for the small camera, but the heat from the lamps played havoc with the model. Once, the glue on a pipe-cleaner hedgerow melted, and it sprung from the board at one end. It was most disconcerting to fly around a two-hundred-foot-long hedge rising from a field near the airport.

The press was invited to the grand opening of this modern marvel. The VC10 taxied towards take off. The field of view was limited, and the image was blurred and jerky.

"You are number two for take-off." the controller stated.

The VC10 turned the corner, and a horrific gargantuan monster was waiting on the runway ahead of them. A dead fly had been pinned on the centre of the runway with its multi-faceted eyes staring lifelessly towards the horizon.

The press laughed.

The fly was removed, and they took off. To simulate entering the cloud at two hundred feet, the camera was simply switched off.

At the end of the demonstration, the VC10 commenced its approach. The reporters peered through the windows to watch the landing. The camera was turned on again at 200ft. Two titanic tits materialised out of the gloom at the far end of the runway like barrage balloons. The centre page of Playboy had been taped on the church spire near the end of the runway, and the surprise of seeing those 100 metre humongous hooters shocked the press into stunned silence.

The 747 was equipped with digital visuals which were very realistic. I was in the simulator during my training course when one of the simulator engineers suggested that we taxy into a hangar at Shannon without explaining why. We slowly taxied towards the building and rolled into its cavernous interior. In the corner there appeared to be an oversized television set, and as we got closer, we realised that a pornographic film was playing on its flickering screen.

Rosemary agreed to let me take Matt out on Saturday with the stern proviso to bring him back by 11pm. I parked at the Mews and took him to the movies. Dinner in the cheap pizza parlour afterwards was not a great success and unfortunately, the tube broke down on the way home. We didn't arrive back at the Mews until 1130.

Incandescent with rage and frustration, Rosemary attacked me as I stood in the doorway. I did little to protect myself from the tirade of insults and the rain of blows and scratches. I turned away into the soft drizzle, leaving her slumped on the floor sobbing.

'How could I be so heartless and cruel?' I thought as I walked off into the night.

I was half-way through an examiners course run by the CAA at Gatwick. It covered a multitude of topics including; skills assessment, situational awareness and crew coordination.

The topic for the lecture on the Monday was recognising stress in candidates.

The instructor wandered into the classroom wearing a crumpled tweed suit and brown brogues. He sat down at his desk, looked at his notes and peered at us over his half-moon glasses.

"Gentlemen," he said in a very posh accent, looking bored and disinterested. "Gentlemen. It is important to recognise stress in your candidates, as stress can adversely affect your victim's, sorry, candidate's performance."

He swung back on his chair and put his feet on the desk and stared at the ceiling.

"Stress can be caused by many factors; finances, health and personal problems for example. Did you know that divorce rates rose nearly 30% last year?" he asked rhetorically, picking his teeth with a pipe cleaner, "indulge in a little small talk, probe a little before you start. Try to establish some sort of rapport, you could learn a lot. Look at them and ask yourself, do they seem stressed?"

I faced him with a black eye, my face covered in scratches and laughed.

I had my 6-monthly medical and managed to scrape through as usual, except that I had a problem with my eyes.

I used the same aviation medical examiner for years and had memorised the eye chart. For some unknown reason he had a new chart and I could hardly read it.

I don't know of any other profession which has to undergo so many tests each year in order to keep current. We had four simulator sessions, two medicals, one line-check, one technical test and a safety procedures exam each year. A failure in any of these could lead to dismissal.

I believe doctors should be assessed for competence regularly in the same way. Imagine how they would react!

Keir had become a trainer the year before and I flew to New York with him as part of my course. We rarely flew together but he was assessing my performance in the right-hand seat as a trainer. He had put on a bit of weight, had streaks of grey in his hair, but was the same old Keir. Flying with him made me realise how much I missed the old days.

He flew the leg from London to New York while I was his co-pilot. New York, Kennedy is one of the world busiest airports, but Keir navigated around thunderstorms and threaded us into the landing patterns with great skill. He flew an immaculate approach, and perfectly aligned, pulled back on the controls for what should have been a flawless landing. Except, I had my knee behind the controls, and he couldn't flare quite enough. We hit the ground with a thump.

We turned off the runway in silence, and the chief steward came running in with an ice bucket of water.

"You've planted it, you might as well water it!" he trilled.

I grinned from ear to ear.

Keir glared at me.

"You bastard!" he growled.

Changing fortunes

I met someone who I really liked.

I flew a trip to Caracas.

Before the passengers boarded, I wandered around the cabin to introduce myself to the cabin crew and check out the talent. I drew the curtain to the first-class galley and peered in. A slim girl was on her knees looking into the lower larder with her backside in the air.

I addressed the Botticellian bum.

"Hello, I'm Colin." I said with my best Top Gun accent.

She grunted without looking at me and continued to move trays and cutlery around in the metal box.

"The crew are meeting in my room for a drink this evening if you'd like to join us?"

No response.

She reached further into the larder and I caught a glimpse of her dark hair in a short bob.

"What did you say your name was?"

"I didn't" came the muffled reply.

She continued to ferret about.

I skulked back to the flight deck.

The hotel was on a spit of land not far from the airport at Maiquetia. My room was unremarkable generic Sheraton but was spacious and faced the sea. I ordered a bucket of ice and soft drinks and opened the sliding doors leading to the little balcony. The curtains billowed in the balmy tropical breeze and surf crashed on the beach beyond the circular swimming pool. I was dressed to kill in my trendiest grey fine corduroy trousers and pink floral tropical shirt.

The mystery girl was the last to arrive. She was young, slim and very chic in a simple white shirt and jeans. Her bob was immaculate, her fringe framed her slightly freckled, tanned face. She wore little make up apart from bright red lipstick and nail polish.

There was something about her.

She didn't acknowledge me at all, so after a few drinks I decided to say hello. As I approached, I heard her tell a steward that she was going for a run the following afternoon.

She turned to me.

"Lucy" she said, looking at me with her dark eyes, before I had a chance to say anything.

"I'm sorry?" I replied baffled.

"In answer to your question this morning, my name is Lucy."

She smiled, her teeth were pearl white with a small gap in the front. She held out her hand.

I shook her hand; her fingers were warm.

"I'm here with my brother and I have to phone my boyfriend, so I can't stay long," she continued, taking a sip of rum punch, "nice shirt, by the way."

I looked down and fingered the garish material.

"If you were carrying a parasol you might be mistaken for a strawberry daiquiri!" she chortled and sauntered off.

I arrived in the lobby in my running kit and sat in a chair hidden behind a flower pot. I didn't have to wait long before I spotted Lucy striding purposefully across the lobby towards the beach. Her tight-fitting training shorts accentuated her slimness and she looked very sexy. I waited five minutes and walked out to the jogging trail. I could see her jogging towards Caleta beach in the distance and I started after her. It was hot and it took me a long time to catch up. I ran alongside, drew my stomach in, and adopted what I thought was a gazelle like trot. More likely it resembled a silverback-gorilla, knuckle-dragging, scamper.

"Hello, Lucy." I said breezily, trying to disguise my breathlessness, "what a surprise. Do you mind if I join you?"

"So long as you don't talk!" was her terse reply, "I can't run and talk at the same time."

We jogged past Coconut Beach to Caleta and back without a word. Holding my stomach in for that length of time was pure torture. We neared the hotel and Lucy ran up a breakwater towards a small lighthouse at the far end. I followed and we sat down on the rocks facing the rippling sea. I turned to look at her. She sat on a rock with her eyes closed facing the sun. Her knees were bent, and she leant back with her arms outstretched behind her. Her freckles were accentuated by the warm evening sunlight, her tousled black hair was tugged by the capricious breeze, and a bead of sweat lined her upper lip. She was panting softly, sensuously, with her mouth slightly open. Her shoulders rose and fell with every breath. I closed my eyes. I could hear the sea lapping on the beach, seagulls squabbling, and faint sounds from the hotel.

I hoped Lucy couldn't hear the tattoo of my heart.

I was smitten.

The muddy grey Thames in Goring was in full spate, swollen by recent heavy rain. A family of swans was trying to swim against the current and two fuzzy feathered cygnets were unable to keep up. The leafless trees stood silhouette to a sombre scudding sky.

Rosemary and I were contesting the divorce, and it dragged on.

My hi-fi was tuned to BBC Radio One.

"Time is flowing like a river, to the sea" sang Alan Parsons.

So true, as I watched the Thames flow inexorably past my window.

"Who knows when we shall meet again, if ever?" the song continued.

It had been three months since I met Lucy, and I couldn't get her out of my mind. I telephoned her a few times, but we'd had nothing more than an affable chat.

I frequented the 'Miller of Mansfield' pub in Goring and I made a few friends. We played darts, bar billiards and drank warm beer. None of my new chums were involved with aviation and it was pleasant not to be part of a flying clique.

Baz was a saw sharpener. He was short with dark hair, lively twinkling eyes and he was fascinated by my flying tales.

I was certain that he had never been out of Oxfordshire, let alone anywhere near an aeroplane.

One of the perks of being an instructor was that I could fly the simulators when they were not being used for training. Late one night I treated my five pub pals to a flight round New York in the simulator.

The air conditioning in the dimly lit hall hummed, and our footsteps echoed off the walls as we approached the simulator. It looked like a Martian from HG Wells' 'War of the Worlds', crouching, waiting to pounce. Baz fidgeted nervously.

We traversed a gangway to the box and opened the door. Like Narnia's wardrobe, we walked into a magical world. We were in the cockpit of a 747. Baz stared in amazement at the dials, switches and flashing lights. I told Baz to stand behind my seat as he would have a better view. I loaded JFK into the simulator computer database and sat in my seat. The visual flickered, and through the front windows, we could see that we were on the threshold of runway 31 Right at JFK, with the Empire State Building just visible in the distance. The computer-generated image was incredibly realistic.

I retracted the drawbridge and switched on the motion. A klaxon sounded as the miscreation awoke from its slumber and lurched up on its hydraulic limbs.

Baz held grimly on.

I explained what I intended to do.

"OK guys. We'll take off straight ahead, climb to 400 ft and accelerate to 350 knots. I'll try to fly between the Empire State Building and the Chrysler Building. It's a bit tight but we should be OK."

Baz looked decidedly uneasy.

"Then we'll turn south west descending to 100ft," I continued, "and knock the head off the Statue of Liberty. We'll descent to 50ft and fly under the Verrazano-Narrows Bridge, then we'll zoom climb to 1,500 ft, pull the engines back to idle and glide to a landing back at JFK on 13L. Anybody got any questions?"

Nobody did. I started the four engines, and with a roar we shot off down the runway. The machine tilted back to simulate acceleration, and we leapt into the air. We soon reached 400ft heading towards the Chrysler Building. The buffeting from the speed and a cacophony of warnings added to the sense of impending doom. I steered for the Empire State Building rather than the gap and just before we hit it, I yelled out above the din.

"Oh No! We're not going to make it!"

I heard a screech.

We flew through the image like a phantom and I turned south west. I looked behind me. Baz was curled up in a ball with his arms over his head at the back of the simulator shaking like a leaf.

He wouldn't speak to me in the pub for a long time after that.

Lucy

It was official, I was having a mid-life crisis, Lucy was 14 years younger than me.

I bumped into Lucy a couple of times in the crew reporting centre and I finally managed to pin her down for a date.

Lucy lived in London and we met half way at the 'Crown Inn' near Burnham Beeches. The meal was mediocre, but the wine was excellent. The bright sunshine filtered through the iridescent green leaves as we strolled through the woods. Lucy wore a short-pleated skirt and a navy-blue sweater over a white blouse. She took my hand as we noisily kicked our way through the old dry leaves. We sat on a gnarled old log, a cuckoo sang its song in the distance and a squirrel rustled in the leaves behind us. We talked and talked, we had so much in common, there was so much to share.

The scent of peat and humus borne by a damp zephyr wafting aimlessly among the new leaves, embraced us. The woods were alive with sounds of industry; squirrels scratching in the leaves, birds nesting in the branches, insects buzzing in the sunshine.

Cuckoo.

Cuckoo.

The sounds of Spring.

The sounds of renaissance.

I edged closer to her and gently put my arm around her. She didn't move away. She turned towards me and kissed me on the lips. Surprised, I pulled her closer and kissed her passionately. Time lost its meaning. We kissed, exploring each other's mouths with the tips of our tongues, and I slid a hand under her sweater. She moaned gently.

"Not here" Lucy whispered, "over there," pointing towards a large tree surrounded with bushes.

I led her towards the tree and Lucy leant against the trunk of the immense Beech. I pulled her to me and kissed her again. Gently we made love as the sound of the cuckoo faded to a murmur in the distance.

Pearls of dew dripped from the tip of a leaf, sparkling in the shafts of sunlight, as they fell.

I met up with Lucy as often as I could.

She was so full of energy and vibrant enthusiasm She took everything in her stride, she was funny, witty, naughty and wild.

Why is sex so powerful?

I was a child of the swinging sixties, the progeny of a tumultuous social upheaval. The beginnings of sexual equality sprouted exuberantly from the drab 1950's, and by the 60s the Pill had transformed attitudes to sex. Sexually transmitted diseases were all but defeated, the younger generation had more money to spend and new-found freedom exploded in a profusion of promiscuity on a generation thirsty for radical change. During my early years there were no holds barred and normally no hard feelings. I was chosen as often as I chose, but my relationships were hollow, without substance or emotion. I didn't know what I was looking for, I felt purposeless and depressed.

I had hoped that settling down with Rosemary and raising a family would banish the demons and fill the void with purpose and direction, but that was not to be.

I couldn't see what Lucy saw in me. There was kudos to be with a Captain, maybe it was that? Perhaps it was my ineffable charm and wit? I doubted it. The money? The divorce stretched me financially, so it was probably not that.

The ticking biological clock? That was a possibility too.

I'm not sure that I wanted any more children, but at least it would be good fun trying.

It had been more than a year and still the divorce was nowhere in sight. Poor Rosemary was taking it very hard and I felt very guilty to have caused her so much grief.

If I closed my mind to my problems, I was blissfully happy for the first time in my life.

Lucy moved in.

Her little red Peugeot 205 full of suitcases and clothes laboured up the lane scattering inquisitive Canada Geese waddling by the water's edge. Lucy opened the door of the car and climbed out clutching an arm full of clothes. She walked up the path with a huge grin and kissed me. I wanted to carry her over the threshold.

Two years later we moved to a bigger house in Cray's Pond near Henley. We enjoyed our time in the little cottage by the river, but I hoped that Matt would soon be allowed to stay with me, and the cottage was just too small.

I started a conversion course onto the Boeing 747-400. Outwardly the aircraft looked the same as the older version, but it was radically different. It had very efficient wings, advanced avionics and more powerful engines.

The greatest advances in aircraft design during my 25 years were in the electronics or avionics. Integrated navigational systems rendered the navigator obsolete. A flight engineer was no longer required, his complicated systems had become fully automated and the engines were controlled by solid state computers. I was sorry to see the engineer go, they knew the best bars, the cheapest restaurants and had the casting vote in the aircraft or on the ground. I was difficult to imagine that such a large aircraft could be flown by only two pilots.

The conversion course was three months and I was on basic pay once more. I was still in debt and had worked as much overtime as possible, but I couldn't imagine ever being able to afford a house of our own.

I wished Rosemary would agree to the divorce terms and end the misery.

The Collyweston slates on the roofs of the pale stone cottages basked in the warm afternoon sun. Children played noisily on the small green by the pub under the sign of a Lion which squeaked as it swung gently in a light breeze. The doleful sounds of bells drifted through the window from the pointed church spire on the far side of the village.

My brother John's thatched cottage wasn't far from where I used to go to school.

Despite the upheaval at home, Matt had done very well at school. He was forecast to achieve high grades in his GCSEs, and I decided to apply for a scholarship for him from my old school.

I called the Bursar.

"Mister Portman is not here this morning, but he can see you at three this afternoon if that's acceptable?" the reedy voice replied.

I was surprised.

"Is that Mister Ralph Portman? Did he used to teach at Langham's years ago?"

"Why yes, I believe so. Do you remember him?"

"Vaguely, I think he used to teach me biology. Three this afternoon is fine"

I was lying.

I remembered very clearly the three painful strokes of his cane on my arse all those years ago during hockey practice.

At three he ushered me into his stuffy office. He was instantly recognisable even though his curly black hair was now grey, and his once slim athletic body was now podgy and cumbersome. He waved me to a seat and sat down opposite, scrutinising me through thick horn-rimmed glasses. He flipped through a rolodex muttering.

"Fairdale. Let me see. Fairdale". He gave up and sat back.

"So, you're an Old Boy?"

I nodded,

"1960 to 1967. You taught me biology and coached the second hockey team, I think." I replied

He stared at his finger nails.

"Sorry. I can't really remember. So many boys. What can I do for you?"

I explained my request for a scholarship.

He droned on about the school and the exams Matt would need to sit to qualify for a bursary. After a few minutes he asked me if I had any questions.

I asked him about the academic success rate, the new sports hall, the new laboratories and finally,

"What is the school's position on discipline, Mr Portman?"

He put his elbows on the desk with his fingertips touching in front of his face.

"Ah yes, discipline. For minor infringements we make them write lines. After that, it's detention and then gating. Confinement to house if you remember?"

I nodded.

"What's after gating?"

"Well, that would be expulsion I'm afraid."

"And that's it? Nothing higher than that?"

"No, that's it." He replied peering at me through his bottle-bottom glasses.

"What about corporal punishment, caning, beating, that sort of thing?"

"Caning! Good God no!" he blustered. "Caning hasn't been allowed for years. Well before my time!"

"You never caned anyone Mr Portman?"

"Absolutely not!" he spluttered.

I put my hands on the desk and moved forward to face him closely.

"Mr Portman, you beat me three strokes on my backside and it bloody-well hurt!"

He looked at me wide-eyed, with his mouth open.

I turned and strode out of the room feeling very pleased with myself, leaving him doing an excellent impression of a monstrous goldfish out of water, with a stick up its arse.

Lucy shepherded a tipsy, busty blonde onto the flight deck. Lucy and I were flying to Chicago together, and this was the fourth visitor she had brought up to see us. I explained a few things in the cockpit to the visitor, but she was clearly more interested in my young co-pilot and draped her voluminous self over the back of his seat.

Eventually she left and I returned to my crossword.

Half an hour later Lucy called me on the interphone.

"Colin, you're not going to believe it. That woman chatted up a club class passenger on her way back to her seat and they've gone into the club loo together. I'm sure she doesn't know him."

"What a laugh" I said, "I'll come down."

I left the co-pilot in charge and went downstairs. The rumble of the engines mingled with the hiss of the air-conditioning as I opened the curtain of the line of toilets. Two or three of the crew were standing in the dimly lit aisle laughing.

"They're shagging" sniggered one of the girls

"How do you know?"

"If you look along the door you can see it bulging."

Sure enough, the honeycomb door was bulging rhythmically. More crew joined us

"How can we get them out?" I asked Lucy

"You could put the seat belt signs on?"

"Good idea," I pushed through the curtains and picked up the phone by a door and dialled the flight deck.

"Dave, put the 'seat belt sign' on, will you?"

"Why? There's nothing on the radar and we're clear of weather!"

"Do me a favour and just do it please, Dave"

'Ding' The seat belt light came on and I walked back to the loos. Two more crew were there watching the fun. I decided that it was time to leave and returned to the flight deck. As I climbed the steps, I heard Lucy on the PA.

"Ladies and Gentlemen the Captain has switched on the seat belt sign, could you return to your seats and fasten your seat belt securely."

The crew banged on the door of the loo telling them to return to their seats. The woman was the first to emerge and she scuttled back to her seat. She had lost her bra and as she strode past, her ample chest wobbled like a couple ferrets in a sack of blancmange.

A few moments later a sheepish looking man scrambled out and slunk back to club class. As he approached his seat he looked down and saw a capacious bra stuck to his foot. Involuntarily, he flicked his foot to rid himself of the bothersome brassiere, it sailed through the air and landed on the head of an adjacent passenger, who sat there looking like a startled, spluttering Deputy Dawg.

Lucy retrieved the bra and brought it up to the flight deck where I hung it from the overhead circuit-breaker panel like fluffy dice.

Shortly before landing I gave it back to Lucy and asked her to make a PA to say that an article of clothing has been found in one of the loos. If she had claimed it, I would give her a bottle of champagne.

She didn't claim it and she ambled unsteadily past Lucy as she left the aircraft with her coat wrapped tightly around her.

On our return to England Lucy told me she was pregnant.

I wasn't expecting that. The biological clock had been ticking after all. I wondered why Lucy kept leaping on me at every opportunity; and I thought it was because she fancied me.

Everything would be different now. Could I afford it? How would Matt react? I had enjoyed a free-wheeling relationship with Lucy up to then and I uncharitably wondered if it all would change.

We visited the John Radcliff hospital for the ultrasound. We were number eight in a queue of people called Patel. Lucy lay down on the couch and a brusque sonographer quickly performed the scan. She was middle-aged with greying brown hair and had glasses perched on the end of her large nose.

"Everything's fine."

I heaved a sigh of relief.

"You're due at the beginning of May."

Only six more months of freedom, I thought despondently.

Lucy looked up. She was visibly relieved and asked in a quiet voice.

"Can you tell what sex it is please?" she so desperately wanted a girl.

Without looking at us, the sonographer replied.

"Without doubt it's a boy."

Lucy burst into tears.

Rosemary finally agreed that Matt could stay with me from time to time. Fortunately, the house in Cray's Pond is big enough for him to have his own bedroom and I would love him to think of it as home, but I know that that will never be the case.

I hope he will welcome his little baby brother.

A New Family

I was a father again! I had another son, he was born five weeks premature in Hillingdon Hospital.

I was in Newark, training a new Captain.

It was a clear crisp day with unlimited visibility, and I went for a jog around Liberty State Park. The watery blue sky was criss-crossed by vapour trails as brightly clothed joggers meandered the paths. The gravel crunched as I ran, and a police siren wailed plaintively in the distance. Across the Hudson river silhouetted by the early morning sun, a brooding Manhattan loomed like an immense Stonehenge with the menhirs of the Twin Towers standing silent sentinel.

It was the calm before the storm.

I did some shopping for Lucy on the way back to the hotel and the concierge handed me a note from BA.

'Your wife has gone into labour and is in hospital. Please call operations.'

I dialled the number. The station manager answered in a heavy New York drawl.

"Ah, Captain Fairdale. London called. Your wife went into labour in the crew shop. I'm sorry, we were going to put you on Concorde home, but we couldn't find you. You've missed that flight, so I suggest we stick to your schedule. It will be the quickest way home."

"Shit, she wasn't due for another 5 weeks. Do you know if she's OK?"

"I only know she was taken to Hillingdon Hospital. I'll find out what I can and let you know at briefing this evening. Are you OK to fly?"

"Absolutely" I replied and told him to load an extra 5 tonnes of fuel for our flight home.

I sat next to the trainee Captain on the crew transport and explained what had happened, and what I intended to do.

"Ignore everything I've taught you so far."

He smiled.

"I'm going to fly home as fast as I can. You never know, we might even beat the Transatlantic speed record." I joked.

In the briefing room the duty manager handed me a slip of paper with the telephone number of the hospital. He wished me luck.

The weather forecast for the crossing was good and all the passengers had checked in, so it looked like we would be on time.

The sun was setting behind us casting long shadows in front as we crossed the coast of Newfoundland. I was flying almost as fast as I could go. At 40 degrees west I contacted the ship-to-shore radio at Portishead and asked for a telephone patch to the hospital. The operator explained to the baffled nurse that I was calling from over the Atlantic.

"Hello, hello are you receiving me? It's Colin Fairdale calling from an aeroplane over the Atlantic. How is my wife, Lucy doing? Over."

The line was heavy with static.

"Over? It's not over yet." Came the confused reply.

"Your wife is doing fine. She's dilated 4 centimetres."

"Fantastic. Thanks. OK. I'll call again in 45 minutes. Over."

I ended the call.

I had no idea what she was talking about.

I called the stewardess in the upper galley and asked if she could come to the flight deck to explain.

"It's the dilation of the cervix," the pretty little blonde said, leaning against the back of my chair, "birth normally occurs at about 10 centimetres."

"Right. Thanks."

"More power," I muttered, and pushed the thrust levers a little further forward.

We nudged 88 percent of the speed of sound. The fuel consumption was off the clock, the wings were vibrating slightly, and I could almost imagine them glowing cherry red with the friction.

Forty-five minutes later, and 10 degrees further east I called again.

"How's it going? Over."

"Ovaries? Did you say ovaries?" The nurse said. "I can't hear you very well. All's fine, she's dilated 5 centimetres."

More power, the speed was creeping up.

I was sweating.

The stewardess had told the upper deck passengers that the Captain's wife was having a baby, and they were rooting for me.

At 20 degrees west, dilation was 6 centimetres.

I signed off with Portishead. The operator had been monitoring my calls.

"The best of luck, I've worn out my carpet pacing up and down all night." He said.

We passed over Ireland, it was still dark. Little pinpricks of lights dotted the ground below, and the first glow of dawn appeared ahead. Above Wales we were handed over to London Control.

I checked in, it was a female air traffic controller.

"I've always wanted to say this." I explained to her, "my wife's having a baby, can you give me a direct?"

There was a short delay.

"No problem," came the reply. "Turn onto a heading of one-zero-zero, you should be number one."

"Thank you, I'm very grateful."

"You're welcome, I know how you feel, I had a baby myself two months ago."

There was very little traffic at that time of the morning, but out of the ether, a voice crackled over the radio. Someone had recognised me.

"Is that you Colin?"

I didn't reply.

"You're not trying that 'my wife's having a baby' routine, again are you?"

I laughed.

We landed and taxied to the stand where a BA car waited. The trainee Captain shut the aircraft down and to tumultuous applause, I rushed from the flight deck, flew down the stairs and drove off to the hospital.

The sun was peeking over the horizon and the birds of the dawn chorus were singing their little beaks off as I arrived at the hospital. I clambered upstairs and staggered into Lucy's room.

Lucy was sitting up in bed with three of her girlfriends around her. They were drinking a bottle of champagne.

I looked around for the baby.

"Hello, you" she said, her coterie turned to look at me.

"They gave me an epidural, Colin. My contractions stopped at 8 o'clock. Come and join the party," she said, turning back to her giggling friends.

I slumped in the chair and stroked the stubble on my chin. I was knackered, I had shot across the Atlantic like a scalded cat, burnt tonnes of extra fuel to get here quickly; and they're having a party?"

I fell asleep.

At two o'clock I awoke to repeated yells of 'push, push' and screams and grunts; Lucy was giving birth.

I staggered to her side, looked into her eyes and helplessly held her hand.

"You bastard!" She hissed in her pain and anguish. "It's all your fault!" With a mighty heave, our little red wrinkled boy came into this world bawling his head off.

He looked very small, helpless and vulnerable.

Our baby suffered from jaundice and spent a couple of days in an incubator. He was discharged and we brought him home.

The house we rented in Cray's Pond was originally two adjoining red brick Victorian farm labourers' cottages with steeply pitched roofs. It was secluded and private at the end of a long gravel track in the middle of a beechwood and its crumbling sand-stock brick facades were patterned in diamonds with dark blue glazed bricks. The ornate olive bargeboards were peeling and covered with green mold, it was gloomy, there was little direct sunlight and haunting muntjac barks echoed in the trees. The cottages had been badly converted into a single building, the large sash windows were rotten, and patches of rising damp dotted the walls. Our bedroom was in one wing with its own staircase. The baby's room and a spare bedroom were in the other wing accessed by a separate staircase.

The previous tenant was an artist friend of ours, and we moved in when he hurriedly left for Spain. Andre was an illustrator and fine artist whose claim to fame was painting pornographic images on toilet seats for rich Arabs. He grew marijuana plants in the greenhouse which he dried in the kitchen and stored in popcorn barrels. He held riotous parties and it wasn't long before the barrels took pride of place on the kitchen table.

The morning was cold, clear and sunny. A heavy dew dripped from the leaves which sparkled in the sunlight as it fell.

There was a knock on the door.

I opened the door in my pyjamas.

An oafish young policeman stood by the door. A police Land Rover was parked on the drive.

"Mr Fortman?" he asked brusquely, looking at me intently.

"No."

"Do you know of Mr Andre Fortman's whereabouts?" he continued, writing in a tattered notebook.

"I'm afraid not."

I did, but I wasn't going to tell him.

The policeman wrote laboriously with the tip of his tongue poking out of the side of his mouth. Out of the corner of my eye, I noticed a young marijuana plant bravely pushing out of the gravel by my foot. I shuffled over towards it hoping he wouldn't notice. Shit! I wasn't sure that that hayseed would have known a cannabis plant from a palm tree, but I needed to distract him.

"Can you check you have the right address?" I asked, pointing to his notebook.

He looked down and flipped the well-worn pages.

I surreptitiously stood in front of the plant.

He glared at me impatiently.

"Mr. Fortman is required by law to present himself to Reading Crown Court in ten days."

He pulled out a summons from an inside pocket and handed it to me.

"If you see Mr. Fortman, give him this."

He walked towards the greenhouse, and I shuffled to hide the offending plant.

"You're quite remote here, aren't you?"

"I suppose so." I replied, shuffling again as he moved to peer into the empty greenhouse.

"Let us know if you hear anything about Mr. Fortman, won't you."

I nodded.

He turned and walked back to the Land Rover.

I shuffled as he went.

He must have thought I was dying for a crap.

He clambered into the Land Rover and drove back down the lane.

By UK law we had to register our babies name within 42 days, but we couldn't decide between Tom and William. Lucy drove me to the airport and before I got out of the car, we tossed a coin.

William won.

"Awww" said Lucy.

"I really liked Tom."

Greenland is stunning. It is the world's largest island and one of the least populated. The mountains in the centre rise to more than 12,000ft but are completely covered by the icecap. Arctic high-pressure systems often mean the views are spectacular. Massive glaciers crawl relentlessly down steep sided, iceberg strewn fjords to the sea.

I had my nose pressed against the windscreen marvelling at the sight. We were en route for Los Angeles with seven hours to go.

The chief steward came onto the flight deck.

"Captain, I'm afraid we have a bit of a problem."

I turned around to face him. He was tall, balding and anxious.

"One of our passengers has gone into labour. Her waters broke in the loo, apparently."

He wiped away a strand of hair from his florid face.

"She's very agitated so we've moved her by the door. I'm not sure what to do."

Passengers are not normally allowed to fly after 32 weeks and I wondered why she was allowed on the flight.

"OK. Make an announcement to see if we have a Doctor on board? Let me know how you get on."

I asked the First Officer to look at the weather for Sondestrom and Gander. If this became serious, we had few options available to us. The nearest airport was Sondestrom, but the weather was poor, and the approach was complicated. Furthermore, I doubted that the medical facilities would be up to much. The next best choice was Gander but that was two hours ahead.

The chief returned shortly afterwards, breathing heavily.

"A young Italian doctor has offered to help but he doesn't speak any English. He's attending to her now"

"Good. Do you have any proof that he is a doctor?" I asked.

Surprised, he shook his head.

"We don't normally ask."

I was concerned. There was a case a couple of years ago when a female passenger complained of severe toothache on a flight to Barbados. A PA was made, and a doctor offered his services. He proceeded to give her a full internal examination.

It turned out he was a Doctor of Philosophy.

"OK, I'll come down."

I walked through the cabin. The passengers looked alarmed, which was not surprising considering the noise she was making. The crew had erected a screen of blankets around door 3 Right, and the pretty red-head was lying on a mattress of cushions and seat rests in great distress. The young doctor seemed to know what he was doing; another female passenger was translating for him.

"I'm afraid our medical kit doesn't really cater for child birth." I told her.

The doctor was swarthy, with a large aquiline nose. He said something to the translator.

"He says the baby is upside down. We need to get to hospital quick."

I thanked her and told the chief steward to prepare for an unscheduled landing.

I returned to the flight deck and we set course for an emergency landing at Gander. The weather was marginal, and we were too heavy to land immediately, so we jettisoned 50 tonnes of fuel.

The turbulence was severe on the descent and Gander was lashed with strong cross winds and rain. During the flare we flew into a wall of sleet, and for a couple of seconds I had no visibility at all. We flew through it and touched down.

Gander did not have steps tall enough to reach a 747, so the pregnant passenger and the doctor, were disembarked by a high-lift catering truck. The back of the truck descended slowly, and a baby girl was born among frozen dinners and dry stores.

I'm passionate about skiing, I love the mountains and snow. I started skiing at 10 years old when my father ran an RAF winter survival course in Bavaria.

I taught Matt to ski from an early age and he became very proficient.

I skied as often as I could when I was on trips. Once I went skiing in Alyeska near Anchorage. None of the crew wanted to ski, so I went on my own. After lunch I stood in line for a chairlift when an elderly American asked me if we could share the ride up.

We chatted on the chairlift. He was skiing on his own and asked if I minded if we skied together for the rest of the day?

I looked at him. He was ancient! He was going to slow me down dramatically.

Reluctantly, I agreed.

"I've lived here for a few years." He said, his frozen breath formed tiny ice crystals in his bushy grey eyebrows. "I know a few back-country routes if you're interested?"

I nodded. God! This was going to be boring.

We arrived at the top of the lift.

He shot off like a scalded cat, executed tight turns around trees in the powder, and gracefully jumped off snow covered rocks. I followed him at half his pace. I almost lost my balance at the first turn and my ski poles flailed impotently in the air. Thankfully he couldn't see me. The second turn was worse. My weight was too far back, I slowly pirouetted, my arse dragged in the snow, and I crashed headlong into a tree. The snow cascaded from the branches in a mini avalanche and smothered me.

Lesson learned.

I went on a ski holiday with Matt to Chamonix. I wanted to see the Hale-Bopp comet from somewhere unaffected by light pollution. What better place than the top of a mountain? I hired a guide and we hiked up the Argentière glacier with skins on our skis. In the late afternoon we reached the refuge where we were to stay the night. The modern wood and stone building on a rocky spur at the confluence of two glaciers was out of place in such a beautiful setting. The sun set in a cloudless pink sky behind the Aguille Verte as seracs tumbled noisily from the cliff on the far side of the valley.

After dinner the generator was switched off, and Matt and I sat in silence on the frozen little terrace, looking at the sky.

I was fascinated by the night sky. I had an office window with the best view in the world and I spent hours gazing at the stars. One night, over northern Canada, I flew between the geographic and magnetic north poles. Concentric rings of Northern Lights shimmered for hundreds of miles in every direction, like diaphanous pale-yellow curtains fluttering and pulsing in the cosmic breeze.

The view from the refuge was extraordinary, it was crystal clear and calm. The nebulous strands of the Milky Way hung in the firmament above, and the panoply of stars glittered brightly. Mars, Jupiter and Venus twinkled in a line towards the last streaks of twilight in the west.

Hale-Bopp was clearly visible above the horizon, its pale bifurcated tail stretched thousands and thousands of miles behind as it continued its silent, lonely odyssey towards the sun. Once round the sun, it would be catapulted back to the far reaches of the Oort Cloud, not to return for another few thousand years.

I sat with Matt in silent awe and shared the spiritual, intimate moment.

Temptation

Lucy finished her maternity leave and returned to flying

It was immediately apparent that we needed child care. Although Lucy had requested to fly short trips, there would be a few days each month when we would both be away. We needed a full-time nanny.

A Dutch girl answered our advertisement in 'The Lady' and we flew to Maastricht to interview her. Mathilda was a chubby, friendly blonde girl in her late teens who had previous nannying experience and could speak good English. She started working for us two weeks later.

It was a disaster.

Mathilda dented the car and didn't tell us, she was lazy, she lied, and we caught her smoking while holding William. Lucy fired her.

The next nanny was Sharon, a young Cornish lass from Truro who was an acquaintance of a close friend of Lucy's. Sharon had been training as a nurse in Plymouth and decided to take a break from her studies. She was a non-smoker and had some child care experience. She had mid-length brown hair, a round face and a sexy smile. I thought she was attractive in a West Country sort of way, but I could sense that Lucy was not too keen on her. We were desperate and she hired her.

Sharon eased into her role effortlessly. She was mature, needed little guidance and genuinely cared about William.

When Lucy was home, Sharon made herself scarce when off-duty, and stayed in her room or visited a girlfriend in Reading.

At least Lucy and I had some time to ourselves.

She tried to be as unobtrusive as possible, she didn't wear makeup and fed William his breakfast in a plain winceyette nightdress and thick cotton dressing-gown. She looked frumpy, dull and unattractive.

Lucy seemed pleased.

However, when Lucy was away on a trip, Sharon was quite a different person. She made an effort with her appearance and followed me around with William tucked under her arm. One morning, she came down to breakfast wearing a skimpy satin baby-doll nightie, even though it was freezing in the draughty kitchen. She purposefully leant forward to feed William revealing her full breasts through the loose-fitting top. I could tell it was cold.

Jet-lag and sleepless nights wreaked havoc on my relationship with Lucy. Financial worries and my frequent battles with Rosemary added to the volatile brew. Lucy was suffering from Post Natal depression and had little time for me, we squabbled, and I sulked.

The attention from Sharon was welcome.

There was no requirement for her to do any housework or washing, apart from Williams or her own. I hated ironing, but

I liked cooking, so I struck a deal with Sharon. When Lucy was away, I would cook, and she would do the ironing.

I enjoyed those evenings. Sharon ironed in the kitchen while I cooked. We shared a bottle of wine huddled around the Aga with our collars turned up against the wintry draughts.

One day when Lucy was in New York, Sharon called me up to William's room. I walked to the bottom of the steep staircase. Sharon stood at the top in her nightie, but without any underwear. She stood with her legs apart with one hand on her hip and the other on the bannister. I hesitated, I wanted to climb the stairs, but I slowly turned away and went back into the kitchen.

Sharon used Lucy's trusty Peugeot 205 as a run-around. I cleaned it one day and found a photo wallet under the front passenger seat. I opened it. Sharon was naked in a shower canoodling with another naked, dark-haired girl. The wallet was so obvious under the seat I wondered if I was meant to find it.

Lucy was away on a long trip and Sharon asked if she could invite her friend from Reading to join us for dinner. I prepared a scrumptious chicken casserole `a la Col` and laid the table in the kitchen, while Sharon busied herself putting William to bed. It was a cold evening, I lit candles in the kitchen and opened the Aga doors. I laid a fire in the sitting room and put 'Candle in the Wind' on the CD player.

The doorbell rang.

A tall thin, androgynous girl in a trench coat, with short black hair, stood under the feeble porch light. She stepped forward and her face emerged from the shadows. It was the girl from the photos.

"Hello." I stammered, "I'm Colin. You must be Sharon's friend?"

"I'm Ruth" she replied with a soft Irish accent, holding out her hand.

I invited her in and took her coat. She wore a royal-blue tight-fitting crushed velvet dress which complemented her elegant figure. Sharon ran down the stairs, threw her arms around her and gave her bottom a little squeeze. Arm in arm, Sharon steered Ruth into the kitchen and sat her at the table.

I served my culinary classic and poured glasses of wine. The girls chatted animatedly across the table during dinner. They had attended the same nursing school in Plymouth and regaled me with doctor and nurse stories from the West Country. They briefly touched hands on the table and burst into fits of giggles as they recounted a juicy bit of gossip. The candles on the tables were guttering, I poured out the last of the wine.

We moved to the sitting room to watch a movie. I stoked the fire and Sharon and Ruth sat next to each other on the sofa. I turned off the lights and sat down on a bean bag to watch 'The English Patient' by candlelight.

Ruth rested her head on Sharon's shoulder while Sharon gently stroked Ruth's arm. Sharon's fingers delicately traced the line of Ruth's arm, and slowly undid the buttons at the front of her dress. She slipped her hand inside and fondled her breasts. Ruth turned, placed her hand on Sharon's thigh and kissed her. They kissed passionately with their mouths open. Ruth had her eyes closed, but Sharon glanced at me and smiled.

Shit it was hot! I didn't know what to do. I wanted to stay but I felt that I was intruding on a very private moment. Red-faced, I got up and stumbled to the door.

"Good night," I croaked and closed the door behind me.

I reached the bottom of my stairs, the sitting room door opened and a partly dressed Sharon approached me. She touched me on the arm and said.

"What would you say if we both came up to your bedroom?"

My head swam. The stakes were so high. I desperately wanted to, but the consequences?

I searched for words and after a few seconds I blurted out.

"I would tell you to fuck off Sharon!"

I slowly climbed up to bed and locked the door.

All night I tossed and turned.

What if?

I felt so guilty, that stupidly, I told Lucy. Incandescent with rage she fired Sharon on the spot.

A week later Lucy intercepted a letter addressed to me from Harrods asking for a reference for Sharon. She had applied for a job as a buyer in the menswear department. To put it mildly, Lucy wrote some disparaging comments on the form, signed my name and sent it back to Harrods.

Lucy hired the next nanny. She was a plain, stodgy Jehovah's Witness with hairy armpits, body odour and a moustache.

Lucy had the last laugh, if there was anything to laugh about.

New Beginnings

Lucy and I finally married, and Princess Di died.

My divorce finally came through, I transferred my share of the house to Rosemary and she took on the mortgage. I continued to pay the school fees; monthly maintenance and she would take a chunk of my pension when I retired. It was a heavy price to pay, but I was free to get on with my life.

We were married at a registry office in Henley-on-Thames. In the middle of the proceedings Lucy burst into tears, we had been through so much to get this far. We held a small reception for close friends in a riverside hotel and Lucy looked stunning in a simple cream Grecian dress with a chiffon scarf. William created havoc toddling around the tables.

We set off for our honeymoon in Bruges leaving William with friends. We stopped just outside Dover to fill up with petrol.

Lucy bought a paper.

'Dodi is killed, Diana badly injured in Paris car crash.' blared the headlines in the Sunday Times. Lucy was visibly shocked and turned on the radio. The news was on every radio channel. Diana had died. Lucy was mortified.

We crossed the Channel to Calais on the hovercraft and drove to the beautiful, medieval 'Venice of the North.' Lucy read the paper repeatedly and listened to BBC Radio 4 on long wave until it faded into crackles somewhere near the Belgian border.

Connected to the sea by a tidal inlet and situated at the cross roads of two important European trade routes, Bruges was the centre of the Flanders wool trade. The imposing walled city became wealthy, majestic churches and large merchant houses were built along the city's canals. Patronage of the arts transformed the business-minded city into a cultural centre. Today, cafés, shops and renovated architectural gems have revived the city.

It is an untouched medieval tourist paradise.

We didn't see much of the city, Lucy stayed in our hotel room and watched the news on television all night.

So much for our romantic honeymoon.

We returned from our honeymoon and a few months later Lucy announced she was pregnant again. She assured me that it was going to be a girl this time as she had made certain. I'm not sure what Lucy meant by that, but I hoped she was right, as she was so desperate for a girl.

She accepted a redundancy package and was due to stop flying in the summer.

We bought an old barn in a nearby village to renovate. We moved from Cray's Pond and planned to rent a flat in Hardwick stables until we completed the renovation. Hardwick House was on the River Thames near Reading, and the Edwardian stable block was 300 metres from the main house. Above the stables, on the north side of a large cobbled courtyard, was a black-and-white revival style accommodation block, originally used by grooms. Horse filled stables surrounded the yard. Poor Lucy was so stoic, the flat was in an awful state of repair, it was draughty, and damp and we could hear the horses farting and kicking in their stalls below. I reminded myself that it was only a temporary situation and it would give us a chance to get back on the property ladder. We watched William like a hawk, one kick from a horse could be catastrophic.

It was very pleasant being near the Thames again. I jogged along the river or walked in the woods on the rolling downs behind the stables.

On a rare sunny day, nothing beats England in the spring.

Lucy did not want a prolonged pregnancy and booked an induction at the John Radcliffe hospital in Oxford.

We were much better prepared for our new arrival. We plotted routes and timings to the nearest hospitals, and tested them out in our new, albeit second hand, Volvo T5 estate. The Radcliffe was our choice, but it was 50 minutes away. However, Wallingford Cottage Hospital was on the route, at about halfway. The quaint, tiny hospital in Wallingford had a maternity unit of only two beds.

I was concerned about another premature birth, so I took extra leave and packed Lucy's hospital bag well in advance. I arranged childcare for William that I could call on at short notice.

The day before the due date we went for a curry in Pangbourne.

Perhaps it was the vindaloo or the jalfrezi, but Lucy woke with a stomach ache. She sat up in bed with her black hair tousled by a restless night.

"I have to go to the loo," she said, peering at me through her dark, scrunched up eyes.

She looked child-like, vulnerable and very pregnant. Her elfin figure was contorted by her impossibly large belly. I felt deeply protective, I wanted to put my arms around her but I'm not sure they would have reached. A cold draught swirled from the window, she shivered and with difficulty pushed herself off the bed to reach for her dressing gown. She waddled slowly across the threadbare carpet to the bathroom.

A few seconds later she cried out.

"Colin! Come here!"

I fell out of bed and ran to the bathroom. Lucy was sitting on the toilet leaning forward, holding her stomach.

"Fuck! My waters have broken!" she gasped. "I think I can feel a contraction!"

I spent my entire adult life learning how to deal with emergency situations in a calm and ordered way and to be methodical and logical.

I panicked and ran down the stairs to the courtyard shouting.

"Help! Help!""

Jenny, the stable manager, emerged from a stall where she had been mucking out the horses. She was in her 30s, blonde and stout. She wore a Barber gilet, riding breeches and her riding boots were covered in horse shit.

"What's happened?" she asked, wiping her hands on her jacket and resting the fork against the wall.

"Lucy's having the baby!" I blurted out, and with my arms flapping, I ran back upstairs. Jenny followed.

Lucy was sitting on the bed, calmly pulling on a pair of leggings.

"Right! I'll get your bag. Let's go!"

"Aren't you forgetting something?" Lucy said gently.

Frantically I searched my mind.

"Um. No."

"What about William?"

Bugger, he was still asleep.

"I'll phone Helen," I said and scampered to the telephone in the kitchen. I looked at it uncomprehendingly. My mind was blank.

"What's the number Lucy?"

Lucy wobbled into the kitchen, took the phone, calmly dialled the number and spoke.

Lucy put the phone down.

"Helen will be here in 15 minutes. Put the kettle on and make yourself and Jenny a cup of tea."

A cup of tea, I thought, a cup of tea? God!

Lucy sat on the bar stool holding her stomach with her eyes closed.

"Another one." she said and doubled up with pain.

I turned to Jenny.

"Jenny, you've had lots of experience foaling horses. Can you stay with us, just in case?"

She smiled.

"I wouldn't want to compare Lucy to an old nag." She whispered.

Fifteen minutes is an eternity, the clock slowed to a crawl and Lucy had two more contractions. I helped Lucy down the stairs to the car. She was panting and a little distressed as she lay on the back seat. Helen arrived and went upstairs to look after William. Jenny climbed into the front seat beside me and we set off for the John Radcliffe. Well, that's not quite true, because I backed into a pile of straw and manure. I revved the car too hard and the wheels spun, showering a couple of startled stable lasses with crap.

It was a Saturday; the traffic was light, and I made it onto the A4074 in record time. Lucy shouted in the back that the baby was coming. Jenny reached over to calm her down.

"I want to push now!" Lucy wailed.

"No Lucy! Hold on until we get to the hospital!"

"You bastard Colin!" screeched Lucy, "it's all your fucking fault!"

'How come it's always my fault?' I thought dejectedly, as I screeched around a corner with tyres squealing. The roadside was a blur, the car bounced as it roared along, scattering gravel in all directions.

"I really have to push! It's coming!" shrieked Lucy.

'I really have to push as well' I thought, flattening the accelerator.

Jenny was leaning over the seat with her bum in the air. The rear-view mirror is aptly named as that was all I could see.

"Fuck It's almost out!"

My mind was racing. Should I stop, or should I continue? Wallingford was three miles, I decided to go there instead. I got lost in the town but after jumping a couple of red lights and nearly running over some pedestrians, we arrived at the little hospital. It didn't look familiar, but we parked the car under the entrance porch in full view of a lady's hairdressers alongside the track.

Like a couple of headless chickens, Jenny and I got out of the car and ran into the hospital leaving Lucy unattended in the car. Horse shit flew from Jenny's boots as we galloped up and down the corridors looking for help. We didn't find anyone. I realised I had driven to the rear entrance of the hospital, no wonder it looked different. We ran back to the car.

Two nurses were with Lucy. One of them looked at Jenny's boots with distain.

"It's almost out!" panted Lucy quietly on the back seat.

"Well, it ain't coming out with yer trousers on is it?" said the nurse.

Lucy shook her head, and with help from the nurse tugged one leg of her leggings off. Exhausted, she lay back, and in full view of a gaggle of blue rinses in the hairdressers, our impatient little baby girl was born.

She was ugly, red, squashed and covered in white stuff. She wriggled and let out a loud bawl. She was the most wonderful thing I had ever seen.

The nurses cut the cord and wrapped the bawling baby in a blanket. Thank God they didn't ask me to do it. Lucy's leggings were removed, and she was helped into a wheelchair. Lucy stepped on the placenta as she climbed out of the car and mashed it into the carpet.

We followed the nurses through the hospital to the maternity ward.

We called our snuffling, squashed-face little girl Eleanor. We brought her home two days after her precipitous arrival, and the sleepless nights began again. I seemed to have spent the whole of my adult life raising children. I needed a break.

Eleanor was not very demanding, in fact she was completely placid compared with William. She had fair hair and big blue eyes, she dribbled a lot and generally ignored me. I wasn't really into little babies, but she was gorgeous

I wrote a letter to Volvo hoping that they might send me a new car.

The Manager   *Hardwick Stud*
Globe Park   *NearPangbourne*
Marlow   *Oxon*
Bucks

December 2ᵈ, 1998

Dear Sir

I am writing to you to express my satisfaction with my Volvo 850 TS Estate. N 770 KBW

Last Saturday, my wife, who was nine months pregnant, unexpectedly, and very rapidly, went into labour. It was soon evident that an extremely expeditious trip to the hospital was required, and with my wife lying prone on the rear seat, I set off with alacrity.

I was able to drive my car to the limits comforted by its meteoric acceleration and the existence of airbags, SIPS and ABS. I felt that if the police stopped me, I had a very reasonable excuse.

Unfortunately, not even Michael Schumacher would have been able to get us to the John Radcliff Hospital in time. and we had to divert to the Wallingford Community Hospital. As we arrived in a billow of smoke, my wife started to give birth.

Two midwives appeared from nowhere, and after marvelling at the cavernous interior of the car, decided to continue with the delivery on the rear seat.

I am overjoyed to tell you, that just five minutes later, my baby daughter, Eleanor, was born weighing in at 8lbs 6oz.

I would like to complement you on the materials used in the construction of the car.

1. The scream-muffling sound-proofing, and lightly tinted windows reduced the number of curious onlookers to a minimum, even though I had parked the car by a busy hairdresser.

2. The tensile strength of the rear window opener and arm-rest resisted every effort of my wife to rip them off during her moments of anguish.

3. The quality of the upholstery was such that the subsequent mopping up was achieved with very little effort.

4. I am happy to say that I did not need to test the efficiency of your splendid looking tyre lever.

My wife and baby are both fit and well and will be returning home tomorrow.

I will be driving them in what I now regard as my Volvo delivery wagon.

Yours faithfully
M Fairdale.

PS. It has been suggested that we christen our baby 'Volvo', but I fear some unscrupulous wags might nickname her Vulva.

A large bouquet of flowers arrived with a note wishing us the best of luck, but sadly no new car.

South of France

We celebrated the Millennium in Dorchester Abbey. The night was crisp and cold, and the moon shone brightly through the ornate 13th century windows of the choir. Smoke from hundreds of guttering candles curled lazily upwards through the shafts of moonlight partially obscuring the oak trussed roof high above. Children skipped across worn pale-yellow flagstones, their giggles echoing in the sepulchral hallowed halls. Parents clustered around a table serving free cheap wine, their murmurs competing with the Rector's droning monologue from the pulpit.

It was fitting to celebrate the new Millennium in the Abbey, it exuded solid permanence. Parts of the building date back over 1400 years to Anglo Saxon times. I imagined 1,000 years ago, superstitious village folk gathering on this very same spot, fearful for what apocalyptic events would herald their new millennium. The Second Coming? Plagues of frogs and locusts? Famines or the end of the world? And all we were worried about was, whether our computers would work or not in the morning.

I glanced again at the moon as it continued its silent peregrination through the ancient stained-glass window of the St Birinus chapel. In astronomic terms 1,000 years was a mere bagatelle, an insignificant mote in the vastness of time and space. How utterly unimportant our lives and struggles were.

We moved into our renovated barn, and at last we had some space and a house of our own. I was glad to see the back of the stables, but it wasn't long before *la malaise Anglaise* reared its ugly head.

Before we bought the barn, it had been used as a rubbish tip. It was in the centre of the village and was covered in rusty corrugated iron. It was an eyesore, but inside was a beautiful oak and elm timber frame which we sympathetically renovated.

The English are good at building people up and take great delight in knocking them down. They are jealous of success.

We weren't made very welcome, and the Parish Council complained about our work, although it had enhanced the village centre dramatically. We felt stifled by the parochiality of our life in England. The bitterness of Rosemary, the petty jealousies of neighbours and the gossipy cliques wore us down.

We decided to start a new life and a new millennium in France. BA had many flights a day to Nice, so we decided to move to the South of France.

We sold the barn, packed the car and set off for Biot. We rented a modern house with views of the sea and enrolled the children into school. It took some time before William settled down and he caused chaos as usual, but Eleanor was too young to understand what was going on.

The terrorist attacks on the Twin Towers in New York changed our lives for ever. Security was tightened, baggage was screened, and thorough searches caused frustration and long delays. Passengers were advised to check in three hours before departure.

It was the death knell for the notion that flying was romantic.

The terrorists took control of four aircraft by gaining access to the flight deck and cutting the throats of the pilots with box cutters. They flew two of the aircraft into the Twin Towers, one into the pentagon and the fourth crashed into a field in Pennsylvania.

Our aircraft were fitted with armoured cockpit doors and no one was allowed onto the flight deck apart from crew. The door was locked at all times and a security camera system monitored the access. I was concerned initially, and I must admit that I kept the emergency fire axe by my side just in case.

We were not allowed into the cabin to talk to the passengers and we became hermetically sealed in our lonely and boring eyrie.

There was always an issue of 'us and them' between the flight deck and the cabin crew, particularly with the older stewards. The chief steward now controlled who on the crew could visit the flight deck, so we rarely saw anyone, and no one saw us. I heard stories of some chief stewards introducing themselves to the passengers as the Captain.

We were preparing a flight to Chicago. It was snowing lightly, and we were de-icing the aircraft as a precaution. The Dispatcher came onto the flight deck, his red cap wet with snow. He looked tired.

"Captain, sorry, but we have a problem. An Indian passenger has the ashes of his grandfather with him in a brass box. It's a security issue."

I looked at him quizzically and wondered how a box of ashes could pose a threat. Someone could hit us with the box or blind us with the ashes I supposed.

The dispatcher wiped the melting snow off his face and sighed.

"Security X-rayed the box and there is a ceremonial dagger inside. We can't have it in the cabin."

"I see. OK. Can't we put it in the hold?"

"Captain, I'm sorry, but he won't have it. He's making a heck of a fuss, so I suggested that you might consider carrying it on the flight deck?"

I turned to the First Officer who was finishing his pre-flight checks.

"Any thoughts, Jim? Seems OK to me."

He shook his head.

"Fine with me, Captain" he replied and continued flicking switches and testing systems.

"OK. Bring up the box up just before we leave." I said to the dispatcher over my shoulder.

Half an hour later the door-bell chimed and the dispatcher came in carrying an ornately etched brass box of about 20 centimetres square.

"Where do you want me to put grandad?" he asked.

I shrugged.

"Um, just put him on the floor under the observers table, he'll be OK there."

Reverently he placed him on the carpet and backed out the door.

It was odd having someone's remains on the flight deck, but we kept granddad entertained all the way to Chicago. We chatted to him, told him jokes and explained what all the instruments did. Thankfully he didn't show much interest in the cheeseboard.

It was the First Officer's turn to fly the aircraft. Chicago is a notoriously busy airport and the tower asked us to land on the shortest runway. The weather was poor with low cloud and a stiff cross-wind. The First Officer did an excellent job and arrived over the runway in exactly the right place, but a sudden gust of wind hit us in the flare, and he had no option but to land the aircraft firmly. The runway was short and wet, so he hit the brakes hard when we thumped onto the ground. Cutlery and glasses crashed in the galley and we came to a shuddering halt like a nodding donkey.

Gingerly, we taxied towards the terminal. I looked around and horror of horrors, Granddad's box had fallen over, the lid had come off, and the ashes were spread over the scruffy carpet. In the middle of the pile, gleamed a small gold ceremonial dagger.

"Shit!" I said to Jim. "Granddad's escaped!"

We parked at the terminal and I kept the door locked while we dealt with granddad.

Two minutes later, I sheepishly handed the box to the handling agent. Inside was the dagger, most of granddad, carpet fluff and a few crumbs of cheese.

I liked living in France and Lucy loved it. William was settling down and Eleanor just went with the flow. We bought a small house and we had somewhere we could call home. Apart from the strikes and the bureaucracy it was a lovely place to live. The weather is very pleasant, and although I wasn't not keen on beaches, we were just 30 minutes from the sea. More importantly we were 45 minutes from the nearest ski station. There is no local industry, the air is clear and apart from the coastal strip, it is sparsely populated.

Everything was looking rosy except for my approaching retirement. My licence allowed me to continue flying until 60 years old, but my contract with BA was until I was 55. A group of pilots were considering suing BA on the grounds of ageism, but I didn't hold much hope. My contract was agreed nearly 35 years ago and was too expensive and restrictive for BA. I could be easily be replaced by someone much cheaper and more flexible.

I wasn't ready to retire, I enjoyed flying and I was good at it. It was such a pity that the wealth of knowledge experience

I had accumulated would be thrown away by an arbitrary retirement age.

The Provençale summer was around the corner. Warm moist winds from the Mediterranean are forced to rise by the mountains to the north and condense into fluffy white clouds. By the afternoon they evolve into majestic towering cumulus, which lead to short, sharp downpours.

Clouds were also gathering at home. Lucy was still suffering from postnatal depression which affects many women after child birth. It is thought that it may be triggered by a hormonal imbalance after the rigours of child birth. The delicate equilibrium of the endocrine system can be affected by external factors as well, and I feared that I was one of them.

My father was a no nonsense, sort-it-out-yourself type of man. He believed showing emotion or seeking help was a weakness to be dealt with by a stiff upper lip. He once pulled out his own tooth rather than visit a dentist. He never showed me any affection and encouraged me to be like him. In consequence, I had little empathy for illnesses unless there was evidence such as blood or broken bones.

I said to myself 'What's the problem, Lucy? Why can't you just deal with it?'

Was I so selfish and unsympathetic?

Sometimes it was preferable to be away on a trip.

I love Seattle.

The sky was clear as we descended across the Cascades, wisps of low clouds in the valleys dramatised the volcanic peaks which marched in a line as far as the eye could see. We passed Mount Baker heading for the snow-capped peak of Mount Rainier. The brooding titans of Mount Hood and Mount St Helens crouched beyond. On the far side of Puget Sound the mountains of the Olympic Peninsular gleamed in the afternoon sun.

Our flight from London was the first time that everyone on the crew, including the First Officer, was female. We settled in the cruise and the chief stewardess requested to come onto the flight deck. We unlocked the door and she came in looking very flustered. It was once fashionable to have a tan, but now her sun ravaged face was lined and deeply freckled. She wore heavy make up to cover the blemishes and her once dark hair was streaked with grey.

"Captain. A passenger in economy is drunk. I would like permission to tie him up."

"Hold on a second, Mary." I replied gently, "we have to give him a written warning. What's the problem?"

Crew are trained in the use of handcuffs to restrain disruptive passengers but the decision to use them is not taken lightly. Legally, we had to deliver a written warning before a restraint was made.

"He's drinking heavily and keeps wandering into the galley and interrupting the service."

It didn't sound like a strong enough reason to physically restrain him to me.

"OK Mary. Stop serving him alcohol and see if you can move the passengers around him to other seats. We're not full, are we?"

"Right. We have space, but I still want to tie him up."

"Well, let's wait and see. Keep me informed."

She marched off the flight deck leaving us to our lunch trays.

Mary stormed back onto the flight deck.

"Captain, he hasn't listened, and he refuses to sit down. I insist that we tie him up!"

I looked at her, she was clearly agitated.

"OK, Mary, OK. What's he like?"

"He's a big man with fuzzy grey hair. I think he's Polish."

The girls on the crew were slight and I couldn't imagine them restraining a big man with ease. This left me in a dilemma, since 9/11 it had been forbidden for flight crew to leave the flight deck, but I was the only male on the crew. I decided to go into the cabin and give him the written warning in person.

The best option was to be as intimidating as possible. I put on my jacket and made myself look taller by wearing my hat. I pulled my crumpled hat from my flight bag and put it awkwardly on my head. I looked like a clown with a sack of potatoes on my head.

I climbed downstairs and made my grand entrance through the curtains of the economy cabin with a flourish.

Captain to the rescue.

There was a sudden hush, everyone turned to look at me highlighted in the sunlight streaming through the windows. On the left side of the cabin, surrounded by empty seats, sat a mountain of a man in his seventies with oafish features and a grey stubbled head. He rocked gently in his seat humming a tuneless tune. He didn't appear to be an aggressive drunk, far from it, he seemed to be having a good time, lost in his own little world. I approached his seat and he turned his turnip head towards me, his bloodshot eyes struggled to focus.

I leant over to read him the riot act, there was a collective intake of breath from the watching passengers.

This inebriated, geriatric dotard was obviously no match for me. I was made from ripcord and steel with a Buzz Lightyear chin and reactions of a cat, for goodness sake.

He caught me by surprise

In the middle of my speech he suddenly reached up and grabbed me by the lapels. He pulled me roughly towards him.

I squawked, and my unloved hat flew off my head into the aisle.

In a heavy East European accent, he said.

"You remind me of my Father!" and kissed me fully on the lips.

The cabin erupted with hysterical laughter and applause, I turned as red field of beetroot, extricated myself, and scuttled back to the flight deck.

I passed a visibly shocked Mary and I snarled.

"Tie him up!"

I stumbled inexorably towards the precipitous cliff of retirement. I had a few months to go before I plummeted into the unknown. I had been flying since 18, it was my soul and my being. I never regarded it as a job, it was a way of life. I wouldn't pine for the long nights out of bed, the time change, or the industrial problems, but I would miss the excitement, the challenges and the opportunity to work with young people.

Since 9/11 our downline social life was a shadow of what it used to be. I used to laugh at the old codgers who said, 'Things were much better in my days.'

I found myself thinking the same.

Perhaps it was time to go.

I returned from Boston on my last Atlantic trip. We levelled off in the cruise for the five-hour crossing to London. Circadian rhythms are lowest an hour before dawn and I was fighting to stay awake.

The doorbell chimed and the monitor flickered on.

The pretty stewardess stood in front of the camera, and with her back to the passengers, lifted her blouse to expose her breasts.

The spirit wasn't dead after all.

Is That It?

It is said that time is linear, but the physicists are wrong. Time is an exponential, it accelerates.

I retired from BA. One second before midnight, the day before my 55th birthday, I could fly 550 people anywhere in the world. Two seconds later I could not. There was no easing gently into retirement, it was brutal and abrupt. Suddenly I wasn't anybody anymore, I had no responsibility, nobody asked me for my advice.

I felt lost.

My retirement from BA was a farce. I had served them for nearly 37 years and yet I was just a number. I arrived from Bangkok on my last trip early in the early morning and nobody from management bothered to congratulate me.

The crew held a little farewell party for me on the upper deck after the passengers had disembarked. They toasted me with a glass of champagne. Little speeches were made, and I was presented with a caricature from Chatuchak market.

I was moved. It was fitting that my adieu was being celebrated by the people who I felt were family, rather than some anonymous disinterested manager.

Deep in reflection, I waited on the tarmac below the huge black shadow of the aircraft for the crew transport. In the east, the sun rose, dispersing wispy smudges of stratus clouds, the orange sky portending a fine summers day.

It would have been more fitting if the sun was slowly sinking in the west.

The transport drivers were on a go slow, so we had to wait 45 minutes for the crew bus. We arrived at the crew reporting centre and I went to help the driver offload the bags. I had unloaded one bag when the driver arrived and said aggressively.

"Wotcher doing?"

"I'm only trying to help."

The crew looked surprised as they ambled wearily towards the rear of the bus.

"Well you're bloody-well not!" he snapped, picking up the bag and putting it back on the bus before offloading it again.

How could he speak to a Captain like that? I was aware that the drivers had been told by their union to try to provoke an incident, so I kept my mouth shut. How embarrassing, especially in front of the crew. This would never have happened when I joined BA, the man would have been fired on the spot. Perhaps it was a good thing that I was being forced to retire.

I dozed in the crew lounge until 9am, waiting for the admin staff to arrive. I returned my identity card, headset, manuals and company credit card to a sullen, gum-chewing self-important girl. She made a big show of cutting up the card in front of my face, symbolically severing me from BA. In uniform stores I handed in my uniform apart from my hat which was in my suitcase.

"Where's your hat?" the young lad said.

"I'm afraid I've lost it."

"Well, I can't sign you off then!" he muttered.

"What are you going to do? Sack me?" I snapped as I turned and walked out the door.

I had to wait 4 hours for my flight home to Nice and I sat in the crew lounge wearing a visitor's identity badge. I looked around at the familiar surroundings and felt I didn't belong, I took a bus over to Terminal 1 and waited there.

I looked in the mirror and wondered who was looking back. My hair was white, and my face was lined and jowly. Where did the time go? How did it happen?

Lucy had hardly aged, she had virtually no grey hair and could still wear the same clothes she wore when I first met her. We weren't as close as we were, and my concern was heightened by our age difference. Before we married, I reminded Lucy that she would be only 66 when I was 80. Was she certain that she could cope with that? She said yes emphatically.

I'm not so sure I still believed her.

I had lived an extraordinary life, I crammed at least two lifetimes into one, but I was floundering. A friend once said that when he retired, he didn't feel important anymore. He felt discarded. In many ways I felt the same.

Lucy and I were not used to spending so much time together. Our relationship was moulded by being apart most of the time. We both liked our own space and freedom to do what we wanted.

Our cat was completely deaf and very frail. It was semi-feral, rarely came in the house and slept on a pile of rags in the garage. I had no idea how old it was, but I didn't think it would last much longer. It walked stiffly past, dragging one leg and I felt sad. It was no longer a cat, it had only two teeth and couldn't catch anything if it tried. It had fulfilled its purpose and was now redundant.

I needed a purpose. I needed a challenge.

I sailed on an ice-breaker from Longyearbyen to explore Svalbard on skis. Svalbard is a desolate, mountainous Norwegian island deep inside the Arctic circle and its northern shores butt up to the edge of the pack ice. Svalbard is sparsely populated, mostly covered with glaciers and is home to polar bears, elephant seals and reindeer.

We went ashore in zodiacs to climb the mountains and ski down to the pack ice. The ice-breaker beached for the night on the pack ice and a continuous watch for Polar bears was kept in the mid-night sun. They are not territorial but will often be aggressive. Thankfully attacks are rare.

It was incongruous to ski following a guide with a blunderbuss slung on his shoulder.

The Russians own a small part of the island where they mine coal. Barentsburg has a population of 400 and is a melange of ancient rotting wooden houses and garish Soviet-era edifices. The drab concrete is brightened by colourful heroic murals which adorn the walls of the streets.

A bust of Lenin glared sternly down at us as we wandered into the 'Red Bear' brewery to try to drink it dry.

It was exhilarating but not enough, it didn't satisfy me.

What was I looking for? I had no idea why I did those stupid things. What was I trying to prove? Was I pretending I was younger than I really was? Perhaps I was subconsciously trying to impress Lucy? Maybe I was hooked on adrenaline?

I had no idea.

I decided to cross Greenland on skis.

Greenland

The crunch of Inuits walking through the snow outside the bright yellow clapper-board community centre masked the yapping of the huskies in the village. Jagged snow-covered mountains surrounded the brightly painted, steep-roofed houses of Tasiilaq situated on an ice-bound inlet in eastern Greenland. Polar bear skins stretched on frames dried in the feeble noon-day sun and pale-yellow huskies chained to posts, barked and frolicked in the deep snow.

Greenland was once a Danish colony and Inuit children were required to complete their education in Denmark. Many did not return, but those who did, failed to make much of an impression on the Inuit way of life. Amauti and mukluks may have given way to colourful North Face jackets and synthetic snow boots, but the Inuit still hunt and fish in the traditional way. Alcohol is a problem and bars are only allowed to open for limited periods at the weekends. Neglected Inuit children were cared for by Danish missionaries in the hall below out dormitory. I read children's stories to a group of the kids each day and one little girl was fascinated by the hairs on my arms. I could only assume that Inuit have little body hair.

We were scheduled to helicopter across the iceberg strewn Denmark Strait to the Hann glacier to start our crossing of Greenland. Our planned route was across the icecap from

Tasiilaq to Kangerlussuaq on the west coast. It was six hundred kilometres and would take about five weeks. We were unsupported and we aimed to drag our provisions, cooking fuel and clothing in orange plastic sledges called pulkas by ropes attached to our belts.

The pulkas weighed about 85 Kg and we would haul them over the 9,000ft high icecap wearing thin Nordic skis with sealskins. We would then descend the very gentle slope towards the west coast, where the icecap terminated in a confusion of tortured ice, melting snow and crevasses known as the ice fall.

We needed to be prepared for a violent catabatic wind called 'the Piteraq' which could sweep down without warning from the ice cap at over 300 kilometres per hour. Each night we had to build a two-metre-high wall of ice blocks around our tents to protect our camp.

Polar bears migrate north in the spring and often take a short cut inland to the west of Tasiilaq.

Our track crossed their migration route, so our guide, Max, and I went to a trading post to rent a gun. We walked down a narrow icy path towards a large snow drift with a chimney stack belching black smoke sticking out the top. The dilapidated wooden trading post was almost hidden in the bank of snow and, under a small porch, fur pelts hung from pegs either side of the deeply scratched door. We pushed our way in and walked into a gloomy, smoky room. The walls were lined with stuffed animals and shelves overflowing with hunting equipment. The flames from an old iron stove in a corner cast dancing shadows among the cluttered bric-a-brac.

I moved towards the stove and gratefully warmed my hands.

"Costs me a fucking fortune!"

An enormous man with long white hair and a bushy grey beard stood behind the cluttered counter, peering at me with his beady eyes. He looked like an albino ferret poking it's nose out of a Polar bear's arse.

He bit off a piece of hardfiskur and chewed noisily.

"You don't get much wood round here." he continued in a heavy Danish accent, wiping his mouth with the back of his hand.

"Can I help?" he asked, spraying us with flecks of dried fish.

Max explained what we wanted, and the trader lifted down a dusty, antiquated rifle and placed it on the counter. He wiped if off, opened the breech and showed us how to use it. He put the safety catch on and handed me the heavy weapon.

He asked us why we wanted it, and I explained.

"For Fanden!" he muttered "are you mad?"

I pointed the gun towards the door and squinted through the sights. I noticed the barrel was significantly bent towards the left.

"No problem" he laughed, "just aim 5 centimetres to the right"

I felt very encouraged.

The bright red helicopter leaped into the air in a cloud of ice and snow and clattered back to Tasiilaq leaving us alone on the ice. We were a team of five including the French guide. Two of the skiers were almost half my age, built like brick shit houses and took part in a race to the magnetic north pole the previous year. I was Methuselah's granddad built like custard pudding and had enough trouble staggering to the local pub. I felt seriously inadequate. I trained for 9 months pulling a tractor tyre around a field, but I had serious doubts.

We started off and I quickly discovered that pulling the pulkas in soft snow uphill was seriously difficult. I had rope, a shovel and an ice axe strapped to the top of my pulka which made it top heavy. Max's sledge rolled over onto its side, slid down the slope and broke the polar bear gun in two.

I hoped we wouldn't stumble across any migrating Polar bears.

I was bloody cold and knackered.

I lay in my sleeping bag wearing my down jacket and a woolly hat. Each time I exhaled, my warm breath rose to the top of the tent, condensed and fell on me as a personal mini-snow storm. Gareth, the doctor, was beside me in the cramped two-man tent boiling water from chunks of ice on the small primus stove. We didn't carry water, we used the stove to melt ice, and we needed eight litres of water each. That's an awful lot of snow and ice to melt in our piddly little one-litre kettle. It took forever.

The food was high calorie, high protein and highly boring. Dinner commenced with an *amuse-bouche* of cup-a-soup followed by the *plat principal* of 'Turmat' freeze-dried expedition food and finished off by *le dessert* of muesli with powdered milk and chocolate. Yum!

After a few days of arduous trekking, the mountains of the fjords of the east coast were no longer visible behind us. We were at the centre of a giant upturned china plate which stretched to the horizon and merged seamlessly with the nebulous, chalky sky. When Buzz Aldrin walked on the moon, he described it as 'beautiful, magnificent desolation'.

Greenland is a cold featureless plain of white moon-dust, nothing grows, and nothing can survive.

A little bird landed on my pulka in a snow storm and sheltered behind the shovel. How could it be so far off course? We tried to feed it, but in the morning, it was gone.

I felt sad.

We averaged 25-30Km each day and made good progress towards the top of the ice cap.

The wind turned southwest, and a snow storm blew up. We had trekked for twelve hours and we now had to build a second wall. I forced the tip of the ice saw into the snow and sawed the ice into 60cm blocks. The blizzard drove the snow into drifts as we made the walls from the blocks. It was back-breaking work and it took two hours to build our defences.

Eventually, I crawled into my sleeping bag exhausted.

The wind was ferocious during the night and tugged at the thin material of the tent relentlessly. The diaphanous layer of nylon was all that was between us and probable death. Part of the wall collapsed in the middle of the night with a mighty woomph. I prayed that we wouldn't have to get up and repair it. Luckily no-one stirred.

In the morning the wind had died down and I had my first ever attack of claustrophobia. Snow had piled against the sides of the tent, making the small space smaller. I felt suffocated, overwhelmed, out of control, everything was closing in on me. There was no way I could continue, what on earth was I doing there? It was time to call it a day. But I couldn't give up, rescue wasn't possible. I would let the team down and I couldn't live with that.

I was suffocating.

I had to get out

Hyperventilating, I scrambled out of my sleeping bag, I threw on my clothes and frantically unzipped the door of the tent. I stepped into a magical world, in the curling mist the sun's pale disk peeked over the horizon and a pavane of ice crystals tumbled and glittered in the early morning light.

I looked up to the sky, opened my arms and took a deep breath. All would be OK.

I had mouth ulcers and my bleeding lips were cracked from frost bite. I slept on my back with my mouth closed and by the morning my lips had fused together with scabs. I gently poked my tongue out through the corner of my mouth and worked it along my lips to open my mouth. God it hurt!

The temperature approached -40C and froze our lungs with every breath. We had rasping coughs and Gareth had frost bite on his face. I ignored severe blisters on my heels, I had no choice.

The routine was always the same. With military precision I had a shit every morning at 6.10am in a snow hole which we dug the night before. The name of the game was to do it as quickly as possible without freeze-drying one's arse. It was a time-consuming ritual to prepare for the dash outside. First, we scraped the ice off our sleeping bags and then pulled on long johns and sweaters while sitting in the sleeping bag. Finally, we donned our parkas, quilted trousers and snow boots and made the dash outside. The secret was to expose your arse to the elements for as little time as possible. Undo belt pull down trousers, long johns and underwear in one smooth action. Squat - shit – wipe arse - pull up clothing, hope your gonads hadn't frozen and dropped off or, in your eagerness, you hadn't commenced the shitting action too soon.

The turds froze before they hit the snow with a thud.

'We must be there soon.'

Gusts of wind tugged at my anorak, hurling clouds of ice laden snow in my face. The matted fur ruff around my hood, crusted with frozen snow and ice, flapped noisily against my steamed-up goggles.

'Just follow the skis.'

'Left-right,-left-right.'

The greasy green anorak of Max was dimly visible in front of me. He pulled his dented orange pulka topped with a bulbous faded blue tarpaulin. The drifting snow piled up under the runners and covered my tarp, adding extra weight and making it difficult to pull.

Max purposely strode forward, the ropes attached to his waist slackened and tightened with each step, jerking the heavy sledge fitfully forward.

'Keep the rhythm.'

'One-two-three-four.'

My lime green skis looked ridiculously narrow and the skins made a metallic sound with each stride as they scythed through the snow. My faded black expedition boots were ripped along one seam and beginning to show the signs of excessive wear. Would they last the distance? A scatter-gun of ice shards hurled by the Piteraq penetrated the layers of my leggings, stung my skin and melted, only to refreeze in my boots.

With our heads bowed against the maelstrom, my three companions were strung out in a ragged conga. Their anoraks were a splash of vivid reds and greens in a landscape utterly devoid of any definition or colour, vibrant ice breakers in a crystallised moonless sea.

'Don't lose the rhythm.'

'The-Grand Old-Duke of York-- he had- ten thou-sand men.'

The blizzard was ferocious. The relentless wind barrelled down from the icecap whipping up the surface of the snow into a frenzy, the wind chill dropped to well below -50C. Capricious gusts of wind found their way into every crevice, every weak spot, the headwind was an invisible hand pushing me back.

I was so tired.

I thought we would be romantic adventurers like Nansen or Shackleton. It seemed like a good idea at the time

How fucking stupid.

Six hundred sodding kilometres pulling an 85 kg sledge in temperatures down to minus 40? Are you mad? My friends said.

They were right.

We'd been battling for twelve hours, we must be there soon. I could no longer feel my legs. My arms ached from the repetitious pulling and striding. I was sweating profusely under my anorak, my merino wool underwear wicked out the moisture which froze instantaneously into a white fuzz of hoar frost. I resembled a lurching, shambling Yeti.

I'm sure the others weren't suffering like me, but I mustn't let them see I was struggling

Each step was a gargantuan effort

'He-marched them-up to the-top of the-hill.'

The sound of the wind was deafening, it roared, flapped tugged and swirled. A cannonade of ice pellets hit my hood with a thunderously disorientating clatter.

'And he-marched them-down-a-gain.'

There was a hardly definable, subtle change in the light, a fleeting moment of texture, a slight shadow. I was sure I could see something in the distance through the crinkled clingwrap of my world. It was an amorphous blur, a smudge in the infinite distance.

Was I mistaken?

'One-green-bottle-hanging on a-wall.'

Doggedly we continued.

Whatever it was, it was large, a brooding intangible ghostly galleon, a murky satanic mill.

The slope increased gently, and the pace slowed. The wind forced the snow between my mask and stung my face, my goggles steamed up inside and there was no way to wipe them. My vision became more and more myopic, there was no horizon no sky, nothing.

'There'd be-no-green bot-tles, and-no bloody-wall.'

In the maelstrom the shape became darker and more defined, the blurred edges sharpened into purposeful angles. It appeared to be a frozen Taj Mahal. The Mughal dome slowly metamorphosed into a multi-faceted, gigantic golf ball, the minarets into ice encrusted aerials.

It was a cathedralic sanctuary from the elements. Majestic organ music filled my befuddled mind as we wearily unclipped our pulkas and clambered stiffly and unsteadily down a steep snow drift to a broken metal door flapping cantankerously on the side.

The abandoned radar station welcomed us into its eerily silent, frigid maw.

It was dark and cold, very cold. Snow drifts filled the corridors and spilled into the bedrooms. Ice hung from pipes in the ceilings and coated the peeling walls. Marie-Celeste-like, mattresses, newspapers and overflowing ashtrays littered the rooms.

We forged through the snow filled corridors and clambered up the stairs to the canteen. The stainless-steel kitchen equipment glinted in the light from our head lamps and a faded poster of a woman in an Hawaiian skirt hung incongruously on a wall. A green plastic Christmas tree stood on a table by the entrance.

Dye 2 early-warning radar station was an early casualty of the thawing Cold War. It was quickly abandoned in 1986 and left to sink ignominiously into the Greenland icecap.

It was so out of place, a blot on the pristine landscape. It would have been nice if the Americans had taken their rubbish with them when they left.

The icecap descends towards the west, and as it changes direction, crevasses form in the bends. It terminates in a tumble of steep, house-sized chucks of ice called the icefall.

Normally the gaps between the ice blocks were filled with snow which made it easy to ski, but the snow had melted prematurely.

We spent a day roped together as we crossed a crevasse field. The dark blue chasms disappeared into the void below our feet as we trudged along. By the end of the day the snow had become wet and slushy.

We broke camp on our last day. We were almost there, it was a heady feeling. Thirty minutes later we were amazed to find a lake in front of us shimmering in the bright sunlight. It stretched as far as we could see. We made a long detour around the lake, but we were forced to cross fast flowing streams of ice-cold water and slush. Max led the way and we followed in his footsteps.

The sound of rushing water filled my ears as I inched towards the stream. My skis, partially obscured by floating slush, slipped below the surface. The resistance of the moving water slowed each step and soon my calf-high boots filled with water. My feet instantly froze. The water gradually rose above my knees as I pushed forward. What if I was dragged under by the pulka? What if I missed the track and stepped into deeper water? I started to breathe heavily with my heart racing. The water was almost to my waist in mid-stream when my pulka followed me into the river. Thankfully it floated, but it shot downstream and nearly yanked me over. The current had carved a steep bank in the snow on the far side where Max waited to help me out. My pulka tugged at me as I tried to negotiate the steep slope and my skis crossed. I grabbed Max's outstretched hand but fell chest deep into the torrent. Max and Gareth dragged me out and I lay shivering and panting on the ice.

We were wet and miserable as we continued towards Kangerlussuaq, aiming for a moraine at the base of the icefall. At the beginning of the day the planned distance was 19.7km. We had trekked for hours, but we weren't far from where we started.

The flat watery icescape slowly gave way to an uneven vista of ice hillocks and crevasses. Streams flowed into the fissures and hollowed out the ice underneath which collapsed into huge holes known as kettles. We crossed the crevasses without a second thought, I became *blasé* and paused with the tips and tails of my skis either side of the gaping crack to take photographs of the bottomless blue-black crevice below.

Eventually we reached the icefall proper and started to navigate the mountains of ice. It was exhausting dragging the pulkas up the steep sides of the mounds. At the top, I continued over the brow and paused with the pulka just below the apex on the far side. As soon as I pulled the pulka over the top it became an unguided missile. I side-stepped and jinked one way or another but my homicidal pulka took me out every time. On one occasion I was certain that I had outwitted it, but it crashed into the back of my heels and knocked me backwards on top of it. We careered down the slope and fell into a small stream meandering between the hills of ice with a splash.

We stopped for dinner on the ice as the sun dipped towards the horizon at 11pm. We had been trekking for 14 hours and still had 9km to go. We voted to continue through the night.

Wispy bands of cirrus clouds in the azure sky radiated from the horizon and embraced the half-moon above. The ice field was clearly visible in the twilight as Max climbed a large mound to survey our route towards the setting sun. It was still and calm.

Our progress was slow, and when the sun rose at 3am, we took off our skis and continued on crampons. We glimpsed the moraine in the distance, I never thought a slab of brown rock could look so welcoming. It was the first piece of dry land we had seen for four weeks.

Seven hours later we reached the base of the moraine after 26 hours of non-stop effort.

It wasn't quite the end, we had to drag our equipment 200 metres up the moraine to meet our transport. At 11am I fell asleep in the middle of the road and was nearly run over by our truck.

We were housed in a faded brown wooden Nissan hut on the old US Airforce base of Sondestrom and it felt better than any five-star hotel I had ever been in.

I have been asked what I wanted most when I arrived. Surprisingly it wasn't a beer, it was a shower. I stood under the hot stream of water and looked down. I was ripped, I could see my feet for the first time in ages. I had lost 17 Kg and even my muscles had muscles.

I felt great.

I had achieved something special, I felt validated.

I had overdosed on endorphins. We walked 1,300,000 steps and burnt 8,000 calories a day. I felt fantastic for a while, but after a few months I was depressed again.

Cold turkey.

Instead of feeling contented, I felt hollow, something was missing.

I needed another hit.

I planned to ski across Corsica from south to north. It is recognised as a significantly difficult route, but I had trained a for it. I felt confident and raring to go.

Perhaps this time I would find what I was looking for?

ABOUT THE AUTHOR

Calvin Shields was an airline pilot for 47 years and lives in the South of France.

38918033R00215

Printed in Poland
by Amazon Fulfillment
Poland Sp. z o.o., Wrocław